SWEET TALK & LIES

INSPIRED BY ACTUAL EVENTS

SANDA DUDLEY

Order this book online at www.trafford.com
or email orders@trafford.com

Most Trafford titles are also available at major online book retailers.

Note for Librarians: A cataloguing record for this book is available from Library
and Archives Canada at www.collectionscanada.ca/amicus/index-e.html

Printed in Victoria, BC, Canada.

ISBN: 978-1-4269-0076-1 (Soft)
ISBN: 978-1-4269-0078-5 (e-book)

*We at Trafford believe that it is the responsibility of us all, as both individuals
and corporations, to make choices that are environmentally and socially sound.
You, in turn, are supporting this responsible conduct each time you purchase a
Trafford book, or make use of our publishing services. To find out how you are
helping, please visit www.trafford.com/responsiblepublishing.html*

*Our mission is to efficiently provide the world's finest, most comprehensive
book publishing service, enabling every author to experience success.
To find out how to publish your book, your way, and have it available
worldwide, visit us online at www.trafford.com*

Trafford rev. 6/22/2009

Trafford. www.trafford.com
PUBLISHING

North America & international
toll-free: 1 888 232 4444 (USA & Canada)
phone: 250 383 6864 ♦ fax: 250 383 6804 ♦ email: info@trafford.com

The United Kingdom & Europe
phone: +44 (0)1865 487 395 ♦ local rate: 0845 230 9601
facsimile: +44 (0)1865 481 507 ♦ email: info.uk@trafford.com

10 9 8 7 6 5 4 3 2 1

CHAPTER ONE

As Cassandra hurried down the sidewalk on her way home from work, the breeze was blowing her long auburn hair across her face... Pausing at the curb to check the traffic signal before crossing the intersection she causally brushed her hair out of her eyes and noticed the department store on the corner had a new window display of lingerie and she spotted one of the most beautiful nightgowns she had ever seen. On impulse, she decided to cross the street in the opposite direction than she had originally planned because she just had to get a closer look at that nightgown.

Soon as the light changed, Cassandra sprinted across the street slowing her stride when she reached the curb so as not to trip. She sucked in her breath when her eyes took in the sheer nylon and lace confection. The nightgown was just what she had been searching for to wear on her wedding night. Cassandra rushed into the store to check out the price to see if she could afford the lovely creation.

Hurrying down the aisle towards the women's department, she rounded a large display of cosmetics. In her haste, she failed to see the couple with a small toddler that was walking down the other side of the display and she collided with them nearly knocking them down, the mishap caused her to drop her purse. Embarrassed because she had only been thinking about the nightgown and not paying any attention to what was going on around her. As she stooped to retrieve her purse, she started to apologize. "Oh please forgive me; I wasn't watching where I was going and it was all my fa---." The words froze in her throat as she took in the couple that she had nearly knocked down in the aisle, her mouth dropped open when she saw Glenn Ogden, the man she was going to marry in two months. He had his arm around the woman by his side that looked to be about seven months pregnant. She was holding the hand of a small boy about two years old.

Seeing that Cassandra was about to bolt Glenn laughed as he reached out and took hold of her arm. "Hold on a minute Cassandra what's your rush is the store having a real fire sale or is the devil chasing you?" He questioned her with a big grin on his face making light of the situation.

Before Cassandra could respond, the woman with Glenn asked. "Do you two know each other?"

Glenn looking all innocence smiled. "Yes dear as a matter of fact we do. You remember me mentioning Frank Benning; well this is his daughter Cassandra." He explained to the woman by his side whom he hugged close as he made the introductions. "Cassandra this is my wife Gail and son Glenn Jr." He said proudly.

Cassandra shocked by this information felt the tears starting to well up in her eyes; she quickly ducked her head, which caused her to make eye contact with the little boy who stood there starring up at her with a frightened look on his face. It was all she could do to hold back the tears so as not to make a complete fool of her self. Looking up she stammered a hasty apology. "I'm really sorry about all this, please forgive me. But I really do have to go."

Then as she started to hurry away, she remembered her manners. "It was nice to meet you Mrs. Ogden." She called back over her shoulder not wanting to make eye contact...

"Goodness what was that all about?" The woman asked Glenn as she stood and watched Cassandra hastily fleeing down the aisle on her way to the front door.

Glenn acting as if he was just as amazed by everything as his wife was shook his head. "Damned if I know honey, don't give it a second thought. You know how teenagers are, always in a hurry." Then he changed the subject to get his wife's mind off Cassandra.

"Come on honey let's go look at those things for the new baby you wanted to show me." Glenn said excitedly.

* * *

BY THE TIME CASSANDRA reached the sidewalk in front of the store, the tears were blinding her; she could hardly see where she was going. She was devastated, she felt like someone had just taken a knife and cut her heart out of her body, leaving only an empty hole where her heart had been. Somehow, she managed to make it to the park across the street and sat down on a bench to deal with the reality of what had just happened to her.

How could Glenn have been so cruel to her? He knew he was a married man when they started dating, yet he continued to lead her on knowing she was falling in love with him and still he said nothing. Telling her how much he loved her as he placed a ring on her finger and asked her to marry him. Knowing the whole charade was just a pack of lies. What could he have possibly gained by stringing her along for the past six months knowing nothing could ever come of it because he was already married? The lie that hurt the most was when he had placed a beautiful engagement ring on her finger Valentine's Day and asked her to marry him. Telling her she would make him the happiest man on earth if she would consent to be his wife. All lies, everything he had ever said was lies.

But the worst hurt of all was the fact that she had believed him when he said he loved her, and had been stupid enough to give him her love in return. Her love for Glenn meant more to her, than life it's self. Her world collapsed around her, as she realized her dreams of a life with Glenn, had just been shattered by all his lies and deceit. Cassandra sat on the bench in the park across the street from Gorman's department store dazed as her whole world had come to a standstill.

While her heart was breaking into a million pieces, she made a vow that she would never fall in love ever again.

* * *

CASSANDRA FINALLY CAME TO her senses and realized that it was getting late and her mother would probably be wondering what had happened to her. Pulling herself up from the bench feeling weak and drained from the tragic heartbreak she had just endured she decided it was time to go home.

When Cassandra arrived home, she found her mother in the kitchen preparing the evening meal. Nora looked up from the potato she had been peeling, giving Cassandra a big smile. "Oh there you are Cassy I was beginning to worry about you when it started getting late."

Then Nora noticed that her daughter had been crying. "Is there something wrong Cassy?" She inquired.

"No mother." She lied and started towards her room, her feelings were just too raw right now and she knew she could not talk about it without breaking down again.

Nora knew that something bad must have happened today to reduce Cassandra to tears because she had never been one to cry. Laying down the half peeled potato and paring knife on the counter top, she hurried out of the kitchen and went down the hall to her daughter's bedroom. When Nora got to the open bedroom door, she could see Cassandra laying face down across her bed crying her heart out. Nora walked to the side of the bed, sat down, and gathered her daughter into her arms.

"There, there Cassy honey, tell mother what's wrong, maybe I can help." She whispered as she cradled Cassandra in her arms comforting her as she had when she was a little girl.

Cassandra clung to her mother's neck and sobbed. "There isn't anything you or anybody else can do mother that will stop the pain and make this hurt go away. I just want to die."

"Surely it's not all that bad dear." Nora consoled her.

"Yes it is mother, Glenn is a liar and a cheat and I never want to see him again as long as I live." Cassandra wailed.

"So that's it, you and Glenn have had an argument and you're just upset." Nora stated as though she fully understood her daughters problem. "This happens to a lot of young couples. But you and Glenn will patch everything up, and after you get married you will look back on this and have a good laugh about it." Nora smiled. "Besides all young couples go through these little spats. They even have a name for it called Pre Wedding Jitters. So come on dear, dry your eyes and let's go finish getting dinner ready, your father will be home soon." Nora was sure that she had solved the problem and made the proper assurances to ease her daughter's worries.

"Mother there isn't going to be any wedding for Glenn and me." Cassandra wailed.

"Surely it isn't something so terrible that you and Glenn can't work it out if you just be patient and give it a little time." Nora coaxed.

"Mother I ran into him with a pregnant woman and a little boy in the department store on my way home from work today and Glenn introduced them to me as his wife and son." Cassandra said heart-brokenly between sobs of despair.

This information rendered Nora speechless; all she could do was hug her daughter close to her trying to ease some of her pain. "Oh baby I had no idea that it was this bad. I'm so sorry honey." Tears were running down Nora's cheeks as she spoke.

Thinking it might help some to get Cassy's mind on something else for a while; she suggested patting Cassandra on the back. "Lets just put this all out of our minds for a little while dear, and finish fixing dinner shall we? And we can talk about it later after dinner when you've had a little time to adjust to all that's happened."

Cassandra, who was trying desperately to control her emotions, summoned up a weak smile as she wiped her eyes with a tissue and blew her nose. "Okay mother." She agreed as she stood up and wrapped her arm around her mother's waist as they headed for the kitchen.

*   *   *

LATER THAT NIGHT GLENN came to see Cassandra, when she opened the door and saw him there on the porch her first thought was to slam the door shut in his face. Glenn must have sensed this and quickly said. "Cassy you have to let me explain." He blurted out.

"There's nothing to explain Glenn! I believe you said it all in your introductions today in the store." She said heatedly, knowing that as long as she was angry she wouldn't cry. Darned if she would give him the satisfaction of knowing how badly she was hurting.

"Come on baby let's go for some coffee, so we can be alone. Once I explain everything to you it will all make perfect sense. " Glenn coaxed.

"I'm not going anywhere with you ever again Glenn Ogden, anything you have to say to me you can say it right here." She told him clearly.

"I can't talk to you in front of your folks honey it wouldn't be right to air our problems in public. Can't we just go somewhere a little more private?" He asked.

"If you prefer some place more private we can talk out on the porch. Because that's as far as I intend to go with you, now, or ever." She stated vehemently.

She stepped out on the front porch and closed the door. "Okay Glenn say what ever it is that you have to say and get it over with, because I want you out of my sight as soon as possible." She ordered him.

Glenn started to put his arm around her, but she quickly stepped back out of his reach. "Come on honey don't be that way." He pleaded.

"Just what way do you want me to be Glenn? Do you really think that after I found out you have a wife and family that I would welcome you with open arms? Well Mister you have another think coming." She informed him.

"You just don't understand baby, I'm asking you to wait until Gail has the baby then I'll ask her for a divorce. I just can't ask her now

6

because it would upset her. You and I can still get married after the divorce is final. Course we will have to move back the wedding date from where it is now because Gail isn't due until the end of July. I figured we could probably get married around the first of November." He said in all sincerity.

Cassandra stood there and heard him out until he finished what he had to say, and then it was her turn. "No Glenn you are the one who doesn't understand. I can't believe you can be so callous. Do you honestly think for one minute that I'm stupid enough to sit around waiting for you to divorce your wife, well Mister you are sadly mistaken." Cassandra jerked off her engagement ring and handed it to him. "I'll never take part in breaking up your marriage Glenn." Cassandra was so mad she was trembling with anger, striving to regain her composure she took a deep breath. "I'm glad I found out what kind of man you really are Glenn before we got married. Just go away and leave me alone, I never want to see, or hear from you again as long as I live. You are nothing but a liar and a cheat, and I wish to God I had never met you." She opened the door to go back in the house, then turned to him and said. "Goodbye Glenn, you really should think about what you are doing to your wife and children, and pray that if they ever learn of your infidelity that somehow they can find it in their hearts to forgive you, because I never will." She entered the house closing the door behind her and leaned against it as the tears came. She was heart broken; she had loved Glenn with all her being. How was she going to manage without him, he had been her whole world.

*   *   *

THE WEEKS WENT BY and Cassandra refused to leave the house except to go to work because she didn't want to run into Glenn. Her parents were starting to worry about her, as she was so despondent and losing weight because she was not sleeping very well, and hardly ate anything. Finally, they decided the best thing for them to do to help Cassandra through this terrible ordeal was to send her to spend some time with her aunt in Missouri. They hoped that the time away from home would help her heal and she would learn to laugh, and be her old self again. They told her to stay as long as she wanted to, and when she felt that she was ready to come home, they would welcome her with open arms.

*　*　*

HAVING STAYED SEVERAL MONTHS with her Aunt Lilly, Cassandra felt like she had her life back on track again and decided it was time to return home. She had made up her mind that what she had with Glenn would never become a reality, so she should just forget about him. As Cassandra started packing for the trip home, she made herself a promise to just have fun in the future and leave love out of it, that way she would never have to go through the torment of suffering another broken heart.

CHAPTER TWO

CASSANDRA GAZED OUT THE window of the bus lost in thought as it traveled across the country taking her back to southern California. Six months had passed since that fateful day she had broken up with Glen. She was coming home, that part of her life was behind her, and now it was time to move on.

*　　*　　*

THE BUS SLOWED DOWN and pulled into the terminal and Cassandra felt a familiar tug at her heart when she saw her father standing there waiting for her. She stepped off the bus and ran to her father's out stretched arms. "Oh daddy I've missed you so much." She confided in a voice choked up with emotion.

Frank Benning wrapped his arms around his only daughter in a bear hug. "I've missed you too baby." He confessed trying to keep his own emotions in check.

Frank gently eased Cassandra away from him so he could take a good look at her and said. "God but you are a sight for sore eyes Cassy; I can't tell you how good it makes me feel to have you back home again."

Smiling through her tears, she looked up him. "I feel the same way daddy, I've missed you and mother so much." She confessed.

Grabbing Cassandra by the hand Frank said excitedly. "Come on honey let's get your bags and head for home, your mother will be anxious to see you."

*   *   *

ON THE DRIVE HOME, Frank filled Cassandra in on what had been happening while she had been gone. Smiling over at her, he said. "You got home just in time Cassy the company picnic is coming up in a few days."

"That's great dad there's nothing like a company picnic for a welcome home party." She teased.

"Which park have they picked for it this year?" She asked interestedly.

"They decided to have it at the beach this year instead of the traditional park, so I guess the first thing for you to do Cassy is go out and buy yourself a new swimming suit." He said wriggling his eyebrows at her.

"Oh come on dad you know how I hate the water, especially the ocean." She reminded him.

"Guess I forgot about that." He winked at her as he pulled into the driveway where they lived.

"Oh look there's mother." Cassandra squealed, as the car stopped she jumped out and ran towards her mother.

They met each other half way and wrapped their arms around each other in a hug; both had tears of joy streaming down their face.

"Oh mother I've missed you so much." Cassandra sobbed.

"Cassy, Cassy, Cassy." Was all Nora could say as she hugged her daughter close fighting back her own tears as she tried to regain her composure "Let's go inside sweetie I've got dinner ready to go on the table, and I even made your favorite desert; lemon meringue pie." Nora informed her as they went indoors.

Frank followed them inside with Cassandra's two bags and set them down just inside the door. "Hey did I hear someone mention lemon pie?" Frank kidded as he smiled at his two favorite girls.

*   *   *

THE DAY OF THE company picnic arrived, and that day Cassandra met Raymond Cartone for the very first time. He was the son of one of the men who worked with her father.

Raymond was very tall, well over six feet, husky build, and had wavy black hair and brown eyes. He was the exact opposite of Glenn Ogden. Cassandra and Ray were the only two young people who didn't have a date at the picnic. They were paired together for different events during the day, and teased incessantly. Everyone called them Mutt & Jeff, due to their size. Ray towered over Cassandra's five foot three stature, and they took the chiding in fun, spending a good part of the day getting acquainted.

Ray told Cassandra that he had just returned from a two-year tour of duty in Japan, and that he was stationed at one of the Air Force Bases near San Francisco a few hours drive away, and he was just home on a weekend pass. Ray seemed like a nice person and he showed Cassandra a lot of thoughtfulness and consideration throughout the day, he was a perfect gentleman, and Cassandra enjoyed herself for the first time in months.

*   *   *

LATE IN THE AFTERNOON, Ray said his farewells to everyone because he had to leave early to make the drive back to the base. Before he left, he asked Cassandra if he could call her when he came home on his next pass.

*   *   *

THREE WEEKS PASSED BY before Ray returned home for another visit, he called Cassandra as soon as he arrived to invite her out for dinner and a movie. However, Cassandra wasn't too sure that she wanted to get involved with him, so she declined.

"I'm sorry Ray but I have other plans tonight." She lied.

Just as she hung up the phone her mother came in from outside. "Who was that on the phone Cassy?" She asked.

"It was Ray mother; he's back in town for a visit, and called to ask me out." She replied nonchalantly.

Nora smiled. "Are you going out with him?" She asked.

"No mother not tonight, I told him I had other plans." Cassandra answered.

"Really Cassy I think it would be good for you to get out and be with young people again. Ray seemed like a very nice young man. Why don't you give him a chance?" Nora suggested.

"Maybe I will next time, that is if he should call me again. To tell you the truth mother there is something about Ray that I can't explain. I just have this strange feeling that I just shouldn't get involved with him." She answered.

"Well you know best Cassy I just thought it would help if you went out once in awhile with someone your age, and had some fun for a change." Nora said shrugging her shoulders, not understanding why her daughter had turned down the invitation to go out with Ray.

"I know you mean well mother, but Ray is five years older than I am and I'm not sure if it is really such a good idea to date him." Cassandra tried to convey her feeling of unease to her mother. She knew her mother meant well. Smiling she said. "I'll think about it mother but I won't make any promises. Okay?"

*　*　*

TWO MORE WEEKS PASSED and Ray returned for another visit with his parents. Soon as he got in town, he dialed Cassandra's number, when he heard her voice on the phone he said. "Hello Cassandra, it's Ray Cartone, I hope you remember me."

"Of course I remember you Ray." Cassandra replied politely.

"I called to see if you would do me the honor of having dinner with me tonight." He stated sounding like a real gentleman.

Cassandra remembered what her mother had said the last time he called, and she thought why not; after all, it was only a dinner date. "I would be delighted to dine with you Ray, what time would you like to come for me?" She responded in the same formal manner he had used.

"Does six o'clock sound okay? I figured we could go somewhere nice for dinner, and then maybe we could take in a flick afterwards." He replied.

"Six will be fine Ray." She agreed. As she hung up the phone she noticed her hand was shaking and wondered if perhaps she had made a mistake accepting his invitation, after all she knew very little about this man other than his father worked with her dad. Cassandra decided she should talk to her father and see if he knew anything about Ray's character and background. It would be wise to stay on the safe side, as she certainly didn't want to have a repeat of her last mistake by getting involved with the wrong man again.

"Dad I was just wondering, do you know anything about Ray?" She asked as she sat down beside him on the couch.

"No baby, all I know is he was stationed in Japan for the past two years, and he will be getting his discharge from the service sometime in October. Why do you want to know?" Frank asked as he patted her hand.

"He asked me for a date, and I agreed to go. Now I'm having second thoughts, because I really don't know anything about him. And I'm wondering if he might be married or has someone waiting for him someplace." Cassandra replied voicing her doubts.

Frank put his arm around her pulling her to his side. "Hey you aren't worrying about lightening striking twice in the same place are you?" He teased using the age old saying. "Stop worrying Cassy, go out and have a good time and put things like this out of your mind."

" I know you're right dad, only I can't stop thinking how Glenn always acted like he was single, foot loose and fancy free, and look how that turned out." She reminded him.

"Okay Cassy if it will make you feel better about dating Ray I'll see what I can find out." Frank assured her.

Cassandra leaned over and kissed her father on the cheek. "Thanks dad I knew I could count on you."

*   *   *

WHEN CASSANDRA WENT TO bed that night Frank gave some serious thought to what she had asked him and he realized that he didn't know a damned thing about the Cartone family either. Frank knew that no matter what job he asked Alex to do, it was always finished on schedule. Up until now that's really all he needed to know about the Cartone's, but if it would make his little Cassy feel more secure then he would certainly do some checking.

*   *   *

CASSANDRA FELT SO MUCH better after she had talked to her father. She knew if he told her there wasn't anything to worry about then everything would be okay. She did sort of like Ray, but was quite sure in her own mind that a few dates was probably about as far as their relationship was likely to go, because she had no intentions of letting herself fall in love again. The last time she let herself fall in love had caused enough pain to last her a lifetime.

*   *   *

DURING THE MONTHS OF July and August, Ray was spending almost all his time home with Cassandra. He was already checking out job prospects as it wouldn't be long now and he would get his discharge, and needed to have a job lined up for when that day arrived.

Cassandra noticed that Ray was starting to get serious and was talking more and more about marriage. She tried to tell him that she didn't feel the same way about him, only he refused to take her seriously. He kept pushing her to make a commitment that she had no desire to make. He kept telling her that when he got married it would be to her and nobody else. Sometimes he frightened her with his possessiveness. In addition, he refused to take her seriously when she told him that she wasn't in love with him. He told her that she just didn't know what she wanted. But one of these days she would wake up and realize that they were in fact, meant for each other.

*　　*　　*

MANY TIMES CASSANDRA TRIED to talk to her mother about Ray's possessive actions, but her mother would just smile and tell her it was all her imagination. In time she started thinking maybe her mother was right and she was just imaging things. Maybe she did have Ray figured all wrong, maybe he wasn't really being possessive. Perhaps it was just his way like her mother said. Slowly as time went on Cassandra started pushing the things that bothered her about Ray to the recesses of her mind so she wouldn't dwell on them.

In her heart, Cassandra knew that no matter what, she could never love Ray the way she had loved Glenn. She liked Ray, but doubted if she would ever love him.

CHAPTER THREE

T HE FIRST WEEK IN September 1957, Frank came home from work and told Nora and Cassandra that his company had transferred him to the Sacramento area to work for the next six months, and they would have to move with his job. Nora was ecstatic about the idea because it would give them a much-needed break, and would sort of be like taking a vacation.

Cassandra could hardly contain herself when she heard the good news that they were going to be a long way away from where Ray and his family were, which would put some much needed space between her and Ray. It was the perfect opportunity for her to sort out her feelings and see how she really felt about him. Being around Ray all the time seemed to keep her mind in a state of confusion. One minute she really liked him, and then he would do, or say something that she didn't especially care for. There were several times, that the way he acted towards her would even frighten her, and she would want to end their relationship.

When Ray came to pick Cassandra up for their date, she told him her father was bring transferred to Sacramento for the next six months, and how much she, and her mother were really looking forward to the move. Ray got so mad she thought he was going to blow a fuse when he started yelling at her. "What the hell do you mean that you are going to move up there with your folks? Good lord Cassandra I can't believe that you are so happy about moving away from me, what about us Cassandra? I thought we had plans to get married. I can't believe you are so stupid Cassandra; I bet you never even thought about that little fact did you?" He accused heatedly, waving his arms in the air.

"Ray, why in the world are you so angry? I never agreed to marry you, so there is, no us." Cassandra informed him calmly.

"Come on honey you know how much I love you, and that I figured on marrying you as soon as possible, so how come you're acting like you don't know what I'm talking about?" Ray questioned.

"Really Ray for your information this fantasy of us getting married is all in your mind. I never agreed to marry you. You got this crazy notion that all you have to do is make up your mind to do something and it's a done deal. Well let me tell you right now I don't even know if I even like you, let alone have any desire to marry you. For your information Mister, I'm moving to Sacramento with my parents, and I could care less if it meets with your approval or not." Cassandra was practically screaming at him by the time she finished.

Ray was stunned; he couldn't believe that Cassandra was actually yelling at him, in all the time they had been going together he had never heard her so much as raise her voice. He couldn't figure out why she was so mad at him, all he wanted to do was just keep her near him so he could take care of her. "Now you listen to me Cassandra, I forbid you to go running off across the country with your folks. Your place is here with me Cassandra, and don't you ever forget that, you'll stay here with me and my family where you belong." He informed her clearly.

"No Ray you listen to me. First, you have no right to forbid me to do anything, and second, I don't intend to stay here with your family or anyone else. I'm going to Sacramento with my parents and that's all there is to it." She said defiantly.

Ray grabbed her by the shoulders and shook her none to gently trying to force his will on her. "Cassandra you are not, I repeat, you are not moving to Sacramento. You are going to stay here with me and we're going to get married, and that's final." He snarled at her.

Cassandra jerked loose from his grasp. "No, that isn't final. You don't own me Ray Cartone, so get that through your thick skull. Since I have never agreed to marry you to begin with, it isn't any concern of yours, where I go, or whom I go with. And as far as marrying you goes, well you can just get that idea out of your head, because right now marriage to you is the last thing on my mind." Fuming Cassandra turned and marched back into the house and slammed the door firmly shut in his face.

The big jerk, she thought as she leaned against the closed door, he sure had his nerve. If he thought just because of a few dates that gave him the right to tell Cassandra Benning what to do. Well he certainly had another think coming, because as far as she was concerned Mr. Raymond Cartone could just go jump in the lake, and the sooner that she and her parents could move to Sacramento, the sooner she could start forgetting all about him and his possessive ways.

* * *

SINCE ALEX CARTONE WORKED for the same company that Frank Benning did, it made it easy for Ray to be able to obtain Cassandra's address in Sacramento. He started writing to her almost every day, telling her how sorry he was for everything, and begging her to forgive him. Ray pleaded with her to give him another chance, telling her how much he loved her, and needed her. How he couldn't live without her in her life. Promising her that if she would only let him come see her, he would prove to her how much he really loved her.

However, as far as Cassandra was concerned she didn't care if he loved her or not, plus she could care less if he ever proved a single thing to her. He was bad news, and she was better off not having him in her life.

Instead of his letters impressing Cassandra the way Ray had hoped they would, they only made her more determined to have nothing more to do with him. Every time she received a letter from

Ray, she would read it, then tear it up in little pieces and throw it away without answering any of them. In time she even stopped reading them at all, she just tore them up unopened. She hoped that in time Ray would get the message that she no longer wanted anything more to do with him, that she just wanted him to leave her alone.

*   *   *

WHEN RAY FINALLY REALIZED that Cassandra wasn't going to answer any of his letters he decided that he would move to Sacramento, that way he would be able to talk some sense into Cassandra. Who knows he thought, maybe he could even find a job in a bigger town. There damn sure weren't any job prospects in the sleepy little southern California town where he lived. He had been looking for the past month since he got out of the service, and so far, he hadn't had any luck in the job department. Moving to Sacramento would solve two of his problems, he would be able to have Cassandra, and if he was lucky, a job too.

*   *   *

WHEN RAY ARRIVED IN Sacramento, it didn't take him very long to locate the trailer park that the Benning's were living in. He drove right up to the front of their trailer space and parked his car. As Ray exited the car, he hoped that it would be his lucky day and he would find Cassandra at home, because he damned sure intended to find out what her reason was for not answering any of his letters. Ray knocked on the trailer door, he was pleased when Cassandra opened the door, smiling he greeted her. "Hi baby, damn you look good."

All Cassandra could do was just stand there in the door speechless. Before she could find her voice, Ray pushed her aside and entered the trailer planting his self firmly on the couch as if he had the right to be there. "Well Cassandra what do you have to say for yourself? Why didn't you answer any of my letters?" He demanded.

Cassandra found her voice and got right to the point. "I didn't answer you letters Ray because I decided it was for the best if we don't see each other anymore, I refuse to be ordered around by you, or anyone else. So looks like you have made the trip here for nothing." She informed him.

Ray jumped up from the couch. "Please Cassandra, don't do this to me, you've got to reconsider, and give me another chance to prove to you how much I love you." He pleaded with her.

"It's just no use Ray; can't you see how you were trying to take over my life? I am a person Ray, not a possession. You want to own me, but I can't live that way. I'm real sorry Ray, but it is all over between us. Now will you please just go and leave me alone." She was trembling as she held the door open for him.

Ray glared at her as he went out the door. "Believe me baby it's not over!" He threatened her.

Cassandra snapped the lock on the door when he left, afraid that he might try to come back in the trailer. She wondered why Ray was just sitting there in his car staring at the trailer. She held her breath until she heard his car start up and he drove away, she hoped he would return home to southern California, and that she would never have to see him again, he frightened her.

*   *   *

HOWEVER, RAY HAD OTHER ideas; he decided to stop at the office for the trailer court to see if they had any vacancies. He found out that there was a small kitchenette apartment available at the front of the trailer park, so he paid for a months rent so he could live close to Cassandra. That way he could see her every day and "Hopefully" he would be able to convince her that they really were meant for each other. Ray figured if he was close by he could wear her down and get her to go out with him again. He was sure that whatever problem Cassandra thought she might have, they could work it out, if only they could be together.

Ray turned on the charm every time he was with Cassandra, and showed her more consideration than he had since they met. Finally, she agreed to have dinner with him. Not once did Ray show any sign of his former possessiveness that he had displayed in the past, and after awhile Cassandra started to see him through different eyes. Ray was like a different person altogether, treating Cassandra with the utmost respect, and never let his anger show when he didn't agree with her plans. He was more like he was in the beginning, when they had first started dating. He actually seemed to put her feelings above all else as though he truly cared for her. She simply couldn't believe the change that had come over him.

Then one night Ray done the unexpected, he actually got down on one knee and proposed to her. Cassandra was speechless; she didn't know what to say because she was uncertain just what her feelings really were towards Ray. She knew that she liked this new Ray, but she also knew, beyond the shadow of a doubt; that she wasn't in love with him. Her feelings for Ray came nowhere even close to what she had felt for Glenn. In fact, she really doubted if she would ever be able to love anyone again. She was twenty years old, and so far her romantic adventures had been very unsuccessful. Maybe she should just forget about finding the kind of love her parents had, and just settle for someone she liked and respected, maybe in time she would grow to love Ray.

Hoping that she was making the right decision Cassandra accepted Ray's proposal.

* * *

THEY SET THE DATE for their wedding for the following Saturday night, December 18, 1957. They planned to live in the small apartment that Ray was renting until he found a job, and then they would look for a larger place later on.

"It's only temporary Cassy, just until I land a decent paying job." He promised her.

Cassandra agreed with Ray that it would be best to stay in the small apartment at the trailer court, the rent was cheap and she could afford it on her salary, since Ray still didn't have a job. Ray had been in the Sacramento area now for about six weeks, and didn't seem too interested in job hunting. However, he was certainly going to have to get busy pretty soon as his money was about to run out. They couldn't live long on what Cassandra made, but that didn't seem to matter a whole lot to him, while he had been wining and dining her these past few weeks.

"Say Ray how are the job prospects coming along for you, does anything look promising?" Cassandra inquired.

"Now don't you worry your pretty little head about things like that baby, I'm sure something will come from one of those last two applications I put in the other day." He assured her.

"That's easy for you to tell me not to worry Ray, but you know that my income can't support two of us for very long." She reminded him.

A frown crossed Rays face but he smiled and said. "It won't be long baby, when I land a good job the pay will be good enough that you can quit your job and just stay home and take care of the big new apartment we're going to get. How does that sound to you?"

"Fine I guess Ray, but I just want you to know that I like my job and I don't plan on giving it up in the near future. In fact I plan on working for quite awhile so that we can get a little nest egg saved for a rainy day." As she spoke, she noticed a strange look appear on Rays face. Cassandra sensed that Ray wasn't too happy about the comment she had just made, but he held his temper in check.

* * *

THAT NIGHT WHEN CASSANDRA told her parents that she and Ray had made plans to get married Saturday night, she could tell that her news had come as a terrible shock to her father, and was surprised when her father said. "Cassy honey I wish you would give this some more thought before marrying Ray; after all you really don't know that much about him. Do you remember sometime back, when you asked me to check into Ray's background?"

"Yes I remember Dad, but that was several months ago and since you never mentioned anything about it, and mother had been encouraging me to go out with Ray, I just figured that everything was okay."

" Well Cassy that is partly my fault, the reason that I never said anything to you or your mother was because it looked as though you had more or less given up on Ray, and I didn't feel that it was necessary. But now that you are considering marrying him there's something I think you should know." Frank proceeded to relate the facts that Alex had told him in conversation. "You see honey Ray had a Japanese girl friend, he lived with her for most of the two years that he was stationed in Japan. According to Alex, Ray has been planning to bring her to the States as soon as he found a job, and was settled in a place of his own. Alex says Ray is planning to marry this girl, and he has been corresponding with her every since he was shipped home. That means that he has kept in touch with her all the time he has been dating you." Frank told his daughter sadly.

"Oh daddy, I never dreamed it was possible that this would happen to me again, I guess all men are just born liars. Ray never told me that he even knew anyone in Japan, much less bother to tell me that he had a girl friend while he was there. In fact, from the way he has been chasing me every since we met, you would think that I was the only single girl left on this planet." Cassandra paused taking a deep breath. " But you can sure bet that I'm going to have a serious talk with Ray about this, and see what sort of explanation he gives me regarding this girl friend he has been keeping a secret from me all these months, and why he hasn't seen fit to tell me about her." Cassandra was so mad and disgusted at the same time that she was beside herself.

While Cassandra was getting ready for bed that night she thought if this was really true, and she had no doubt for a single minute that it wasn't, because her father just wouldn't lie to her about something that was this important, or anything else for that matter. She knew that there was no way that she would go through with her plans to marry Ray. What is it with me, she asked herself. Once again, I am coming between two people. She hated the thought of being in the middle, possibly being the cause of bringing pain to another person. It just wasn't her style, she was the sort of person that would go out of her way to keep from inflicting pain on another human being, no matter what the cost was to her own personal feelings, and she wasn't about to start doing so now.

*   *   *

THE NEXT MORNING AS soon as she saw the curtains open in Rays tiny apartment, she marched herself over there and confronted Ray about his Japanese girl friend. She knew she wouldn't be satisfied until she saw with her own two eyes how he would squirm his way out of this one. Soon as Ray opened the door, Cassandra blurted out her question.

"What's this I hear about your Japanese girl friend that you are planning to bring to the states? When were you planning to tell me about her, or were you just hoping that I would never find out?"

"Look Cassy if I had wanted to marry Susie, then I would have done it before I left Japan. Who told you about her anyway?" He demanded almost shouting at her in his anger.

"Alex told my father during a conversation, and dad mentioned it to me last night. Didn't you think that I had a right to know what the score was with you; and your Japanese girl friend before we got married so that I could make my own decision as to what the right thing was for me to do? You know that I could never be happy if I just stood by and let someone else suffer because of me. In fact; did you ever even plan to tell me about her? Or was it simply your intention to keep it a secret and never tell me a thing about it?" She asked accusingly.

"I didn't tell you about Susie because there wasn't anything to tell. It was over when I shipped home from Japan. So stop worrying your pretty little head about it. I want to marry you honey, no one else." Ray assured her, but the look on his face was as though he would like to do bodily harm to someone if he had a chance, then he ranted vehemently. "Why couldn't my old man have just minded his own business in the first place, and kept his damned mouth shut? Then you wouldn't be having all these doubts floating around in your stupid head."

*   *   *

ONE WEEK BEFORE CHRISTMAS, 1957, Cassandra and Ray were about to be married, the lady who owned the trailer park decided to fix up her patio for the ceremony, and all the residents in the park knew Cassandra and her parents and planned to attend her wedding, about forty people were coming to see her get married.

*   *   *

BECAUSE IT WAS WINTERTIME, Cassandra had not been able to find the powder blue suit she had her mind set on, and since her parents couldn't really afford a wedding dress, she selected a charcoal gray suit, and teamed it up with black patent leather heels, and black kid gloves, and added her grandmothers white pearl necklace and earrings. With Cassandra's natural auburn hair, blue eyes and creamy complexion, the outfit looked quite striking on her slender five foot three figure.

*   *   *

WHILE EVERYONE WAS ASSEMBLING for the wedding ceremony she thought back to the conversation she and her mother had while she was getting dressed, regarding her choice of colors to be married in.

"Cassy honey I do wish that you had chosen some other color to be married in, surely you could have found something besides such a dark color." Nora said forlornly.

"Don't worry about it Mother, it's all right." Cassandra assured her softly.

Tears were forming in Nora's eyes as she spoke. "Oh Cassy, I wish you would have let your father and I buy you a real wedding dress? It would have meant so much to us to see our only daughter married in the traditional white gown." She said wistfully.

" Mother I couldn't let you and daddy spend that kind of money on a dress for me that would only be worn one time, knowing you would have had to go into debt for me, it just wouldn't be right. Besides what difference does it make what color of dress I wear, I will still be just as married even if it were a burlap bag. Please stop worrying about it Mother, honestly its okay, but I love you for the thought." Cassandra smiled to take the sting out of her words as she took her mother in her arms and hugged her close.

Nora stepped back and forced a smile to her lips. "Cassy honey you know very well that they say dark colors on a bride are a sign of bad luck." She teased trying to defuse the tense moment, and bringing a smile to her daughter's face that fell far short of reaching her eyes. Getting married was supposed to be a happy occasion, but for some reason Nora got the impression that Cassandra was far from happy regarding her wedding that was about to take place.

* * *

CASSANDRA SMILED TO HERSELF at the memory as she walked on her fathers arm to the landlady's patio, and thought. Oh, well since I'm not in love with Ray the marriage is most likely doomed anyway. Why should I care if it's starting to rain, and I am wearing dark colors? Then the most awful thought came to her and she had the strongest desire to run before it was too late. Right at that moment she knew she was about to make one of the worst mistakes of her life. With all these turbulent thoughts racing around in her mind, she never even realized that they had arrived at the make shift alter and she was standing beside Ray and the wedding ceremony had already started, until she heard Reverend Thomas clear his throat a couple of times trying to get her attention. When the Reverend asked her if she would take Raymond Cartone to be her husband, she just wanted to scream **No**, wishing with all her heart that she hadn't agreed to this marriage in the first place. She wanted desperately to run and never look back, but she couldn't embarrass her parents, things had already gone too far. She would just have to go through with the ceremony and hope for the best. Finally, she found her voice and whispered. "Yes."

*   *   *

AFTER THE CEREMONY WAS over and everyone congratulated them, they all hurried out in the rain to her parent's trailer for the small reception her mother had planned.

As Cassandra prepared to step off the patio, Ray clutched her roughly by the arm and jerked her around to face him as he snarled at her. "What the hell got into you Cassandra? For a minute there I got the idea you weren't too happy about marrying me, and I fully expected you to tell the Reverend, no."

Cassandra just looked up at him as a single tear slid down her face, then she jerked free of Rays hold on her arm and started walking slowly towards her parent's trailer. Silently she wished that she had swallowed her pride and ran, while she still had the chance, now it was too late.

*   *   *

THE NEXT TWO WEEKS were hectic; the apartment was so small that they got in each other's way every morning in the tiny bath room. Then Ray decided that since Cassandra had a job, and he didn't, that he would just stay in bed until she got ready and left for work. Then he could get up and shower after she had gone, and leave later in the mornings to go job hunting. However, he certainly wasn't trying very hard in the job department, as Cassandra soon found out one evening when she was talking to her father.

"It's none of my business Cassandra; but how in hell does Ray expect to find a job when he doesn't leave the apartment until noon, or sometimes even later in the day?"

Cassandra; just passed it off; "Maybe Ray spends the mornings filling out job applications, and then goes for job interviews in the afternoons."

Chapter Four

ONE NIGHT WHEN CASSANDRA returned home from work, she found Ray sitting in front of the small television in his undershirt drinking a beer, just as he was most every night when she came home. As she closed the door, she asked. "Hi Ray how did your day go, any luck on a job?" She asked cheerfully.

Ray never even bothered to look at her; he just grumbled a harsh, "No."

"Well maybe you should try leaving a bit earlier in the mornings Ray. You know the old saying how the early bird gets the worm." She said teasingly.

Ray glared at her and yelled. " Look Cassy I know how to get a damn job, just get off my back and leave me alone, Okay?"

"Well you don't have to bite my head off, I was only teasing. Anyway I was talking to my father and he mentioned that one of the farmers has a job available, and he thought you might be interested."

"Damn it Cassy why can't your dad just mind his own business? I'm not a damn sodbuster, and I'm not going to spend my life working like some damn dirt farmer. So you just tell your old man I'm not interested, and he can go straight to hell as far as I'm concerned, I'll find my own job."

Cassandra was stunned to hear Ray talk this way about her father.

"Ray you know my father is only trying to help us through this rough time. At least it would provide a paycheck until you find whatever it is that you are looking for. Besides what would it hurt to work for this farmer until something else turns up? After all you don't seem to be having much luck finding the sort of job you want right now, and we sure could use the extra money, my salary just doesn't go very far." She reminded him once again.

Ray jumped up from where he had been sitting every since Cassandra had arrived home, and grabbed her by the shoulders, his fingers digging into her flesh, as he started shaking her so hard she thought surely her neck would snap if he didn't stop. She lashed out and kicked him as hard as she could in the shins, and jerked free of his hold on her and yelled at him. "Ray what in the world is the matter with you? Have you completely lost your mind?" She demanded.

Then Ray hit her, knocking her hard against the wall by the door. "You little bitch; you and your damn family can stay the hell out of my business. I'll get a job when I'm damn good and ready, and not before." He wrenched the door open and barged out of the apartment slamming the door shut behind him.

Cassandra slowly slid down the wall until she was sitting on the floor, wondering what in the world she had let herself in for when she married Ray. Then she thought he was probably just upset because he couldn't find a job, and he was ashamed because she was working and he wasn't, that probably really hurt his pride. Nevertheless, that didn't excuse him in her mind for the way he had just attacked her.

Cassandra decided that if, and when Ray returned to the apartment, they were going to have to sit down and discuss things, so that this sort of abuse did not happen again. Cassandra wasn't in the habit of being knocked around. Ray acted as though she was his own personal punching bag.

*   *   *

IT WAS VERY LATE that night when Ray finally returned to the apartment, Cassandra knew that he must have been drinking as she could hear him stumbling around bumping into everything. When he staggered into the bedroom, she pretended to be asleep. She knew that as drunk as Ray was, now was not the time to be talking to him about anything.

It would just have to wait until she got home from work the next day, because she doubted very much if he would even be awake by the time she left for work in the morning.

*   *   *

IT WAS RAINING VERY hard when Cassandra returned home from work the next night, as she let herself into the dim apartment she saw Ray sitting in front of the television in his underwear drinking beer. She glanced around the tiny apartment and saw what a mess everything was in, and she lost her temper and flew into a rage. "This is disgusting! Ray, when are you going to get off your lazy butt and secure a job of some kind? I would think the least you could do since you aren't working is help keep up the house, just look at this mess you've made, it looks like a pigs sty."

"I'll get a job when I'm damn good and ready, and not before!" He paused and just sat there glaring at her. "And for your information Bitch, I don't do house work, that's what I married you for!"

Cassandra was livid. "Well mister, that's just not soon enough, the rent is due next week, and since you saw fit to spend my hard earned money on beer we don't have enough money for the rent." She paused to take a breath and continued. "And for your information I sure as hell didn't take you on to raise and to wait on you hand and foot; bowing like a damn Geisha girl." Cassandra quickly put her hand over her mouth when she realized what she had just said. She could see that Ray was really angry now.

"To hell with the damn rent, we can move out of this dump, and move in with your folks." He snarled at her.

Cassandra couldn't believe what she was hearing, it only incensed her anger, and she shouted back at Ray. "Well let me tell you buster, if anyone moves out of here and in with my parents, it will only be me. I am getting to hell out of here, and you can sit there in your underwear and rot for all I care. I knew the night I married you I was making the biggest mistake of my life, and you just proved it beyond a shadow of a doubt."

Ray lunged up from his chair and backhanded her across the face before she had any idea what he was going to do. He hit her so forcibly that she struck the wall by the door, and at the same time, he yelled at her. "You will do what ever I tell you to do and don't you forget it. You aren't going anywhere without my permission Bitch. Do I make myself clear?" He said as he held her face in his hand squeezing her cheeks together, then he suddenly let her go.

Just as Ray turned to sit back down in his chair, Cassandra jerked open the door and bolted out in the pelting rain and started running as fast as she could towards her parent's trailer. Half way there she stopped short, she couldn't let her parents see her like this, she was afraid her father would go and confront Ray, and beat the hell out of him for hitting her.

She couldn't stand the thought that her father could possibly even go to jail for what he might do to Ray on her account. She remembered what her father had told her on her wedding night. He had begged her not to marry Ray as he was no good, and asked her not to go through with the wedding for fear that she would live to regret it. "Oh God what am I going to do!" She was too proud to go to her parents and admit that she had made such a terrible mistake, and she certainly couldn't ever let her father know that Ray had hit her, for fear of the consequences. Slowly Cassandra turned around and started walking back to the apartment. But when she got to the door she was afraid to go in for fear that Ray might still be in a temper.

By this time Cassandra was soaked clear through to the skin, she knew she just had to get somewhere dry and out of this horrible down pour. She hurried over to her car and jumped in, quickly locking the doors behind her. She huddled there on the front seat of the car in her wet clothes trying to figure out what she should do about all her problems. Exhausted she fell into a troubled sleep.

*　*　*

CASSANDRA AWOKE JUST AS dawn was breaking; she felt terrible, and was cramped and wrinkled from sleeping in her wet clothes all night. For a few minutes, she just sat there, thinking about all that had happened in the past two weeks. She was horrified to realize what she had let herself in for when she had married Ray. If only she could go to her parents and ask them to help her get out of this mess, but in her heart she knew her pride would never allow her to admit to them that she had made this terrible mistake. She decided that she had made her bed, and now she would have to lie in it no matter what the cost was to her. She simply couldn't ever tell her parents the truth about the relationship she had with Ray.

*　*　*

AS CASSANDRA SAT THERE watching the sun come up she knew that she was going to have to try and talk to Ray and see if they could find a solution to their problems because in her heart she just knew that she couldn't continue living like they were . There must be some excuse for Ray's violent behavior. Was he feeling guilty because he couldn't find a job, and was possibly striking out at her because of that guilt? Somehow all this had to be her fault, there simply wasn't any other explanation.

*　*　*

CASSANDRA STEPPED FROM THE car and walked over to the apartment, just as she slipped inside she noticed that Ray was getting up. He walked over to her and tried to take her into his arms. But Cassandra quickly stepped beyond his reach the fear plainly showing in her eyes.

"Come here baby, I'm sorry as hell about last night, and I promise it won't ever happen again. I know I never should have hit you honey, I just lost my temper. Come on Cassy baby, say you forgive me, I love you baby, and I know we can work this out somehow, only you have to give me a chance."

As Cassandra backed away from him, she said. "No Ray, I don't want you to ever touch me again. I can't stand living like this anymore. The house is always a mess, and you never lift a finger to help me, all you ever do is sit there in front of the television and drink beer that we really can't afford while I am at work every day. Every time I say something to you that you don't like, you seem to think that just because we are married that gives you the right to knock me around any time the notion strikes you. Well let me tell you something, that's not my idea of marriage Ray."

As soon as the words left her mouth, she knew that she had said the wrong thing again. She could see the rage boiling up inside Ray. When he started to reach for her, she made a dash through the bedroom door, quickly slammed the door shut and locked it behind her. She knew she had to get out of these wrinkled damp clothes. She quickly grabbed the first dress she came to and franticly started to change her clothes. All the time she could hear Ray banging on the bedroom door, yelling at her. "If you don't unlock this damn door Cassandra I'm going to break it down." He raged.

Cassandra was terrified that Ray would break the door down before she could get her clothes changed. Quickly she rushed to open the window, thanking God that it was a ground floor apartment. She jerked off the screen, and grabbed her purse just as the bedroom door crashed open. Ray made a grab for her as she went out the window and hit the ground making her escape. Jumping up from the ground where she had landed, she made a mad dash for her car. She dived into the front seat snapping the lock on the door, a good thing too because Ray was right behind her. He was so mad, she could see his face starting to turn red, and he was calling her every vile name he could think of, while he was ordering her to unlock the door, or he would smash the window in.

Cassandra quickly started the car and threw it into reverse, as she backed the car away from him, she yelled. "You just stay away from me Ray Cartone; I never want to see you again. I hate you!"

CHAPTER FIVE

W HEN CASSANDRA RETURNED HOME from work that night Ray's car wasn't there, so she knew it would be safe to enter the apartment. When she opened the door, the sight that greeted her almost made her sick. Ray had vented his anger by trashing the entire apartment.

Willing herself not to sit down and cry when she saw what a horrible mess the place was in she got busy cleaning everything up and putting things back into their proper place. All the time she was working she hated the fact that after putting in eight hours on her job she had to come home and find all this extra work to do before she could even sit down and relax for a few minutes. She realized that the only way to solve the problem of this terrible situation she found herself in was to divorce Ray; otherwise, one of these days during one of Ray's horrible rages he would probably kill her. If only she could go and talk to her parents, but she was afraid to do that for fear of what her father might do when he found out how Ray was abusing her. Frank Benning would never stand by and see any woman mistreated, and if the woman was his only daughter, there was no telling what he would do to protect her from a person like Ray. She was so afraid that her father would do something terrible to Ray and end up having to go to jail because of her, and she just couldn't let that happen. So going to her parents was simply out of the question, and not an option. She was just going to have to find someway out of this farce of a marriage by herself, and figure out a way to divorce Ray. If only she had a better job and could make enough money to support herself, and be able to save a little back each week to pay for a divorce. She knew that if she didn't have the rent on the apartment she could afford to pay for a divorce, but she couldn't move back in with her parents, not now that she had been married, it just wouldn't be right. She would just have to find another way.

*　*　*

LATE THAT NIGHT SHE was startled awake when she heard the key unlocking the door, she was terrified at the thought that Ray must have come back. Just as she reached up to turn the lamp on by the bed, Ray walked up to the side of the bed and just stood there smiling down at her as though nothing had happened that morning, and boldly stated.

"Guess what Cassy honey, I finally got lucky today and landed a job with a big construction company that is building a new runway at the airport outside of town." He leaned over and started to reach for Cassandra, but she shied away from him.

"Oh come here baby, I'm not going to hurt you. In fact, I've thought a lot about what I did to you last night, and this morning. I want you to know that I'm sorry as hell about everything. I know what I did was wrong and unforgivable. I just don't know what got into me. I promise you that things will be better between us from now on. It was all just a terrible mistake, and it will never happen again. I promise I will make it up to you. Please just give me another chance baby, don't shut me out honey, I need you." He begged with tears in his eyes.

Cassandra just laid there on the bed, her frightened eyes staring up at him, afraid to speak, shaking her head in a negative motion. She just simply couldn't believe what she was hearing. She finally got up enough courage to speak. "It's no use Ray; it just won't work between us."

"Sure it will baby, just give it a try, you'll see. It's just this damn dinky little apartment, I feel smothered here. Now that I have a good job we can afford to move to a bigger place, somewhere closer to my job. Then as soon as we get on our feet, you can quit your job and just stay home and be a little homemaker. How does that sound to you baby? I only want what's best for my little sweetheart."

Cassandra lay there on the bed looking up at him, hating the fact that she was at such a disadvantage flat on her back with Ray towering over her. She was so afraid that if she didn't agree with his plans then all hell would break loose again, and she didn't like the thought of what he might do to her, so hesitantly she answered. "Okay Ray I'm willing to give you another chance, but only if you promise me that you won't ever hit me again."

From the look on Rays face, she could tell he wasn't too happy about her giving him an ultimatum. As he stood there beside the bed glaring down at her she was so frightened, she was holding her breath and praying that she hadn't said the wrong thing once again.

Relief washed over her when Ray smiled down at her and said. "Okay, okay, I promise. I just don't know what got into me, but I promise you things will be better this time, you just wait and see. Now that I have a good paying job everything is going to be just fine."

* * *

LONG AFTER RAY HAD fallen asleep, Cassandra laid there beside him in the dark wondering if she had done the right thing by agreeing to stay with Ray and give their marriage another chance. Could she really trust him to keep his promise to her? Finally, she fell into a troubled sleep, soon to be awakened by the noise Ray was making banging around the tiny apartment. She glanced at the bedside clock; it was only four o'clock in the morning. She jumped up in bed asking. "Ray what on earth is the matter? Why are you up so early?"

Ray walked over and shoved her back down on the bed, then leaning over her with his face close to hers, he bellowed. "What the hell does it look like I'm doing Bitch? You were the one harping on me to get a job; well I got one, and it so happens that I have to be at work at five o'clock. So shut your damn stupid mouth, and get your ass out of bed and fix me some breakfast, and make it snappy I don't have all day."

Ray grabbed her by the arm and jerked her off the bed, as Cassandra started to step past him to go to the tiny kitchenette, Ray suddenly backhanded her and sent her sprawling back across the bed. He stood there by the bed glaring down at her with hate-filled eyes, and Cassandra thought that he was going to hit her again. All of a sudden, he turned on his heel, and grabbed up his jacket from the chair. As he opened the door to leave, he glanced back over his shoulder. "Forget the damn breakfast Bitch; I'll buy myself something along the way." Then he barged out the door slamming it behind him.

* * *

CASSANDRA JUMPED OFF THE bed and ran to the window to be sure he really was leaving, and not just pulling some trick on her. When she saw his pickup driving away, she was so relieved that her knees buckled and she slowly slid down the wall to the floor and started crying. She knew in her heart that things were never going to change, Ray had already broken the promise he made to her only a few hours ago. Never in her whole life had she ever felt so alone and confused. She knew she had to leave, and never look back, but where could she go that Ray wouldn't find her? She only knew that her job didn't pay enough for her to support herself. She didn't have enough money to leave town, and staying here in the city Ray would just find her and bring her back. She couldn't go to her parents and borrow some money from them because then she would have to tell them about Ray. Cassandra felt trapped in this farce of a marriage, knowing she had no one in the world that she could turn to for help. Too afraid to tell her parents about how badly Ray treated her for fear of what her father would do if he ever found out that Ray was abusing her. There wasn't a doubt in her mind that her father would kill Ray, and all because of her stupid pride. She should have said no when she had the chance, instead of trusting Ray to keep his promise.

Not that Cassandra cared a hoot what happened to Ray, she just didn't want to see her father go to jail on her account. She wished desperately that she had never gotten herself into this mess in the first place. She never should have married Ray to begin with, when in her heart she knew it was the wrong thing to do because she didn't love him; and now she knew beyond a shadow of a doubt that she would never be able to love such a mean and hateful person no matter what. "Stop it Cassandra!" She screamed aloud to herself. "Get a grip on yourself girl and stop crying like a baby, and start trying to figure out a way to get your-self out of this impossible situation."

My God, thought Cassandra, now I'm talking to myself, I must be slowly going out of my mind. Gently she eased herself up off the floor; her face was throbbing from where Ray had backhanded her. She decided to take a shower, when she entered the bathroom and looked in the mirror to see how badly she was hurt, she almost passed out when she saw all the blood from her split lip, and a large bruise was already starting to form on her cheek around her eye. It crossed Cassandra's mind to stay home from work today, but that idea was out of the question, she needed the money.

While Cassandra was in the shower, her mind was racing trying to figure out how she could cover up the nasty bruise and her split lip so everyone at the office wouldn't know that Ray had hit her. If anyone should ask her what happened she would have to give some kind of excuse. She really hated the fact that not only did Ray beat her, now she would have to lie to her friends to cover up for him. That left an ugly taste in her mouth, because she wasn't in the habit of lying to people.

* * *

SOMEHOW, CASSANDRA MANAGED TO make it through the day without too many people asking her questions. It had been one of the longest days of her life, not knowing that her troubles were only just beginning.

*　　*　　*

WHEN CASSANDRA ARRIVED HOME from work that night, she saw Ray's pickup; she thought he must have got off work early. When she entered the apartment and saw all the mess, and Ray sitting in front of the television drinking beer, she was so angry that she lost her temper.

"I don't believe this Ray; you must have been home all day from the looks of things around here. What happened to the good job you told me you had?"

"Damn it get off my back Cassy, I've had a rough day. The boss fired me almost before I got started. Who the hell needs their damn job anyway, I told them they could stick it up their ass." He roared tipping the beer bottle up to his mouth.

"For your information Ray, just in case you haven't realized it yet, you need their damn job to help out around here. I don't make enough money to pay the bills, and rent on what I bring home, much less pay for all the beer you guzzle every day. I'm getting pretty damn tired of supporting you while you sit around on your lazy ass doing nothing, and the only thanks I get from you for my efforts, is getting the shit knocked out of me every time I turn around So either you get a job, and keep it. Or you get your sorry ass out of here, and stay out!" Cassandra realized she may have said too much, but she was not going to back down, so she braced herself for whatever Ray might do. Instead of becoming extremely angry, he surprised her.

"Just don't you worry your pretty little head about it, okay? We'll do just fine because for your information I've figured out a way to solve our problems baby." He fired back at her.

"How?" She sneered. "The rent is due and there's hardly any food in the house."

Lowering his voice Ray said smugly. "We'll just move out of this dump and go live with your folks, that way there won't be any rent to pay period, and they damn sure won't let their darling daughter starve."

"No way Ray, we've been over all this before and we definitely are not going to move in with my parents. If you remember the last time we had this same discussion, I made it very clear that there would be **no us** moving in with my parents, it would be only **me**, and you can go straight to hell for all I care!"

Ray jumped up, making a grab for Cassandra, but she yanked open the door, and calmly said. "Go ahead and hit me Ray if that's your intention, only this time my father will hear me scream, and that will be the last time you hit me, or anyone else."

As Ray strode through the open door shoving Cassandra aside, he made a parting threat. "I'm getting to hell out of this damn hole, but rest assured I'll be back, after all you are my dear little wife so just don't think for a single minute that you have gotten away with anything."

"Good! You go ahead and leave Ray, and stay away, and don't bother to come back because I don't want you anywhere near me ever again, it's over!" She hissed at him then slammed the door in his face and shoved the dead bolt home. All the time fear coursed through her, afraid he would kick the door down to get at her.

⋆　　⋆　　⋆

RAY STAYED AWAY ALL night, and hadn't returned by the time Cassandra had to leave for work. She just hoped that meant that he was gone for good. At the end of the day as she was preparing to leave work for the day, her boss called her into his office and asked if she would mind staying overtime to type up a response to an urgent letter he had just received by special delivery. She quickly agreed to stay, as she knew it would mean extra money on her paycheck.

When she finally arrived home, she saw Rays pickup parked in front of the apartment, her first thought was to turn around and leave, but where would she go, this was the only home she had right now, for better or worse. When Cassandra entered the apartment her eyes took in the clutter everywhere, and as usual, Ray was sitting in front of the television with a beer in his hand. She just could not believe it; they were back to square one. Nothing had changed. She could feel the anger raging inside of her, so she decided to just walk past him and not say a single word. As she walked past him, he suddenly reached out and grabbed her by the wrist, jerking her around to face him, and yelled at her.

"Where the hell have you been slut? You're two hours late!"

Cassandra, shocked by Ray's accusation, just ignored him, and pulled free from his grasp. Then ran into the bedroom, slammed the door shut and locked it. Ray started pounding on the door yelling at her. "You little tramp, who the hell have you been screwing around with behind my back?"

Cassandra couldn't believe her ears; this was the first time she had ever been late getting home from work. "Just go away Ray, and leave me alone." She responded through the closed door.

The quiet was deafening as she sat there on the bed wondering what Ray was going to do next. When she heard the front door slam shut, she knew that Ray had left, and she heaved a deep sigh of relief.

Chapter Six

Ray had been gone for almost two weeks, and Cassandra had no idea where he was, and could care less, just as long as he stayed away from her. She was starting to relax, and had settled into life on her own without Ray, and she found that she liked it very much. She couldn't get over the fact of how great it was, to come home from work every night and find her house nice and clean. Just the way she had left it when she went to work. It was wonderful not having someone there to yell at her the minute she stepped in the door, and knock her around for no reason at all. She sure didn't miss Ray, or his abuse.

Every night after she finished her meager supper she would wash up the few dishes. Then she sat down at the table and tried to work out a budget, hoping to somehow figure out a way that she could make ends meet, and still be able to save enough money so she could pay for a divorce from Ray. She finally arrived at the conclusion that she would have to find some sort of part time job. With what she brought home from her regular job, she would have enough money to pay the rent and what few bills she had. In addition, if she really scrimped, she just might be able to save around twenty dollars a week; it would take months before she would have enough money to pay for her divorce. However, if she could find a part time job then all that money could go towards the divorce and shorten the time considerably.

When Cassandra crawled into bed that night she really felt good about herself, she finally had a plan, and a goal to reach, and "Hopefully" life would be less stressful for her from now on.

*　　*　　*

SEVERAL WEEKS LATER JUST as Cassandra was preparing for bed there was a knock on the door, she tensed up and called out. "Who is it?" When she heard Rays voice as he identified himself she froze for a second. At that moment, she was happy that she had the good sense to have the locks changed on the door when Ray had not returned the day after he left. She shook off her fear knowing that the new locks made her feel secure for the first time since she had married Ray. Taking a deep breath she walked over to the door, but opened it only as far as the dead bolt chain would allow. Ray was standing there on the step with a big grin on his face acting as though he had only gone down to the nearest store for a pack of cigarettes.

"What do you want Ray? It's late and I was just going to bed." She stated flatly.

"I want to talk to you baby, let me in so I can tell you the good news."

Cassandra shook her head in a negative way, not trusting Ray for a single minute, as long as he was outside, and she was inside, she felt safe. No way was she going to let him in the house. "No Ray, it's just no use, we've been over all this before. I have finally started to get my life back to normal again, and I happen to like things the way they are now. So please just go away and leave me alone."

When Cassandra started to close the door, Ray stuck his foot in the crack to prevent her from closing it. "No wait baby; you haven't even heard what I have to tell you. Please just open the door like a good girl and we can sit down and talk like two adults. I just know that things will be better this time, I promise you." He pleaded with her.

Cassandra didn't feel like she could trust him enough to open the door, so she just stood there not saying anything. How many times had she heard this sorry line before? Taking a deep breath, she calmly told him. " Do you really believe that you can knock the hell out of me, take off for almost six weeks, then show up on my door step in the middle of the night, and expect me to open the door and welcome you back with open arms like nothing in the world ever happened? Well the answer is not only **no,** but **hell no!** You can just go back to where ever you've been staying these past weeks, because I don't want anything more to do with you. All I really want is for you to just leave me alone, and stay out of my life!" While Cassandra had been, talking Ray had relaxed being so sure of himself, that he had removed his foot from the crack in the door, and Cassandra quickly slammed the door shut shoving the dead bolt home.

"Oh come on Cassy baby, will you please just open the door." He pleaded. "I just want to talk to you, and then I'll leave if that's what you want me to do. I promise. I won't ever hurt you again, I love you Cassy, and I just want to start over. I want us to be together again, only this time we will do it right. Please believe me baby, I need you in my life because it's no good without you."

Still Cassandra remained silent, thinking of all the other times Ray had said these very same words. She refused to open the door because Ray had tricked her before with his sweet talk and promises, and she wasn't about to give him the opportunity to do so again.

"Look honey, I know you must think badly of me, but I just want you to know that I've really given this a lot of thought. I realize what I did to you was wrong, and I can't begin to tell you how sorry I am for what I did. Please baby, just give me another chance, and I'll prove to you that I'm a changed man. I have a great job now, and I'm making real good money. What do you say babe, will you please forgive me, and give me another chance to make things right between us? Please baby, just open the door so we can talk. I promise that's all I want to do." He begged.

Finally, Cassandra told him. "Ray it's very late, and I really have to get to bed. I need some time to think about this before I can give you an answer. So will you please just go away?"

For some reason Ray decided not to pressure her on the issue, and he quickly agreed to give her the time she asked for to think things over. "Okay baby, anything you say. How about me coming over Saturday night, say around seven, and I'll take you out to some nice place for dinner and we can discuss it then?"

Cassandra agreed to the dinner arrangements for Saturday night. She leaned back against the door listening for the sound of his pickup as he drove away. Thinking she must be crazy even to consider taking him back again. She had been afraid to tell her parents that they had split up, and she was planning to get a divorce. So when her parents had asked where Ray was, she had told them that he away trying to find work. She hated to lie to her parents, but she couldn't tell them she and Ray were separated, because then she would have to tell them why, and she was so afraid of what her father might do if he ever found out the truth about how Ray treated her.

Cassandra wondered if perhaps during their time of separation that Ray had come to his senses, and finally realized how wrong he had been in his treatment of her, and maybe things really would be different this time now that he had a good job that he liked, and was making decent wages. Perhaps all their problems stemmed from the fact that she had a job, and he didn't. She even considered that it could be some kind of an ego thing with him. She had heard that people sometimes did peculiar things when they thought that their life was a failure. Whatever the reason, Cassandra decided it would be best to wait until after their meeting to make a final decision.

*　　*　　*

RAY ARRIVED FOR THEIR date Saturday night promptly at seven o'clock on the dot. He took her to a splendid restaurant for dinner, one of those places that had dim lights, and didn't show any prices on the menu. He even ordered champagne, and all evening he treated her as if she was really someone special. Cassandra felt like

Cinderella, with all the charm Ray was lavishing on her. In fact, he was treating her like the way he had when they first met, before he became so possessive. He bestowed every consideration on her, even letting her choose what she wanted to eat. Over dinner, he told her about his new job, what sort of work he was doing. About his big beautiful apartment, and how empty it was without her. He let her digest that for a few minutes, then asked her if she had reached a decision about them getting back together, and trying to make their marriage work. Once again, promising her that this time things would be quite different. He even went so far as to tell her that if she would try it for a few months, then if she still wasn't completely happy then he would comply with her wishes, and agree to a peaceful divorce and get out of her life for ever.

Cassandra finally agreed to give their marriage another chance, to find out if they could possibly work out their problems. She received his assurance that if it didn't work out, they would just go their separate ways; just make a clean break with no strings attached.

In the back of her mind Cassandra had the uneasy feeling that she was about to make another terrible mistake. She just couldn't find it in her heart to believe that Ray would really keep his promise.

* * *

WHEN RAY TOOK CASSANDRA home they agreed that since the next day was Sunday, and they both had a day off work that he would come over early and help her pack and move her things to his apartment, since it was larger than the tiny apartment she had, plus it was a lot closer to his job.

* * *

DURING THE NEXT THREE months, everything seemed to be going along real good. She was happy because there hadn't been any harsh words between them, not even a single argument between them. One night when Ray came home from work it all started to change when he told her what his plans were.

"I've been thinking about this all day long baby, and I've decided now is a good time for you to quit your job, and stay home and just be a regular little housewife. Do some of the things that you never had time to do while you are working. I figure we can get along fine on what I bring home every week, and your measly little check won't even be missed." He sneered.

"But I like my job Ray; I don't want to give it up just yet. Besides there just isn't enough for me to do around here to keep busy. I would simply go crazy being cooped up all day in the apartment, and not being around other people." She hoped that he would understand her feelings and let it pass. However, that wasn't going to happen, she could tell from the look on Ray's face that he wasn't too happy with her answer. Then she noticed his face was starting to turn red, and the vanes in his neck were starting to stand out, she was afraid that he was about to blow a fuse. Then he replied in a harsh voice that she remembered from the many times before when things didn't go the way he wanted them to. "You will quit your job tomorrow like I said Cassandra, or else I will personally go down and tell your boss for you. Do I make myself clear Cassandra?"

"Ray don't do this to me, I need my job. If we can't solve our problems, we could end up getting a divorce anyway. Which could very well happen from the way you are acting right at this moment? I simply can't take that chance, because good jobs are hard to find these days, and I've had this job long before I ever married you, and I have no intention of quitting my job until I know for sure that I won't need it."

For a minute, she thought that all hell was about to break loose as Ray stood there glaring at her, and then all of a sudden, he got a big grin on his face. "Sure baby if that's what you want to do. I just thought you would be happy about not having to go to work every day. After all, you've worked hard all your life, and I just figured this would give you a chance to relax and have a little time to yourself. Go shopping, or anything else you want to do. Take life easy for a change." He paused before he said. "Besides we have been getting along so well the past few months that I figured you had given up the idea of us ever splitting up."

Cassandra was afraid that by her refusing to give up her job, and letting him be the sole breadwinner, then it would be another threat to his ego, and soon all hell would break out again, so she reconsidered. "Okay Ray, I'll talk to Mr. Garret when I go to work tomorrow, and give him my two week notice."

"Great baby, I just knew you would see things my way." He responded smugly.

Cassandra just nodded her head in agreement. Hoping she was not contributing to her long list of mistakes. If things didn't work out for them down the road, she would just have to cross that bridge when she came to it and find herself another job. Maybe if she approached Mr. Garret the right way tomorrow, just maybe she could leave the door open just in case she did need a job sometime in the distant future.

CHAPTER SEVEN

Early the next morning when Cassandra arrived at work, she went straight in to see her boss and told him that she would be leaving in two weeks time. Ray wanted her to quit working to take care of their home. She could tell that Mr. Garret wasn't too happy to hear that she was leaving his employment. When he spoke, he really surprised her.

"Cassandra you are one of the best employees I've ever had working for me. However I must say that every since you married Ray I've seen a tremendous change in you. Before you got married you seemed so vibrant and carefree, always had a smile and a kind word for everyone. But for the past several months I have noticed that you rarely smile, and you pretty much keep to yourself. In fact, you look so unhappy it breaks my heart. You have a haunted look in your eyes that was never there before you married Ray, I wonder why. What terrible thing has happened in your life to cause such a change in such a sweet girl? You don't have to confide in me Cassandra if you don't want to. I just want you to understand that if you ever need someone to talk to you can come to me; my door will always be open for you. I have always had the greatest respect for you Cassandra, you are like my own daughter, and I just want you to know that I will always be here for you if ever you should need me, no matter what." Then he held out his hand and said. "I wish you only good luck Cassandra, and I sincerely hope that everything works out for the best, for your sake. Please remember what I said dear, I'll always be here for you if you ever need me."

Cassandra shook his hand, then threw her arms around his neck and hugged him as tears welled up in her eyes, she whispered. "Thanks Mr. Garret, I will never forget you, or your kind offer; I have made such a terrible mess of my life it's nice to know that I have a place to come back to if I need to."

When she stepped back, he could see the tears shimmering on her long lashes as she told him. "I really do hate to give up my job, but Ray insists." Then she turned and left his office.

*　*　*

SEVERAL MONTHS AFTER CASSANDRA had stopped working, and her parents moved back to Southern California, and her life with Ray had settled into a sort of routine. They seemed to be getting along quite well together, not having any disagreements. In fact, it seemed as though their marriage may be going to work out after all.

Cassandra made sure that their apartment was always kept spotless, she done the washing, and ironing every week, and was always cooking and baking. She had even learned how to make homemade bread. She would do just about anything she could think of that would keep her busy, because she couldn't stand to be idle. She was starting to think that perhaps Ray had changed, they were able to talk about all sorts of things now, and Ray never seemed to let anything she said upset him the way he used to.

Then Cassandra discovered that she was pregnant. She was excited beyond her wildest dreams about the thought of having her very own baby. She could hardly wait for Ray to come home from work that night so she could tell him the good news. All of a sudden, the thought came to her that they had never gotten around to discussing anything about having a family. Ray may not even want children.

Cassandra was afraid to tell Ray because she had no idea how he would react to the news, so she decided to wait a little while before she said anything about the baby, it would give her a chance to feel him out about the prospect of raising a family. Then she could get some idea of what his reactions were likely to be before she just sprang it on him.

*   *   *

TWO WEEKS PASSED BY and still Cassandra hadn't told Ray about the baby. Every time she tried to bring up the subject of children, Ray would skillfully change the subject without answering any of her questions. Therefore, she still had no idea of how he really felt about having a baby. If she didn't find some way to tell him soon about the baby, she wouldn't have to bother, because before long he would be able see for himself when she started to show.

Then she started having morning sickness, she was so sick most of the time that she spent a good part of the day laying down, and her house work was starting to pile up because she was just too sick to keep up with everything. Each day she seemed to get worse, and she had to let more, and more of the household chores go, hoping that she would get through this faze of her pregnancy and feel more like doing something besides throwing up all the time. Most days the morning sickness would ease up around one or two o'clock in the afternoon, then she would hurry around trying to get everything done before Ray got home from work.

Then one day her morning sickness was so extreme that she couldn't even get out of bed because she was so weak. Ray came home early that day because they were rained out on the job, and he found everything just as it had been when he left for work that morning, and Cassandra was nowhere in sight. He flew into a terrible rage and started knocking things off the table and shelves, and calling her every vile name he could think of. Then he yelled at her. "Where the hell are you, you lazy Bitch?"

Cassandra was so weak from hardly eating anything for the past several days because she couldn't retain anything on her stomach, and figured if she just didn't eat she wouldn't get so sick. She moaned when she heard Ray yelling at her, and tried to rise up off the bed, but just wasn't strong enough to do so. About that time Ray burst into the bedroom, ran over to the bed, grabbed Cassandra by the arm, and jerked her off the bed and onto her feet in front of him. At the same time, he started slapping her across first one side of her face, and then the other, all the time yelling at her. "You lazy good for nothing Bitch, think you can lay around the house all day doing nothing. But this time I caught you Bitch. You never expected me to come home early and find out, thought you could get away with it, didn't you Bitch?" He ranted on and on, all the while he continued to slap her.

Cassandra realized how faint she was getting, and she felt her knees starting to buckle under her, so she grabbed onto the front of Rays shirt to keep herself from falling when he finally released his hold on her. She pleaded with him. "Please don't do this to me again Ray. I'm sorry, please don't hit me anymore." She panted. "I'm just so sick I simply couldn't help it." Then she slid the rest of the way to the floor, lying in a crumpled heap at Ray's feet.

"What the hell have you got to be sick about? You're just a lying, lazy Bitch." He raged as he jerked Cassandra off the floor with one hand, and slammed the doubled up fist of his other hand into her stomach as hard as he could, knocking her back down on the floor again.

While Cassandra was grabbing hold of his pants leg trying to pull her self up, she screamed at him. "I'm sick because I'm pregnant with your child Ray!" She was almost on her feet when Ray grabbed hold of her again.

"You rotten lazy Bitch, I never said you could get pregnant. I don't want any lousy brats in my house, so you can just get rid of it." With that out burst, Ray hit her again in her stomach with his doubled up fist, this time knocking her unconscious. Then while she lay in a crumpled heap at his feet he kicked her several times in the mid section just for good measure. Then Ray strode out of the apartment slamming the door shut behind him.

*   *   *

WHEN CASSANDRA REGAINED CONSCIOUSNESS, she had no idea what time it was, she just knew it must be late because the bedroom was dark. She had no idea how long she had been laying on the floor. The apartment was quiet so Ray must have gone out somewhere after he had beaten her so bad. She tried to move but it was difficult because she was in so much pain. As she tried to raise herself up from the floor everything in the room started spinning, and she prayed that she wouldn't pass out again. It was then that she realized that the floor all around her was soaking wet. She wondered where all the water had come from, but it was too dark to see if the roof was leaking. Since she was unable to get up, she started to crawl towards the bathroom. Fatigued from her terrible ordeal, and with considerable pain from all her struggling to crawl, she finally made it to the bathroom, and managed to trace her fingers up the wall and finally found the light switch, and turned on the lights, only to discover that there was blood every where she looked. She panicked, and then started screaming aloud. "Oh please dear God, don't let me die!"

Realizing that she had to try to clean herself up, she managed to drag herself over to the bathtub and run some warm water into it. Then through a lot of painful struggling, she dragged herself into the tub of warm water. By this time, the tears were streaming uncontrollably down her face, for she knew in her heart that she had lost her precious little baby.

Cassandra started to feel faint again, and hoped she wouldn't pass out and drown in the tub of water, wondering if this was what it felt like when you were dieing. "Don't you dare pass out again Cassandra Benning?" She berated herself aloud. Holding onto the side of the tub until the dizziness subsided, and her eyes started to focus again. Then somehow she managed to pull herself out of the tub of water, wondering where in the world her strength was coming from, she just knew that it would be better for her if she passed out on the floor, rather than in a tub full of water.

As Cassandra sat there on the floor beside the tub, she looked in the floor length mirror, shocked by the horror she saw, her face was almost swollen beyond recognition, and both of her eyes were black; and partly swollen shut. No wonder she was having such a hard time trying to see. Her lips were very puffy, and split, blood was still oozing out, and trickling down her chin. The sight of her face almost made her pass out again, but she willed herself to hang on.

Cassandra thought if only they had a phone she could call her parents and beg them to come and get her. But deep down in her heart she knew she could never let her parents see her in this condition. She would just have to manage the best she could by herself and hope for the best. She knew she would eventually have to tell her parents about losing the baby; but she knew beyond a shadow of a doubt she could never tell a living soul how she lost it. If her father ever found out, he wouldn't stop until he had killed Ray for doing this horrible thing to her, and killing his unborn grandchild. The thought of her dear father having to go to jail because of her was more than she could bear, and she started crying again. She would have to keep this to herself for the rest of her life.

Somehow, she just had to leave Ray, but that would have to wait until she was stronger. Right now, what she needed more than anything was some rest. Through sheer need, and determination, she managed to drag herself back to the bed and crawl up on it, as she wrapped the blanket around her, she asked God to let her live, and not punish her for losing her baby. Then just before she lost consciousness again her last prayer was that Ray wouldn't return while she slept.

Chapter Eight

Ray hadn't returned to the apartment by the next morning, so Cassandra had to drive herself to the doctor. When she walked slowly into the office, the nurse took one look at her and ushered her straight through to the examining room where she could wait for the doctor in private and not have everyone staring at her. Cassandra figured the nurse must have explained her condition to the doctor because he came right in to see her.

When Doctor Martin entered the room, he closed the door behind him. She could tell that the sight of her had shocked him, as the color drained from his face. "Good grief Cassandra what in Gods world has happened to you?" Evidently, the nurse had not taken time to explain her full condition to him.

Cassandra sat there trembling, she was afraid to tell the doctor what had really happened to her because she was terrified of what Ray would do to her if he should find out she had told anyone the truth. Putting on a brave face, she valiantly tried to smile as she made up an excuse. "I was playing ball with some of the children in the apartment complex and guess I wasn't too good at it because I fell and landed flat on my face." Cassandra was certain that Doctor Martin didn't believe a single word she had told him when he replied.

"Yeah sure!" He continued with his examination not saying anything to her, and when he was through, he told her politely. "You can get dressed now Cassandra, and when you are ready please come to my private office I would like to talk to you."

*   *   *

WHEN CASSANDRA ENTERED THE doctor's private office and closed the door softly behind her, she knew in her heart what the doctor wanted to talk to her about. Without speaking, she walked over to the chair in front of his desk and sat down.

Doctor Martin looked into her sad little face. "Cassandra there is no easy way for me to tell you this. You know that you have lost your baby, don't you?" He questioned softly.

Cassandra nodded her head yes, and a single tear slid quietly down her swollen face.

"I don't know for sure what happened to you Cassandra, but I have a pretty good idea. I do know that this was not all caused by a fall as you said it was. So would you like to tell me about it?"

Cassandra sat quietly with tears streaming down her face. "No Doctor Martin, it's kind of you to ask, but it wouldn't do any good. It won't bring my baby back." Then she jumped to her feet and ran from his office. She didn't stop running until she reached her car in the parking lot. She got in the car and just sat there staring blankly out the windshield. All she could think about was losing her baby. Her poor little unborn baby who never had a chance at life because it's father had murdered it with his bare hands.

Cassandra had no idea how long she must have sat there in her car, finally she realized she had to do something. Shaking her head to clear her thoughts so she could figure out what she needed to do, she finally decided that the only thing there was for her to do was to leave Ray once and for all, and this time it would be for good, before he killed her, like he did their unborn child. In her heart, she knew that she would never forgive him for what he had done. Not this time, his sweet talk and promises, would never be able to undo, this terrible thing he had done to her and their unborn baby.

Having made her decision she started up the car and headed for home, wishing that she had never quit her job, and hoping against hope that Ray wouldn't be there when she arrived.

* * *

NEVERTHELESS AS LUCK WOULD have it, Ray was home. Cassandra was ready to turn and run in the opposite direction; instead she slowly entered the apartment glancing around expecting Ray to pounce on her the minute she closed the door.

Ray having heard her come in rushed towards her, and she cringed away from him in fear. "Cassy baby what in the hell happened to you? I really have been worried about you every since I came home and saw all the blood all over the bedroom and bathroom. I didn't know what to do, so I just sat here waiting. I figured if you didn't show up pretty soon that I would go down to the office and call the police." Ray tried to take her in his arms, but Cassandra was afraid of him, and she kept backing up until she felt the wall behind her, fear overtook her and she started to scream.

"Don't be afraid of me baby, just tell me who the hell is responsible for this and I will kill the bastard."

Cassandra slowly inched along the wall trying to keep out of his reach, her eyes darting around the room looking for something she could use to protect herself, and her fear of him showed clearly in her eyes as she spoke. "Don't touch me Ray, you are the bastard that needs to be killed, you did this to me Ray, and you brutally killed our poor little unborn baby. For that I will never forgive you Ray as long as I live."

Ray just stood there as if he had no idea what she was talking about, so she continued while she had his attention. "I tried to tell you the reason I was in bed, but you wouldn't listen, you just kept hitting me, and when I told you I was pregnant you were in such a rage that you started punching me with your fists in my stomach until I passed out. You killed our baby Ray, and left me laying on the floor alone to die, bleeding to death. And you never done a single thing to try and help me."

It was hard for her to go on but she knew she must. "You are an animal Ray; you killed our baby, and nearly killed me as well. But you won't ever get another chance to do this to me again Ray, because I'm leaving you just as soon as I can get a few of my things. I want a divorce Ray; I just can't live this way any longer, you have made my life a living hell, and killed our baby, and all your sweet talk and promises will never bring my baby back."

Ray just stood staring at her with a doubting look on his face as if he couldn't believe what she was saying. Then he slowly put his arms around her and drew her close to him softly crooning to her as if she was a small child. "Oh baby I'm so sorry if I done this to you, I must have been out of my mind. I never really meant to hurt you. Please forgive me honey. Promise me you won't leave me. You know how much I need you in my life. Baby, you are all I've got in this world, and I swear I will never hurt you again as long as I live. You have to believe me baby, just promise me you won't leave me." He begged as the tears rolled down his face. This time he seemed genuinely sincere in his apology.

Cassandra stood stiffly in his embrace, wanting so desperately to be anywhere but near him. She was afraid to move for fear that he would strike out at her again, and her body was already so battered and bruised, that she knew she simply couldn't endure another one of his tyrannical rages. She decided it would be best for now to let him think she believed his lies and meaningless promises.

Ray felt confident that he was winning her over to his way of thinking. He didn't realize that Cassandra was petrified and scared out of her wits. He continued in a cajoling voice. "Guess I had a little too much to drink, I was pretty upset honey because I had just gotten fired from my job. And after a few drinks I was already half out of my mind by the time I got home, and then when I couldn't find you, and saw that none of the house work was done, I guess I just lost it. Then when you screamed at me that you were pregnant that threw me over the edge, and I just snapped. Honest baby, I swear I never even realized what I was doing. I felt smothered, and guess I struck out at the first thing I came to, and it just happened to be you." He stopped talking and gazed down at her, she could see the horrified look on his face when he actually noticed for the first time how really swollen her face and eyes were, and all the bruises that were starting to turn purple. Cassandra's face looked very much as if it had just been run through a meat grinder.

"God Cassy you've got to believe me, I love you so much baby, please say you will forgive me, and give me another chance so that I can make it all up to you. I swear I will never hit you again baby, I promise." He pleaded in a tearful voice as he hugged her close to his chest.

Still Cassandra said nothing, so Ray started to plead with her again. "Please just have a little patience with me sweetheart, we can work this out. I just know we can if you will only give it another chance. Please, please baby, promise me you won't leave me. I love you so much."

Cassandra pulled as far back from him as he would allow her to, looking up at him she finally spoke. "It's no use Ray, I simply can't live this way any longer, never knowing from one day to the next when you will lose your temper again. This time you killed our baby, and nearly killed me too. Next time I may not be so lucky to survive. I can't trust you to keep your word, and I simply refuse live the rest of my life in constant fear."

Ray refused to accept this for a final answer and continued to talk as though he hadn't heard a single word that she had said. "Listen baby while I tell you the great news I've got. I called my old man this morning from a pay phone in the bar down the street. He said there's a real good job waiting for me on a ranch just outside of Hollister, with a furnished house that goes with the job. In addition, we can have all the milk, eggs and produce we want for our own use, free, it goes with the job. Cassy honey do you realize this is the break that we have been looking for. This is a chance for us to start all over again as though nothing ever happened. What do you say baby, will you take this chance? Go with me, and give our marriage another try?"

Cassandra stood as though in a trance, afraid to disagree with Ray, for fear she would say the wrong thing and cause him to go off on her again. Ray continued trying to convince her that going with him to Southern California was the right thing to do, seeming to forget what he had done to her and their unborn child, as though it had happened to someone else. "I know things will work out this time honey. I really do need you baby, so please just say yes. I promise you won't ever be sorry. I love you baby, and I just can't stand the thought of not having you by my side."

Cassandra knew that she should say no, and run like hell in the opposite direction. She also knew that without a job, and some money; there simply wasn't anything else she could do right now except agree to stay with Ray and hope for a miracle., Her parents had transferred back to Hollister a couple of months ago, and the only way she could get back to where her parents were was to stay with Ray, and make the move with him. Then if he went back on his word again and started abusing her, at least she would be close to her parents and could ask them for help, even if she had to swallow her pride to do it. In her heart, Cassandra knew it was going to be awful hard for her to pretend that she was willing to try one more time to make this farce of a marriage work. Nevertheless, if she wanted to get back to where her parents lived she would have to agree to give their marriage one more chance. If it doesn't work out this time, then she will just have to cross that bridge when she came to it.

Looking up at Ray she hoped that she was convincing enough when she told him her decision. "Okay Ray, I'll agree to give you one more chance, but I warn you, if you ever do this to me again, I promise you there will be no more chances. I will leave you in a heartbeat, and never look back! In fact wild horses won't be able to make me change my mind next time."

A look of anger passed over Ray's face for a brief second, then he must have had second thoughts, he put his arms around her, hugged her up next to him, and whispered softly. "Thanks baby, you won't ever be sorry, I can promise you that. I'll make it all up to you honey, and you will forget this ever happened. I love you Cassy with all my heart."

Cassandra could hardly endure his embrace, and hearing all his sweet talk and lies all over again made her want to throw up. If Ray thought for one minute that she would ever be able to forget what he had done to her and their unborn child, he was sadly mistaken. Right then she vowed that she would never forget that precious innocent baby, and he would never have her forgiveness, ever!

CHAPTER NINE

Cassandra and Ray moved to the ranch located just outside of Hollister about ten miles from where her parents were in the spring of 1958, hoping to start over. Their life seemed to be going along rather smoothly for the past few months; they hadn't had a disagreement of any kind since their reconciliation. Ray really did appear to be a changed man. He seemed content with the work he was doing on the ranch. He often talked about how he would like to save enough money to buy a ranch of his own someday.

Cassandra even managed to save back a little money out of Ray's paycheck every week trying to build a nest egg for the ranch that Ray was always talking about owning down the road. He had even stopped drinking, and treated her with the utmost respect, never once getting angry with her the way he did in Sacramento. He even let her drive into town two or three times a month to visit her parents, he rarely ever went to see her parents with her, using the excuse that he was too busy on the ranch to get away.

Rays parents came a couple of times on a Sunday to see him, but they always done their visiting outside with him alone, and never invited her to come out and join them, using some pretext to get Ray off by himself away from her, but she really didn't mind because she wasn't too fond of Rays parents anyway. Therefore, she just stayed out of their way.

* * *

THEN JUST BEFORE THEIR second anniversary, Cassandra discovered that she was pregnant again. She was so excited about the coming baby she was beside herself, bursting with happiness she could hardly wait for Ray to come home so that she could share this wonderful news with him. She decided that she would wait and tell him after their evening meal when he would be relaxed, and hopefully be more receptive to the news that he would be a father in a few months. The doctor told her that her baby was due in mid July, so that would give Ray plenty of time to get used to the idea of having a baby in their life.

* * *

SOON AS DINNER WAS over Ray went into the living room and turned on the television, then settled back in his easy chair while Cassandra cleared the table and washed the dishes. When everything was finished Cassandra went in to join Ray, waiting patiently for a commercial because she knew better than to interrupt Ray's program. Soon as the commercial started, Cassandra told Ray about the coming baby. However, as soon as the words died on her lips she could tell the news had really upset him. Instead of flying into a rage as she had feared, Ray never uttered a single word, he just glared at her as he stood up and walked out of the room, and then she heard the front door slam shut behind him as he left the house.

When she heard his pickup start up and he revved the engine a couple of times, she ran to look out the front room window, just in time to see him roar off down the dirt lane leaving a cloud of dust in his wake. Cassandra hoped that when he had a few minutes alone to adjust to the news of the coming baby, that he would accept it and return in a good mood. Lord, she prayed, please don't let Ray turn violent again as he had done when they were living in Sacramento. She couldn't stand the thought of losing another baby in a blood bath, like the last time she had gotten pregnant. This time she might not be lucky enough to survive such an ordeal.

* * *

AROUND MIDNIGHT CASSANDRA GREW tired of waiting up for Ray to return and she decided to go to bed. However, she was afraid to go to sleep for worrying about how Ray would be when he finally did come home. So she just lay there in the darkness of the bedroom afraid to even close her eyes.

It was around two in the morning when she heard Ray's pickup return. She lay there in the darkness trembling, listening for him to enter the house. Several minutes passed before she heard the squeak of the rusty hinges when the front door opened. She knew that Ray had been drinking from all the noise he was making. Finally, he stumbled into the bedroom, and when he got to the side of the bed, he just stood there glaring down at her. She started to tremble more as fear took over her body, she could almost feel his deep seated anger reaching out at her there in the darkness of the bedroom, so she pretended that she was asleep hoping that he wouldn't jerk her out of bed and give her another pounding like before. Several heart-stopping minutes passed and she prayed that Ray wouldn't touch her. God must have heard her silent prayers, because without a single word Ray turned around and stumbled from the bedroom.

Almost immediately, she heard a loud crash coming from the direction of the living room. She started to tremble more visibly and was afraid to move, she was holding her breath for fear that Ray could hear her ragged breathing, and come back. Oh God, she thought, please don't let this be happening again.

The house was quiet, too quiet. Finally when she couldn't stand not knowing what was going on any longer, she silently crept out of bed, tiptoed over to the bedroom door, and peered out into the living room, all the time holding her breath for fear Ray would hear her. She could see Ray passed out on the sofa, and the glass lamp lay broken on the floor. That must have been the reason for the loud noise she heard earlier.

Cassandra was relieved to know that the danger had passed for now, and without making a sound she silently crept back to her bed, and thanked God for sparing her from Ray's violence. After awhile she finally drifted off into a troubled sleep.

* * *

THE NEXT MORNING WHEN Cassandra woke up, she had an eerie feeling; the house was extremely quiet for some reason. Holding her breath she walked into the living room, but there was no sign of Ray, she checked out the other rooms carefully, but he wasn't anywhere in the house. Cassandra walked over to the front room window and looked out on the driveway, there was no sign of Ray, and his pickup was nowhere in sight. She didn't know what to think, she only knew that in her heart she was glad he was gone. She didn't even wonder where he had gone; she simply hoped that he would never come back.

* * *

THREE MONTHS PASSED AND Cassandra hadn't saw Ray, or had a single word from him since the night she had told him about the baby. Rays boss had stopped by a week ago and told her that he couldn't hold Ray's job open for him any longer, and that he had hired another man to replace him. He told her that he needed the house for the new man, and his family. He asked Cassandra to pack up her belongings, and vacate the premises within seven days.

* * *

CASSANDRA HAD BEEN BUSY packing for the past five days, all the time wondering where she would go, and still didn't have a clue how she was going to be able to move all the boxes by herself in her present condition, but somehow she would manage to get out in the allotted time. Cassandra looked around, saw that she had just about finished the packing. Except for the few item's she would need to keep out until she found a place to move. She only had two days left before the new people arrived. She decided that she would take a little break and rest while she had a cup of coffee.

While she was pouring herself a cup of the fresh coffee, she heard a vehicle drive up in front of the house. She ran to the front room window and looked out, afraid that Ray had returned. The fear vanished when she saw her father coming up the front walk to the door. Excitement bubbled over in her at the sight of her beloved father. She jerked open the front door and practically knocked him down when she hurled herself into his arms knowing that he was the answer to her prayers.

"Oh daddy; am I ever glad to see you. Come on in and have a cup of coffee with me, I just made a fresh pot. Bet you could smell it, huh?" She teased.

"You look real good honey, putting on a little weight too, bout time, you were too skinny to suit me." Frank said smiling down at her.

"Well I am gaining some around the middle daddy; looks like you will be a grandpa around the middle of July." She responded proudly patting her stomach.

"Oh Cassy, you've made me so proud. I really am going to be a grandpa at last? I can hardly wait. How come you haven't told your mother and me about the new arrival?"

"I wanted it to be a surprise, and was just waiting to tell you and mother at the same time, guess my secret is out now though." She apologized.

As Frank walked through to the kitchen, he noticed all the packed boxes stacked all over the place. "What's going on around here Cassy? Looks like you and Ray are in the process of moving."

"Well that's partly right daddy, I don't know about Ray, but I certainly am in the process of moving; only I haven't a clue of where I will move to." She said sadly.

When Frank saw the sadness in her eyes, he knew something just wasn't right in his daughter's world. "Are you okay baby?" He asked gently as he placed his hands on her shoulders and looked her directly in the eyes.

Seeing the worried look on her fathers face pulled at Cassandra's heart and the tears welled up in her eyes. She almost broke down and told her father everything, but instead she said. "I don't really know dad, when I told Ray that I was expecting another baby, he went into town and got stinking drunk. He came home around two o'clock in the morning and passed out on the sofa. When I woke up the next morning he was gone, and I haven't seen or heard from him since. That was three months ago. Mr. Lancing has been kind enough to let me stay on here until he was able to find a replacement for Ray. He just hired a new man, and he gave me a week to move out. I only have a couple days left before I have to be out of here." She explained truthfully. "Ray never even had the decency to let Mr. Lansing know that he was quitting, so I don't know if he planned to leave, or what. I have no idea if Ray has been in an accident, or what has happened to him. It's as though he has just vanished off the face of the earth."

Frank Benning put his arms around his daughter and hugged her close to his chest, patting her on the back saying. "There, there honey, I'm sure everything will be alright. And when Ray comes back I'm sure he'll be able to explain everything to you."

Standing there in the protection of her fathers arms was more than Cassandra could bear "Oh daddy, I'm not even sure if I want Ray to come back. This isn't the first time Ray has pulled a disappearing act. He's done it a few times in the past."

Frank was surprised to hear Cassandra make that comment. "What do you mean by that remark Cassy, are you and Ray having some problems?"

"I'm not sure daddy, it was just so embarrassing when Mr. Lancing came by the week after Ray left to find out why he wasn't showing up for work, and I had to tell him that I didn't even know where my own husband was. He has given Ray every opportunity by holding the job open for him, and has let me stay here rent-free. However, he's finally hired a new man to replace Ray. He came by a few days ago and gave me notice to vacate the house by Friday as he needed it for his new foreman, and that's the day after tomorrow."

No matter how hard she tried, she couldn't hold back the tears any longer. Once again, her life was falling apart.

Finally, Cassandra managed to get a control of her emotions, she stopped crying and reached for a tissue from the box on the counter and blew her nose. In a choked up voice she wailed. "Oh daddy what am I going to do? I don't even have a place to move to."

"Everything will be okay honey, I promise." Frank assured her. "Come on now dry you eyes like a good girl, we'll figure out something. You know your mother and I will do all we can to help you." Frank hugged her close again trying to comfort her, and he was glad that Cassy couldn't see into his eyes, because right at that moment if he could get his hands on Ray, he would probably beat him to a pulp.

"I promise I won't be any trouble dad; I do have a little money that I have been saving back for the baby that Ray doesn't know about. It should be enough to pay rent on a place for a couple of months until I can find a job."

Wanting to relieve his daughter from anymore stress than she was already under in her condition, he suggested a solution to her problems. "Don't you worry Cassy honey, daddy is here and everything's going to be okay. While you finish your packing I'm going to go talk to a man I know who has a small trailer for sale in the park where your mother and I live. I'll see what kind of a deal I can make with him for you to buy his trailer. That way you will be close to your mother and me, so we can help you out when you need us."

Knowing how proud and independent his daughter was, Frank knew that with the coming baby, Cassandra would never consent to moving back in with him and Nora, so this trailer idea was the only way to go, and he would secure that trailer for her if he had to buy it himself.

Frank figured he had better get started for town, so giving his daughter a big hug he said. "Now you stop worrying honey, you just leave everything to your old daddy, so dry your eyes and finish your packing, and I'll be back before you know it. Just think by tonight you will be the proud owner of your very own trailer house." Kissing Cassandra on the forehead, and telling her once more not to worry, Frank left the house and walked outside and got in his pickup, and drove away, waving to Cassandra standing in the doorway watching him leave with tears running down her face.

* * *

AS FRANK BENNING DROVE to town he thought about his daughter, and how proud and independent she was, and he knew that what ever he done to help her, had to be done in such a way that she didn't think that he was trying to run her life. After all, she was a married woman now and expecting his grandchild. She had the right to make her own decisions. He also knew that right now Cassandra needed someone strong to lean on, even though she would be the very last one to admit it. She sure as hell deserved better than what she was getting from Ray.

Suddenly Frank banged his fist down on the steering wheel, and vented his anger aloud. "Damn that no good son- of-a-bitch for the way he was treating Cassandra. If I could get my hands on that bastard right now I would beat some sense into him, or know the reason why!"

* * *

EARLY THAT AFTERNOON CASSANDRA's father returned to tell her about the deal he had worked out for her on the trailer house. "Well Cassy looks like you have a place to live in for as long as you want. I made the deal with Tom Hicks on the trailer. Tom wants twenty-five hundred dollars for the trailer, five hundred down, and fifty dollars a month, until the balance is paid. The space rent is only twenty a month and that includes all the utilities. The trailer is twenty-eight feet long, and eight feet wide. It has everything you need including a bathroom. It was in such good condition that I took the liberty of giving Tom the five hundred dollar down payment, and you can hand it back to me when you get on your feet."

Suddenly the weight of all her worries lifted, and for the first time since Ray had left her she could find hope in her heart again knowing that everything really was going to be okay. Smiling she gave her father a big hug hanging on for dear life, and now her tears were for the happiness that was filling her heart.

"At least that is one worry behind you honey, you now have a place for you, and the baby when it comes, just in case Ray doesn't return. Your mother and I will be close by to help whenever you need us." Frank smiled, it done his heart good to see some sparks of life back in his daughters pretty blue eyes again. He had to admit that the old sparkle suited her far more than the sad little eyes he saw when he first arrived here this morning. "Oh before I forget Cassy, your mother said to tell you that she is looking forward to her new grand-child, and that she fully plans on babysitting for you when you get back on your feet and find a job."

"Thanks dad for all your help and understanding. I don't know what I would have done if you hadn't come by when you did this morning. You must have sensed that I really did need you. You don't know what a huge relief it was when I saw your pickup drive up out front."

"You don't have to thank me for anything baby, that's what fathers are for."

Frank was getting ready to leave and Cassandra remembered that she hadn't paid him the money for the down payment. "Just a minute dad while I get my purse." Cassandra said, as she ran to the bedroom for her purse. Returning she counted out the five hundred dollars, while her father was protesting that she should wait until she was better situated. However, Cassandra didn't want her father paying for something that she was able to pay for. Making her self a mental note, she only had four hundred dollars left to live on until she found a job. Hoping she could at least work part time until after she had the baby.

*   *   *

CASSANDRA WALKED OUTSIDE WITH her father, as Frank opened the door and got in the pickup, he said. "Well Cassy honey, guess I better be getting on to work now. But I'll be back early in the morning to help you move all those boxes to the trailer house."

Cassandra gave her dad a radiant smile that reached all the way to her eyes. "I love you dad, see you tomorrow. Don't you worry dad, I'll be ready and waiting for you, I can't wait to see mother, and my new home. It's going to be great to live close to you again."

This was the first time in months that she actually felt happy and glad to be alive. Finally maybe her life would amount to something after all.

CHAPTER TEN

AFTER CASSANDRA'S FATHER DROVE off down the lane and she could no longer see his pickup, she decided that she would finish the last minute packing so that she would be ready when he came back in the morning. As Cassandra worked she started whistling a little song she used to sing, suddenly the tune died on her lips as she realized this was the first time she had really been happy since the day she married Ray.

By five o'clock, she had finished the last of the packing, and was standing in the middle of all the stacked boxes wondering if she might have forgotten anything. The sound of the front door opening behind her startled her, she swung around to see who the intruder was and almost fainted when she saw Ray standing there in the open door starring at her. He just stood there not saying anything, and fear welled up in her chest, she wanted to run but there wasn't any place to run to as he was blocking the only door to the outside.

Finally, Ray walked into the house taking in all the packing boxes stacked in the middle of the room, and then suddenly he seemed to explode in anger. "Just what the hell are you up to now Cassandra?"

How dare Ray come in here after all these months that he had been gone and start making demands on her. Who did he think he was anyway? Cassandra's fear had turned to anger. "What does it look like I'm doing Ray?" She snapped at him. "Not that it's any business of yours, but I'm packing to move out of here, so if there's anything that you came back for just tell me and I will set it aside for you. Because I damn sure don't want anything; that belongs to you."

Rays face was starting to turn red, the way it always did when he was extremely agitated. "What do you mean that you are moving? You aren't going anywhere unless I say so." He snarled at her.

"Well big man, since you never bothered to let me know where you were, or what you were doing these past three months, why in the hell are you suddenly concerned about what I do now?" She hesitated, and drew in a deep breath to calm her self. Cassandra wasn't going to let Ray start telling her what she could, and couldn't do again. So much for happiness, she thought.

"But if you really want to know, Mr. Lancing stopped by last week and told me he found a new foremen to replace you, and he said that I would have to move out, so that is exactly what I'm doing!" She informed him.

Ray just stood there looking at her for a few seconds. Cassandra watched the expression on his face turn from anger to elation before he spoke. "Gee whiz baby, no need for you to get yourself all worked up. I came back to tell you some good news. I met this man in the bar right after I left here and he offered me a real good job in his plant. It is about a mile north of town. He has been good enough to let me bunk at his place the past three months until I could find a place close to the plant. Believe me it sure beats the hell out of living way out here in the sticks, and driving that dirty tractor for old Lancing for dirt wages."

Cassandra was having trouble making any sense out of what Ray just told her. It was hard for her to comprehend that Ray just comes waltzing back in here acting like he had just left that morning, and springs all this crap on her again. She was about to speak when Ray said. "Aren't you happy baby about my good fortune to land such a great job? I did it all for you sweetie." He looked around him once more. "By the way honey, where are we moving to anyway? I hope you found us a nice place that will be close to where I work. I've just been so damn busy that I haven't had much chance to even look for us a place in town yet."

It took Cassandra a full minute to realize that Ray was fully expecting her to take up where they left off three months ago and continue living in this farce of a marriage.

Cassandra stood there not knowing just what to say. She was afraid to tell Ray that she hadn't planned on them living together because she was afraid that he would fly into one of his violent rages, and she simply could not endure going through that again.

Taking a deep breath Cassandra told Ray about the trailer her dad had bought for her. As she talked, she kept a constant eye on Ray's expression and she could see that he was getting angry. Then he yelled at her.

"We don't need your old man, or anyone else to get us a place to live. We can find our own damn place. So get that through your stupid thick skull."

Not caring that Cassandra was pregnant; Ray swung around and backhanded Cassandra, sending her sprawling into a pile of boxes that blocked her fall.

"So get busy you lazy good for nothing bitch, and get these boxes loaded in the truck so we can get to hell out of this filthy tumble down dump." He raged out of control.

However, Cassandra stood her ground. "It's too late Ray, I've already gave my dad five hundred dollars for the down payment on the trailer, and I also signed the contract."

"Well you can just get your down payment back, and tear up the damn contract. I refuse to let you do this. Do I make myself clear, bitch?"

"I can't do that Ray. I am not renting this trailer, I'm buying it so that I will have somewhere for the baby and I to live. It's a done deal Ray, and there isn't a single thing you can do about it, because it's in my name only."

Ray looked positively livid, his face was beet red, and there was a mean look in his eyes. "Where the hell did you get that kind of money, you lying bitch?"

Cassandra was shaking with fear, but she looked him right in the eye. "I have been saving back some out of every one of your paychecks since we moved here. It started out to be a nest egg for a place of our own. Then when I found out that I was pregnant, I decided to save it for when the baby comes."

Before Cassandra had any idea what Ray was planning to do, he lunged at her and slapped her hard across the face, knocking her a little off balance, but she caught herself against the boxes preventing her fall, but she was more than a little dazed.

"Who the hell gave you the right to give my hard earned money to your old man?" He yelled at her, and then struck her again, this time knocking her to the floor.

As Cassandra regained her feet, she quietly told him. "You do what ever you want to do Ray. But I'm moving into my trailer, with, or without you."

Ray made a lunge for her again, but she quickly stepped out of his reach, all the time keeping an eye on him because she no longer trusted him. Suddenly Ray threw up his arms in defeat, and said. "Okay, okay, have it your own way. We'll move into the damned trailer, and when I get sick and tired of it, I'll burn the son-of-a-bitch to the ground with both you, and the brat in it." He threatened.

Cassandra couldn't very well tell him that she didn't want to live with him anymore, and since they were still legally married by law she couldn't prevent him from moving in the trailer with her. However, she would have some protection from his violence, living so close to her parents, and she felt compelled to inform him of this fact.

"By the way Ray, I think in all fairness you should know that the trailer is parked in the same trailer court that my parents are living in, and they will only be two spaces away from us. So if you have any intentions of knocking me around in the future, you best get them out of your mind because you will have my father to contend with." There she had said her piece. Seeing the murderous look on Rays face, she added a little insurance to protect her tonight. "Oh! I almost forgot Ray. Daddy will be here at five in the morning to help me move, so you better make damn sure that I'm in one piece, without a mark on me when he gets here, or I'm afraid you will have to answer to him."

For a few weeks, after they moved into the trailer things went along fairly well, with exception of the few nights that Ray never came home at all. Until the night, that Ray came home from work with one of the men that he worked with.

"Where are the keys to your car Cassy?" He demanded as soon as he stepped in the door.

"Why do you want my car keys Ray? Is something wrong with your pickup?"

Ray glared at her. "Stop with the thirty questions and just give me the damn keys Cassy, Joe wants to take it for a test drive, and he hasn't got all night." He snapped.

Cassandra put her hands on her hips in exasperation. "So tell me Ray, just why is this guy I don't even know, wanting to test drive **my** car?" She demanded to know.

Ray looked livid, that she had dared to question him, and he snarled. "Because I'm selling your damn car, that's why. We need the money now that you are having a brat for me to support."

Cassandra was stunned, this had to be some kind of a joke Ray was pulling on her. "You can't sell my car Ray. My dad bought me that car long before I even knew that you existed. Therefore, since the car is only in my name, legally you cannot sell my car unless I sign off on the title. Which I have no intention of doing. So I suggest you go out and tell your friend that my car is not for sale." Feeling proud of the way she had stood up to Ray, Cassandra grabbed up her key ring from the hook by the door to keep Ray from getting them, and held them behind her back.

However, Ray was too fast for her, and he reached around her back and jerked the keys out of her hand, cutting her fingers in the process, and was out the door giving them to Joe before she could stop him.

Cassandra watched as Joe drove off in her car, and Ray came back in the trailer with a smug look on his face.

"Ray how can you do this? I will never sign off on my car, I need it to get back and forth to the doctors office."

Ray became extremely angry yelling at her. "Like hell you need a damn car. You can walk to where ever you need to go, at least that way I know you can't go far, and won't be able to take a hell of a lot with you."

As the tears started to well up in Cassandra's eyes, she willed herself not to cry as she said. "Why are you doing this to me Ray? I don't understand why you are always so mean and hateful to me all the time. I'm starting to hate you more with each passing day, and I constantly wish to hell that I had never married you in the first place. You have made my life a living hell from day one, and I want a divorce!"

Rays only response was to smack her across the face as he snarled at her. "If you know what's good for you, you will stay in the trailer until after Joe leaves. Do you understand me bitch?" He hissed, and then he left, slamming the door behind him, just as Joe drove up in Cassandra's car.

Ray came back in the trailer and told her quietly in a hushed voice, not wanting Joe to hear their conversation. "Get me the title to your car Cassy. Joe has decided to buy it, and you had better not forget to sign the back if you know what's good for you. Do I make myself clear bitch?"

Cassandra jumped up from the chair; and screamed at him.

"I won't let you do this Ray, the car is **mine**! You have no legal right to sell it. I owned that car long before I met you. It's mine, and I don't intend to sell it to Joe or anyone else!" How she wished that her parents were home, they had left just before Ray came home, so his timing was perfect. She knew that if her dad had seen Joe driving her car, he would have come down to see what was going on. However, with her parents away there was no one else to help her. She made for the open door, but Ray was too fast for her. He grabbed her by the arm and jerked it behind her back making her wince with the sudden pain as he twisted her arm up between her shoulder blades, bringing tears to her eyes. Before she could scream out Ray clamped his huge hand over her mouth, and hissed at her. "I warn you bitch, if you make one single sound I'll break your arm. Do you understand me?"

All Cassandra could do was nod her head yes. "Good, now that we understand each other, you can pick up that pen and sign that damn title the way I asked you to. Then Joe can get to hell out of here before your daddy comes home." He grinned smugly to show her this had been his plan right along.

"And just for the record if you value your life, and the life of that brat you're carrying, you better make damn sure your daddy doesn't ever find out what went on here today. Do you get my drift bitch?"

Under duress, Cassandra signed over the car title to Joe. Nevertheless, deep down she hated Ray just a little bit more for forcing her to do it.

* * *

NO MATTER HOW HARD she tried, Cassandra couldn't figure out why Ray treated her as he did. Slowly he was stripping her of all her rights and independence. What was he trying to prove? Why did he make her stay with him? He couldn't possibly love her, or if he did love her, he had a sick way of showing it. If only Ray would just give her the divorce that she so desperately wanted. "Oh God she thought, how am I ever going to be free from Ray, I'm trapped out of fear in this marriage made in hell. I'm afraid to leave, and I'm afraid to stay."

Ray left right after Joe did; he never came home at all that night. As Cassandra lay in bed alone, she made herself a vow, that no matter what, somehow, someway, she would find a way to get away from Ray. Her only hope was that it would be soon. She decided to just bide her time until after she had her baby. Then she would start saving every penny she could get her hands on, and when she had enough money saved up, she would simply take her baby and disappear.

CHAPTER ELEVEN

Five weeks had passed since Ray had forced Cassandra to sell her car, and tell her parents the lie he had made up about why they sold it. Cassandra hated having to lie to her parents, but she was afraid of what Ray would do to her if she told them the truth, and even more afraid of what her father would do. She was well into her seventh month of pregnancy and was so afraid for the life of her baby. Although to outsiders it appeared, they had a normal marriage, so no one suspected that she lived in constant fear of Ray

She was never sure from one day to the next when he might revert to being violent again, so she could never relax. Her nerves were always on edge, and near the breaking point. Her doctor had already warned her that she needed to take things easy, and to stop having sex period, or she wouldn't carry her baby to full term.

*   *   *

Then Ray started going to his parent's house every night after work instead of coming home. Some nights when he did come home to eat, he expected his dinner to be ready to set on the table as soon as he arrived. But most of the time he ate at his parents house and never let Cassandra know ahead of time; so she always had dinner ready just in case, and if he didn't show up on time she would always try to keep it warm. When Ray came home she didn't know if he had eaten with his parents, or if he intended to eat what she had prepared. Most of the time she ended up throwing everything in the garbage after all her efforts cooking a meal, because he had already eaten. Cassandra really hated wasting so much good food. However, she kept her mouth shut about it to Ray; for fear that she would make him angry. She sure didn't want him to have any excuse to get violent; and cause her to lose her baby again. Therefore, she just kept silent and figured to hell with the wasted food. The cost of the food was a small price to pay if it would save her unborn baby.

*　　*　　*

ONE NIGHT WHEN RAY came home later than usual; all of the food on the stove that she was trying to keep warm for him, had started to congeal in the pans. Just as she started to dump everything into the garbage can, she asked softly. "Have you already eaten Ray, or would you like me to fix you something? This food has been sitting here warming for so long that I am afraid it is beyond eating now. But it will only take me a few minutes to fix you something decent."

"Forget it." Ray snapped. "I ate at my folks hours ago."

Cassandra's nerves were so on edge, and being pregnant sure didn't help. She just knew that things had to change, as she simply couldn't continue on like this much longer.

It was almost as though Ray was bating her like a cat would a mouse. She decided it was time to try to talk to Ray calmly, and see if they could work out a compromise

"Why can't you ever call me Ray and let me know when you don't plan on coming home for dinner? At least then I could go ahead and eat my dinner while everything is still fresh and hot."

Without any warning, Ray suddenly grabbed Cassandra and spun her around so that she was standing in front of him with her back crushed against his chest in front of the stove. At the same time, he grabbed a handful of spoiled food from one of the pans on the stove, and yelled at her. "So you want to eat do you, well let me help you by all means." Then he started to try to stuff some of the congealed food into Cassandra's mouth, causing her to gag on the vile stuff. Disgusted, Ray gave her a violent shove away from him causing Cassandra to crash into the cupboard next to the stove. Because of her pregnant condition she was unable to keep her balance, and fell to the floor at Ray's feet.

Cassandra was terrified as she lay there helplessly on the floor at Ray's feet. So afraid that he would start kicking her again and injure the baby. Horrified Cassandra watched as Ray lifted up his foot, but he only stepped over her swollen body and went over and opened the door, throwing it back so hard against the outside of the trailer that the whole trailer shook. Without so much as a backward glance at her, Ray went out and slammed the door shut behind him. Then she heard the roar of the engine as Ray peeled rubber as he drove away.

*   *   *

CASSANDRA SLOWLY STARTED TRYING to pull herself up off the floor by using the drawer handles until she got into a sitting position. Then she just sat there on the kitchen floor rocking back and forth with her arms around her swollen stomach, while tears were running uncontrollably down her face. Suddenly she felt a horrible pain in her side that had her gasping for breath. "Please dear God, don't let this happen a second time. Please let my baby live." She prayed aloud.

The pain in her side was so bad that she couldn't pull herself up, so she just slowly scooted her behind on the floor down the short hall until she got to the foot of the bed, where she was finally able to pull herself onto the bed, and just lay there trying to regain her breath. She was hungry and tired, but decided she would just lay there quietly for a little while, and then she would get something to eat after the pain let up some.

Lying there in the dark of the room she knew that she had to get away from Ray, but that was out of the question in her present condition. She had to stay with Ray until the baby was born, and she had a chance to save a little money, she was flat broke. Ray had taken the four hundred dollars out of her purse, and had been going to the grocery store with her and paying for the groceries himself. He made sure that she never had any money at all. The odds were stacked against her, almost eight months pregnant, no job, no money, and no transportation. She prayed for the strength to get through the next two months, and the birth of a healthy baby. Then after that, she would do everything in her power to take her baby and escape from Ray.

* * *

CASSANDRA HAD NO IDEA how long she had been laying there in the darkness, but the pain in her side had eased considerably, and now she didn't hurt so bad. She felt sure that the fall hadn't hurt the baby, but just to be on the safe side; she would call the doctor the first thing in the morning, right after Ray left for work.

* * *

CASSANDRA GLANCED AT THE bedside clock, it was two in the morning, and Ray hadn't returned. She found herself hoping that Ray had done one of his famous disappearing acts again. Oh God, how she hated Ray, if only he would leave for good. She would never have to endure his touch again. However, that just wasn't going to happen!

* * *

IT WAS ALMOST DAYLIGHT when Cassandra heard the soft click of the trailer door as it closed, she stayed real still and pretended to be asleep. Praying that Ray wouldn't decide to have his way with her again as he often did when he came home late and found her sleeping. He didn't care that the doctor had warned them how dangerous it would be for both her, and the baby, if they continued to have sex.

However, Ray refused to take the doctors advice, insisting that no one was going to tell him when he could have sex with his own wife.

Every since they had gotten married, Ray had never been gentle in his love making, he was like an animal, forcing her to do things she didn't want to do, and only seeking his own satisfaction. Cassandra never enjoyed his lovemaking, she hated the things he done to her, and she grew to hate him as well. In fact, he was worse than an animal. Every time he touched her, it made her skin crawl.

Lately he appeared to get the most pleasure from hitting her during the act of making love. Always when he was through with her he would roll over on his back, then go right off to sleep. There were no tender words, or touches, only abuse, and the string of vulgar words coming from his mouth through the whole, humiliating ordeal.

*   *   *

CASSANDRA HAD NO IDEA what Ray was doing while these thoughts were dancing through her mind, but he never came near her. Suddenly she heard the trailer door close; she lay there listening for the sound of his truck to start up. However, she heard nothing, she was afraid to get up for fear that he was playing a trick on her. It wouldn't be the first time that Ray had faked closing the door, so that she would think that he had left, and when she got up he would pounce on her and start knocking her around, laughing like a jackass enjoying a good sport.

Cassandra decided to lay quiet until she was sure Ray had left. Soon she heard the engine start up on his truck, and heard him drive away then she knew for certain that Ray was gone and she was safe. She breathed a sigh of relief, and turned over, deciding to try to go back to sleep for a while longer. Knowing that now she could truly relax, and not have to worry about Ray pouncing on her while she slept.

* * *

CASSANDRA WAS WELL INTO her eighth month of pregnancy now, and she was getting bigger by the day. Ray hardly spent any time at home anymore, but that was okay with her because she wasn't very quick on her feet anymore, and it was hard to stay out of Rays way in the small trailer, so she was glad that he wasn't around very much. She hoped it would continue that way at least for another month, and it would be time for her to have the baby. What little time that Ray was home, he was always angry and in a foul mood. And the bigger that Cassandra got with the baby, the worse Ray would treat her.

Every time Ray looked at her, he would taunt her, saying. "I hope that baby dies, and you die too. Then I can get rid of both of you. You are so fat, and ugly Cassandra, it makes me want to puke just looking at you." Then he would barge out of the trailer, jump in his truck and drive off to some bar, and come home late, drunker than a skunk, and as mean as they come.

Sometimes Cassandra wondered how in the world she had managed to stay alive this long. Nobody should ever have to endure the amount of pain, and humiliation that she had suffered for so long.

The one thing that kept Cassandra sane was her dream of one day being free from Ray, and never again having to put up with all his mental and physical abuse. With each day that passed she was getting closer to having her baby. Then she would find a way to leave Ray, once, and for all. She prayed to God that Ray wouldn't kill her and her unborn baby before she could find a way to escape.

Cassandra prayed every day that her parents would come home. They had been gone now for almost seven weeks. Her father was checking out a new location for the company he worked for, as they wanted to open another branch location.

Ray seemed to treat her worse when he knew her parents were out of town, knowing that she was at his mercy when there was no one she could turn too, and no place for her to go.

Frank and Nora had promised Cassandra they would be home long before the baby was due, and now there was only four more weeks to go, so Cassandra knew that it shouldn't be to much longer before her parents came home, because they had never broken a single promise to her in her life.

It was her parent's promise that gave her the strength to make it through each passing day just knowing they would soon be home. Every single day Ray seemed to be getting more agitated, and angry with her. His abuse was boarder line to the point that Cassandra was afraid he was going to do something terrible to her. Each day Cassandra prayed it would be the day her parents came home before it was too late for both her, and her baby. She was so stressed out with worry that Ray would do something horrible to her before her parents returned that she was nervous and jittery, didn't feel like eating and was afraid to go to bed at night because she was sure Ray would try to kill her in her sleep. The strain was really starting to take a toll on her; she had dark circles under her eyes from lack of sleep, and she jumped every time the trailer door opened afraid that it would be the last day she would ever be alive. Cassandra just couldn't help but take Rays threats seriously.

Finally, her prayers were answered. Her parents arrived home a few days later, just three weeks before the baby was due.

*   *   *

THAT NIGHT WHEN RAY came home from work, he saw Frank and Nora's car in front of their trailer. Knowing that they were close by again his moods changed considerably, he started to whistle as he walked from his truck to the trailer, acting like a happy husband, just in case they might be watching when he came home. He was really putting on a great act for their benefit, and Cassandra felt she was going to get sick, watching him saunter along pretending to be the happy husband, instead of the monster she knew him to be.

Carrying his act even further, knowing that it was summer and everyone had their windows open and could hear him plain as day. "Hey baby, I'm home. Come give your hubby a big kiss." Then he closed the door, and sneered at Cassandra. "Impressive, don't you agree?"

"It's going to take a lot more than that to convince my parents. I doubt if that sham act you're putting on of being the loving husband will fool them for a single minute." Cassandra hissed at him.

* * *

FOR THE NEXT FEW days, Ray went out of his way to try to treat her nice. He even offered to do a few things around the house to help make things a little easier for her. However, that little crumb of kindness sure didn't last for very long.

CHAPTER TWELVE

ONE NIGHT RAY CAME home late from work, and he was stinking drunk. He ordered Cassandra to strip, as he wanted to have sex. "Get your clothes off bitch, you know what I want. So make it snappy!"

"We can't have sex Ray. You know what the doctor said." She refused, all the time watching his face, as she slowly backed away from him.

Ray made a lunge, and grabbed her, jerking her up close, right next to his face, and the foul stench of his breath made Cassandra gag. She just couldn't help herself, and she threw up; she tried to back a little distance away from him but still managed to get some on his pant legs and shoes.

Ray reached out grabbing her again, jerking her close. "I don't give a damn what the doctor said. I'm the boss around this house, not your damn doctor. And when I tell you to do something Bitch; you damn sure better do it. Understand?" He growled at her, and then he slammed his fist right in to Cassandra's face. Somehow Ray had left the door ajar when he came home, and when he hit Cassandra, she lost her balance and fell out the door, landing on her back on the wood patio.

Ray didn't even look down at her laying there, much less offer to help her to her feet. He just stepped over her swollen body, and walked towards his truck, and got behind the wheel. He started it up and peeled rubber as he backed out of the trailer court

* * *

THE FALL HAD DAZED Cassandra a little, and it took her a few minutes for her head to clear before she tried to get up. Being flat on her back, she felt like a beached whale, no matter how hard she tried, she simply couldn't roll over and get off her back. Suddenly she knew that something was terribly wrong when the pains started racking her body, and she felt like she was going to pass out. She decided that she would just lie still for a few minutes. When she tried again to raise herself, she could feel moisture all around her on the patio, and she knew that she had started to hemorrhage. Terrified that she was about to lose another precious baby, she started to scream. "Oh God not again, please won't someone help me before it's too late." Evidently, the people next door to her trailer weren't home, so she started screaming louder this time. "Daddy, daddy, where are you? Please daddy, come help me, I need you so much." Then she silently waited to see if her father had heard her plea for help, and whispered a prayer. "Please God; don't let Ray kill another innocent baby."

* * *

LUCKILY CASSANDRA'S PARENTS WERE home and had heard her screams for help, they came running through the trailer court, along with just about everyone else in the court who had heard her screams for help. Her father got to her first, as he kneeled there beside her, he said. "Baby, baby, daddy's here. What happened did you fall? We saw Ray leave in a big hurry, was he going for the doctor?"

Cassandra changed the subject, she was afraid to tell her father what had really happened. "Oh please daddy, just help me. I think I am bleeding. Please don't let me lose this baby too."

Someone must have turned on the porch light and Frank could

see the blood pooling around Cassandra where she lay on the patio. Without saying a word, he picked Cassandra up as gently as though she were made of glass. As he started to carry Cassandra up the step into the trailer, he called over his shoulder. "Nora, hurry and go call the doctor, and tell him to come as quick as he can, Cassandra is in a pretty bad way."

*   *   *

A SHORT TIME LATER, the doctor arrived. "Frank would you and Nora mind stepping out side for a few minutes while I examine Cassandra." When he was finished he went out and assured them both. "Frank I want you and Nora to know that both Cassandra and her baby are going to be just fine, they were shaken up a bit. And I'm afraid Cassandra will have to remain in bed from now on, until after she delivers." Then the doctor stepped over and laid his hand on Franks shoulder and spoke softly. "Frank I don't know what happened here tonight. But I sense that Cassandra is afraid of something or someone. So I don't want her to be left alone for a single minute. She's going to need someone with her around the clock if we intend to save this baby."

Frank nodded his head. "You can rest assured Doc, I promise you that Cassy won't be left alone. In fact I'm going to take her down to stay with Nora and me until the baby comes, and I fully intend to keep her with us until she gets back on her feet after the baby is born."

The doctor smiled knowingly, he figured that was what Frank Benning would do. In his heart, he knew that something just wasn't right in Cassandra's house; he just wasn't sure exactly what the problem was, but he had a pretty good idea what had happened here tonight. He just didn't have any proof. He knew that Cassandra and her unborn child would be all right, now that she would be in her parent's safekeeping. Because he had a good idea that Frank would make damn sure of that.

"Well Frank, you take good care of our girl in there, I've gotten the bleeding under control for now, but you call me immediately if anything changes."

"I'll do that Doc. Is it okay to move Cassy now?"

"Yes, but just be damn sure to keep her off her feet."

While Frank Benning was carrying Cassandra down to his trailer, he had a gut feeling that Cassy wasn't telling him everything; she had ignored him when he had asked her if Ray had gone for the doctor. He didn't know what she was holding back, but he sure intended to find out when Cassy was feeling better. Now wasn't the time for him to probe into her affairs. He was quite certain of one fact though, he wasn't going to leave her alone around that no good husband of hers while she was in this condition. He had no idea what had taken place tonight between Cassandra and Ray, but he had a gut feeling that Cassy didn't fall out of the trailer by herself. Right then Frank made himself a promise; he damn sure was going to keep a closer eye on Cassy in the future when Ray was around. If he ever found out that no good bastard had hit or pushed Cassandra out of their trailer tonight he would kill him with his bare hands.

* * *

TWO WEEKS HAD PASSED since Cassandra's fall, and not once had Ray even bothered to come and see her. That just proved to Frank, that Ray knew all along what had happened to Cassandra, and that he could care less. Frank couldn't do anything about that now, but as soon as Cassandra was back on her feet after she had the baby, he was damn sure going to have a long talk with Ray.

* * *

CASSANDRA WAS FEELING BETTER, so she told her mother. "I really do think that I should go back to my own trailer mom. Ray is probably wondering why I don't come home."

Nora Benning was starting to have some suspicions of her own by now, and she was in complete agreement with her husband, that it was very strange that Ray hadn't been down to check on Cassandra's welfare once in the two weeks she had been with them. Frank and Nora had both agreed that under the circumstances they were no way going to allow Cassy to be alone with Ray before she had the baby, and a chance to regain her strength, and get back on her feet again. Hoping by then that she would be more able to cope with whatever the situation was with her and Ray. "Your father and I don't think it's wise for you to go against your doctor's orders, honey. He advised us not to let you go home until after you have your baby." Nora smiled to ease the tension. "It will only be for a little while longer dear." She assured her.

Cassandra was elated to hear her mother say that, she really didn't want to go home; she just felt that she had been here for two weeks, and thought she should at least make the offer to go to her own home. Deep down she was really dreading when the time came that she had to go back home, where Ray would do who knows what to her next time. She knew in her heart that Ray really didn't want this baby or her either for that matter. She was not only afraid for her own life, but for the life of her unborn baby as well.

"Thanks mom. I guess you're right, and I really should stay here where it will be so much easier on you. It wouldn't be fair for you to have to run back and forth between our trailers to check on me everyday."

Nora had seen the look of fear in Cassandra's eyes when she was talking about going back home, and after she had told Cassandra that they didn't want her to go home, she had saw the fear vanish. "Good, that's settled then, because when your pains start honey, I will be right here to time them, and take care of any phone calls. All you will have to do is just concentrate on the baby. And I will take care of everything else."

*   *   *

ONE BY ONE THE days passed, it was getting closer to Cassandra's delivery date, Frank, and Nora found it very strange that Ray still hadn't come to see his wife. In fact they hadn't even seen Ray at the trailer or any where else around town. They wondered just what sort of man their daughter had married. They soon found out.

On the morning of July 5, 1959, at nine o'clock Cassandra went into labor, Nora timed each pain as they came. When they were ten minutes apart, Nora called the doctors office to let them know. The nurse told Nora that the doctor was on vacation, but it was only a short distance out of town, and he had left instructions for her to call him as soon as Cassandra went into labor, and he would meet her at the hospital. The nurse told Nora that when the pains were five minutes apart they were to drive to the hospital and the doctor would be there. When Cassandra's pains were eight minutes apart Nora called the plant where Ray worked and asked him to come home and drive Cassandra to the hospital. She was astounded when Ray gruffly informed her. "You will just have to get someone else Nora, I'm way too busy right now. Besides my boss won't let me take any time off the job for personal matters. Sorry." Then he hung up, not even asking how Cassandra was.

Nora was beside herself, she couldn't believe anyone could be that callus regarding their own wife, and she didn't believe that crap he said about his boss not letting him off for a single minute. As Nora stepped away from the phone she muttered under her breath, hoping that Cassandra wouldn't hear her. "The nerve of that good-for-nothing man, who does he think he is anyway?"

Nora was wondering what she was going to do; they lived in such a small town that there wasn't any taxi or bus service. Just bad luck that today of all days, there wasn't even a single car at home in the trailer court, and Frank was several miles away from town today checking on some things for his boss.

Poor Cassy, Nora thought, her pains were really getting bad, and she was in no condition to walk the ten blocks to the hospital. Nora tried the doctor's office again to see if there was anyone there that might come and take Cassy to the hospital. Maybe the doctor had arrived, and he might be able to come help them. The nurse told her there wasn't anyone there with a car, and that the doctor was still in route from his vacation spot, and hadn't arrived in town yet.

"Damn that sorry husband of Cassy's, deliberately putting them in this terrible predicament, leaving them stranded when he could so easily help them." Nora fumed under her breath, trying to keep from screaming. She sure didn't want Cassy to learn how bad things were, and get her all upset. Nora was getting more nervous by the minute; she had to do something, and it had better be soon, that baby wasn't going to wait forever to put in an appearance. She decided to see if maybe she could get a hold of Frank on his car radio, and he would be close enough to his truck to hear it. Hoping that he would be able to come help them, or at least be able to get a hold of someone he knew to help them. Time was running out fast!

Nora was glad that the phone was in the bedroom, and with Cassy on the sofa she wouldn't be able to hear what was going on with all these frantic phone calls. She dialed the operator and gave her the number for Franks radio, and relief washed over her when she heard Franks voice on the phone. "What's up Nora? Is Cassy doing okay?"

"Oh Frank, thank God I was able to reach you. I didn't know what else to do."

Nora was talking so fast that Frank could barely keep up with her. "Hold on honey, take a deep breath, and slow down and tell me what the hell has you so upset."

"Frank, Cassy went into labor this morning, and when her pains were eight minutes apart I called Ray at work to ask him to come and drive us to the hospital. And he told me flat out to get someone else because he was just too busy, and his boss wouldn't let him off work for personal things. Now Cassy's pains are six minutes apart, and I don't know what to do Frank, I'm so scared."

"Isn't there someone there in the trailer court Nora?"

"No Frank, that's why I called you, I've been on the phone for an hour and I can't find a single person home that has a car. I even called the doctors office to see if the doctor could come take us to the hospital, but he's been on vacation, and is in route now to meet us at the hospital." Frank could tell by the sound of Nora's voice that she was almost in tears.

"Now just take it easy Nora, calm down or you won't be of any help to Cassy she needs you now more than she ever has. Now you go tell Cassy to just hang on, I am on my way. Honey, you tell Cassy that her old daddy has never let her down before, and I sure don't intend to start now. You two just stay calm, and I'll be there before you know it."

Frank was furious when he hung up the car phone; at the same time he romped down on the gas peddle. He wondered how in the hell Ray could be such a total jackass at a time like this. How could Ray ignore the fact that Cassy was having his baby, and she depended on him to be there when she needed him? "I know one damn thing for sure; when I see that sorry bastard I'm going to give him a piece of my mind." Frank said aloud, as he banged his fist down on the steering wheel.

*　　*　　*

NORA HAD BEEN SITTING by the window watching for Frank; soon as she saw his truck drive into the trailer court entrance, she ran out to meet him.

"Thank God you're here Frank. Please hurry, Cassy's all doubled up with pain, they are coming three minutes apart now, and I don't know what to do for her." Nora sobbed, the tears running down her face.

Frank ran into the trailer scooped Cassandra up in his arms; and rushed out to his truck with her, while Nora ran along beside him trying to keep up. Cassandra moaned as Frank lifted her over into the middle of the seat so that there would be room for Nora.

"Everything's going to be all right sweetheart. Daddy's here, so you just relax baby, we'll have you at the hospital in no time."

CHAPTER THIRTEEN

CASSANDRA'S WATER BROKE JUST as they were putting her in a bed at the hospital, the doctor was there and waiting for her when they arrived, seeing her water break the doctor commented that it shouldn't be too long and she would deliver. He couldn't have been more wrong. Cassandra was in hard labor for the next forty-six hours. During that time, Frank and Nora never left the hospital. They remained by her bedside. There was no sign of Ray at all. Frank Benning would have went and hunted him down like a dog, but he just couldn't bare to leave his daughters side for more than a few minutes at a time, as Cassandra was really battling to just stay alive, and bring her baby into the world.

* * *

TWICE DURING THE LONG night, and into the early hours of the morning, the doctor thought that he might lose Cassandra due to the very difficult birth. For the life of him, he didn't know what power kept her rallying back. She was a fighter that was for sure.

Once the doctor had even told Frank and Nora that he was sure he could save the baby, but he wasn't too sure if Cassandra would come through the ordeal, she was terribly weak, and exhausted, and she was out of it most of the time. When Cassandra foggily heard what the doctor said, she knew somehow she had to find the strength to hang in there and come out of this alive, and fight for her baby. Because no way could she leave her precious baby's life in Rays care. Then everything went black.

*   *   *

AS THE HOURS PASSED by, Cassandra valiantly struggled to stay alive; she was in and out of consciousness. Then just before noon on July 7th, she delivered her baby, she was so tired and weak, she vaguely heard the doctor tell her. "Cassandra you have a beautiful baby girl, do you want to hold her?" Then he gently laid the baby on Cassandra's stomach.

"She's so beautiful, my little angel from heaven." She whispered weakly, and then drifted off to sleep, holding her precious baby.

There wasn't a dry eye in the place, everyone was so relieved that both mother, and baby survived the long ordeal. Even the doctor had tears in his eyes when he went out to tell Frank and Nora that they had both a beautiful daughter, and a beautiful granddaughter.

"Cherish this grandbaby Frank; Cassandra won't be able to have anymore children. The way this birth went, the next time it could be her life, the baby's life, or both." He said sadly.

*   *   *

CASSANDRA AND HER BABY remained in the hospital for ten days due to the difficulties of the birth. Not once did Ray put in an appearance. But that was no great loss. Cassandra could care less if she ever saw him again, or not. Because in her heart she knew she would never forgive him for pushing her out of the trailer door and leaving her lying helpless on the patio. Then refusing to come home and help her when she so desperately needed someone to take her to the hospital. How she hated him for all the horrible things he had said, and done to her over the past two and a half years. She had no idea what fate awaited her when she finally left the hospital, but one thing she knew for sure, she would protect her precious little baby from Ray, or die trying.

* * *

CASSANDRA DECIDED SHE WOULD name her baby Jamie Marie Cartone, after her dear father, whose full name was James Franklin Benning. Cassandra could tell that her father was pleased when he heard the baby's name for the first time. He was so proud; she thought the buttons would burst off his shirt if he were not careful.

Frank and Nora visited Cassandra and little Jamie every day. Frank was so happy that they were both doing so well. He even came by on his lunch hour, bringing Cassandra flowers, and candy, and a tiny toy, or book for Jamie.

If Cassandra had ever seen a more proud, dotting grandfather, her dad took the prize. He would tell her funny jokes that he had heard at work, and was always making her laugh. He kept telling her how happy he would be when she was able to go home, because then he could hold his granddaughter anytime he wanted.

* * *

FINALLY, THE DAY ARRIVED for Cassandra to leave the hospital. Her parents came to take her and little Jamie home. Cassandra was really dreading the thought of having to go back home, and be at the mercy of Ray's abuse again. She hoped that she was strong enough to cope with him, no telling what she was in for when she and the baby were back in the small trailer alone with Ray. She hoped that Ray had come to terms with being a father, and that their life would be different from the way it had been before she went to the hospital, but she knew that was probably just wistful thinking on her part; as she very much doubted that thought would ever become a reality because Ray would never change, not in this lifetime anyway.

Frank saw the sadness in Cassandra's eyes, and something else that appeared to register fear. "Doc said in view of all that's happened he still wants you to have complete bed rest for at least another ten days or so Cassy, so mother, and I are going to take you and Jamie to our house until you get back on your feet again." He paused and watched the look of fear leave Cassandra's eyes. "Besides new babies need a whole lot of care Cassy, and your mother can barely contain herself. She wants to get home, and get started right away." He laughed, making light of the situation.

"Oh daddy, I don't like putting you and mother out. I should just go to my own trailer so I won't be such a burden on you. After all you've been taking care of me for quite awhile now, and I think it's high time that I start taking care of myself again."

"Now listen here young lady, you aren't a burden on us, and we want to take care of you and Jamie right now. Honey, you have been through a lot these past weeks, and you need plenty of rest to regain your strength. So please let your mother, and I do this for you. Okay?"

"Alright daddy, you win. For now anyway, but as soon as I'm stronger, I'll have to return to my own trailer. I don't want to wear out my welcome." Cassandra smiled to take the sting out of her words. She was secretly excited, that she would have a chance to get stronger, and used to taking care of Jamie before she had to face the situation at home that living under the same roof with Ray again was bound to prove to be more than she could possibly handle right now as weak and vulnerable as she was.

* * *

CASSANDRA WONDERED IF RAY was still living in their trailer or not. However, she wasn't about to ask. She hoped that he was gone forever. She hadn't seen, or heard from him since that near fatal night when he had knocked her out the door of the trailer, then he had just walked away, leaving her to whatever fate had in store for her, as though he could care less if she died or not. If Ray hated her so much why did he keep coming back?

Cassandra felt relieved to know that her parents were going to have her and Jamie stay with them until she was stronger, and better able to cope with life again. But the main reason she felt relived was she really needed some time before she had to face Ray again.

"Oh thank you daddy, you don't know how much I appreciate all that you and mother have done for me, and my baby. I don't know what I would have done if you two hadn't been there for me." She said tearfully, as she threw her arms around Frank's neck and gave him a hug. "You two are the greatest parents in the whole world."

"We don't want you to worry about a single thing Cassy. We just want you to concentrate on regaining your strength, and getting well. There's no rush for you, and little Jamie to go back home until you are sure that's what you want to do. Just keep in mind that your mother and I will always be here for you and Jamie. Your mother and I want you to know honey; that we will help you in any way that we can. Okay?" Frank was giving Cassandra a chance to open up and confide in him. He knew damn well things in Cassandra's and Rays marriage just weren't right by a long shot. But he just couldn't do a damn thing about it if Cassandra wouldn't tell him what her problems were. Maybe in time she could bring herself to confide in him or Nora. But this was a personal and private matter between Cassandra and her husband and he had no right to interfere, unless Cassandra asked him for help. Meantime all he could do was to be patient and wait and not push his daughter into answering questions that she may not be ready to answer.

"You have no idea how much I appreciate knowing that dad, and I will never be able to thank you enough for all that you and mother have done for me. I love you both dearly, and I mean that from the bottom of my heart."

"We love you too baby, and don't you ever forget that for a single minute." Frank said as he hugged her tightly to his chest.

*   *   *

CASSANDRA COULD TELL WITH each passing day that she was getting stronger. She was well enough now to be able to take care of all Jamie's needs. She loved holding her little daughter anytime she wanted. Those ten days in the hospital, the only time she had been allowed to hold Jamie was at feeding time. How she loved looking at her new baby daughter. Jamie was perfect in every way; from her cap of curly black hair, to her tiny little toes. Every inch of her was so very precious.

"You know you are going to spoil her don't you Cassy?" Nora teased, smiling.

"Yes mother, but I just can't help it. Jamie is so perfect, and lovable. I never dreamed that having your own baby could be so fulfilling." Cassandra paused as a look of sadness came over her. "For the life of me mother, I just can't understand how a man can show so little interest in his own child."

Nora could hear the sadness in her daughter's voice, and knew how much Cassy must be suffering over the fact that Ray had never came to see her, or even inquired once about her and the baby. He hadn't even bothered to ask whether the baby was a boy, or a girl. Strange way for a new father to act, but she and Frank had promised each other that they wouldn't interfere in Cassandra's marriage unless she asked them to.

Nora decided it was best if they talked about something more pleasant. "Well I don't really think it will hurt for you to spoil little Jamie a tiny bit, considering the long struggle she endured entering this old world. Lord knows you put up a pretty good fight yourself, so I guess you've earned the right to spoil her if you want too." Nora smiled as she reached out and gently ran the back of her finger down her new granddaughters soft little cheek, then leaned down and kissed Jamie softly of the top of her head.

*   *   *

FRANK BENNING HAD JUST driven up in front of the trailer in time to witness the tender scene through the front window. He smiled with love and gratitude for the three most important people in his life, he was so proud of all of them.

As Frank entered the trailer, he smiled. "So how are my three favorite girls doing today?" Then he held out his arms for little Jamie, who was his pride and joy. At the same time as he cradled Jamie in his arms; he leaned over and gave Nora a kiss on the lips.

Cassandra's heart swelled with pride to see her parents so happy together, and still so much in love. If only I had a husband like my father to love and cherish me, my life would be perfect, Cassandra thought. Then she had another thought. It had been nine days since she came home from the hospital to her parent's house. She had regained her strength, and now it was time for her to return to her own trailer, and Ray. She dreaded it a little more with each passing day. She knew she had to go back, even though she really didn't want to. She wished desperately that she could just swallow her pride and confide in her parents; but somehow she just couldn't summon up the courage to do so. She never realized that she was crying until her mother spoke.

"Cassy dear you are crying, don't you feel well?" Nora asked, as she gently put her arm around Cassandra's shoulders and led her over to the sofa.

"I'm okay, mother, honest. I guess they are just tears for happy seeing my father, holding my daughter." She lied; it wouldn't do at all to tell her parents that she would prefer to stay here with them, rather than return to the life she had with Ray.

"Well of course you are happy dear, and you have good reason to be. Dad and I are very proud of you for blessing us with this wonderful little granddaughter." Nora smiled, and hugged Cassandra close to her.

*　*　*

THAT NIGHT AS CASSANDRA watched television with her parents, she was fretting so about having to go back and live with Ray again that she couldn't keep her mind on the program. If only she could just tell her parents about the abuse she had suffered at Ray's hands the past two and a half years. She knew beyond a shadow of a doubt that they would never dream of letting her go back. She also knew she couldn't do that, because she was so afraid that something terrible would happen to her father if he ever learned the truth about Ray. In her heart, she knew that her father would probably beat Ray half to death or worse, and end up in jail. She just couldn't take that kind of a chance with her parent's life. After all she had gotten herself into this mess when she married a man she knew she didn't love; and she was just going to have to find some way to get herself out of the situation on her own, and not burden her parents with her problems. It was just something she would have to deal with alone. And the sooner she took care of the problem concerning her marriage to Ray the better off things would be; because now she not only had herself to look out for, she had her precious baby to protect from Ray as well.

* * *

THE FOLLOWING MORNING WHILE they were all three having breakfast, Cassandra broached the subject of moving her and Jamie back to their own home. "Well I guess it's time that I give you back your privacy again, and take Jamie and get her settled in our own home today. After all I've been camping on your door step for long enough now, and I don't want to wear out my welcome." Cassandra smiled, trying to appear happy, and excited about going home Hoping that her parents would not suspect that she was telling the biggest lie of her entire life.

Frank was the first to speak. "Are you sure you feel up to it baby? You're not in our way Cassy, we love having you here. Why don't you stay a few more days just to be sure you are ready to go home?" He suggested, hoping she would reconsider.

"Thanks dad, but it just isn't fair to you and mother, having Jamie and I under your feet twenty-four hours a day. After all you raised your family and now's the time in your life when you should just be enjoying each other, instead of being a nursemaid to your grown daughter with a new baby."

"Honey, you just let your mother, and I, be the judge of who is under our feet, and who isn't. Besides Nora and I decided that we sort of like having a new baby in our house again. It brings back fond memories of when you first came into our life. Doesn't it Nora?" Frank smiled at his wife and wiggled his eyebrows.

"I know dad, and I really do appreciate the offer, but it just isn't right that you and mother should have your sleep interrupted off and on every night when Jamie wakes up for her two hour feeding. So I really do think its best that I return to my own home, please try and understand." She pleaded.

Frank Benning wanted to give Cassandra a chance to change her mind about moving back home. He had a gut feeling that she really didn't want to go back home to live with Ray, but unless she decided to confide in them what sort of problems she and Ray were having, his hands were tied. He and Nora had no business butting into Cassandra's affairs; she was a grown woman with a child of her own. She was no longer a little girl that they could make decisions for. "What ever you decide to do Cassy, your mother and I will back you a hundred percent. We would like you to promise us that if you discover that things are still too much for you to handle yet, that you and Jamie will come back and stay here with us for as long as you want."

Cassandra smiled at her father, but he noticed that the smile didn't quite reach her eyes. "Thanks dad, I'm so grateful for all that you and mother have already done for Jamie and me. In fact if it hadn't been for you both, there probably wouldn't even be a Jamie and I right now." Cassandra took a deep breath, and felt chills run down her spine remembering how close she had come to dieing a few short weeks ago. "You do know that I'll never be able to repay you for saving my life. Without the two of you staying by my bedside, praying, while you held my hand, willing me to hang on and fight, I might not be here today. In reality you both made it possible for me to bring Jamie into this world. I never could have done it without your love and support."

"Nonsense Cassy, your mother and I just done what needed to be done, because we love you with all our heart. We are just thankful that we were close by when you really needed us. So you don't owe us a thing. We just want you to always be happy, and safe." Frank pushed his chair back from the table. "Guess I had better go to work." He said, as he leaned down and kissed Cassandra on the cheek, hugged, and kissed his wife, then went out and got in his pickup.

* * *

RIGHT AFTER CASSANDRA FED Jamie and helped her mother clean up the breakfast dishes. She gathered up all of her and Jamie's things, stuffing them into paper bags. Boy they sure had accumulated a lot of stuff in the short time they had been at her parent's house. Mentally she was wondering where she was going to put everything of Jamie's when they got to her trailer.

"I think I have everything, so guess I better get started hauling these bags down to my house." She smiled at her mother as she picked up a full paper bag in each hand.

"Lord, babies sure do need a lot of stuff, don't they?"

Nora laughed. "Yes, and it gets worse as they get older."

Since she hadn't seen Rays truck for several days now, she hoped that he had gone somewhere else to live and she wouldn't have to ever see him again. Oh how she wished that she could have the trailer to herself and Jamie for the rest of her life.

It had really been great these past few weeks to be able to relax, and feel safe and protected. If only it could last and she could be free of Ray for the last time. Nevertheless, Cassandra had a gut feeling that her wish would be short lived; she doubted that she could ever be that lucky.

Chapter Fourteen

IT HAD BEEN ALMOST two weeks since Cassandra had moved back to her own trailer with Jamie. There had been no sign of Ray at all, and she was beginning to relax, and settle into a daily routine. Life was great, and so peaceful, the way it was supposed to be.

Then when she least expected it, Ray walked into the trailer one night around nine o'clock, and saw her sitting there on the sofa watching television.

"Well look who we have here! The little woman has finally decided to come home. So what do you have to say for yourself, bitch? You know I wasn't too happy when you skipped out on me, so it better be good."

Cassandra was still trying to deal with the shock of seeing Ray again. She noticed that his attitude didn't appear to have changed any since she last saw him. He never even asked about the baby, he just marched in the house and started acting the same way as he did the night he had knocked her out of the trailer. Cassandra just glared at Ray, and never said a word. She could tell by his voice that no matter what she said, it would be the wrong thing. Therefore, she remained silent, refusing to answer him.

"I asked you a question Cassandra, and I demand that you give me an answer."

Cassandra just sat there and ignored him; too afraid to say anything. The look in Ray's eyes frightened her.

"Now Bitch!" Ray yelled at her.

"I'm sorry Ray but I just didn't feel your question required an answer." She responded calmly, watching his expression. "You knew where I was Ray, and you also knew why I was there, so what right do you have to come in here throwing your weight around demanding anything from me?"

"Don't talk back to me Cassandra; you know I don't like it." He snapped.

Then his mood changed, and he grinned. "Guess it's a good thing you showed up when you did baby, because I just came back to get the trailer. I found another job over near the coast in Salinas, and I needed a place to live." Ray informed her of his plans in a smug take it, or leave it manner. "I suppose since you have taken up residence in here again I'm stuck with you. So it looks like you, and that brat of yours will just have to come with me. After all I'm going to need someone to cook, and clean for me. So it might just as well be you. That way it will save me some money because I won't have to pay you a red cent."

Cassandra was speechless by what Ray had just told her. She sat there just staring at him, having no idea what to say. Then she found her voice. "Oh no you don't mister this is my trailer and it stays right here where it is. I want to stay here close to my parents so they can enjoy their grandchild."

Ray grabbed Cassandra by her upper arms and started shaking her. "I don't give a damn what you want bitch. I figure it's high time we put some much needed distance between you, and your parents."

Cassandra managed to jerk free from his hold on her, and spat at him. "And just where would I be today Ray, if it hadn't been for my parents? If I remember correctly you were just too busy at work when I needed to go to the hospital. For your information I came close to dying when I gave birth to your child, but evidently you could have cared less about either of us. You haven't the slightest idea of whether you have a son or a daughter, because you were only interested in yourself and never bothered to ask."

Pausing, Cassandra took a deep breath, she was shaking from head to toe, but she wasn't going to back down this time. "Well I don't intend to go any where with you Ray, I like it here. So if you want to leave then go ahead and leave. But the trailer is staying right here where it is with Jamie and me."

Ray knew that he had the upper hand, and he had made up his mind that he was taking the trailer to Salinas. "You need me Cassandra; this trailer was bought with my money so according to the law that makes it mine. Besides how are you planning to support yourself and that brat of yours? You don't even have a job, and no transportation, and when I leave you won't even have a home because I'm taking the trailer with me."

Ray stood there watching Cassandra like a cat watching a cornered mouse. "And just how long do you think your precious parents can afford to keep you and your squalling brat in that small trailer of theirs?" He sneered driving home his point.

"But Ray the trailer is in my Na…." The words died on her lips as Ray cut her off in mid sentence.

"Just shut the hell up Cassandra. The law says that you are my wife so you will go wherever I say. Understand?"

Cassandra nodded her head yes. She knew deep down that what Ray said was true, California was a community property state and men were the head of the household, and women were no better than another piece of a mans property. She knew she just couldn't move in with her parents with a new baby. It was not their responsibility to have to take care of her and Jamie. It just wasn't right for her to place this burden on her parents. She would have to go with Ray for now. At least until she regained her strength. Then when Jamie was a little older she would find a job, and some one to watch Jamie while she worked. For now she would just have to bide her time and plan for the day when she could take her precious baby and walk away from Ray and never look back.

* * *

THE NEXT MORNING RAY hooked onto the trailer while Cassandra was saying her goodbyes to her parents. Their goodbyes were short, because Ray was sitting in the pickup honking the horn. He wouldn't even walk down to speak to Frank and Nora before they left.

* * *

THE TRAILER COURT THAT Ray pulled the trailer into was quite a ways out of Salinas; Cassandra knew that it would be impossible for her and Jamie to walk into town, so her hopes that she would be able to find a job was out of the question. She knew that this had been Rays plan all along. Not only was she a hundred and sixty miles away from her parents, but her plans to find a job and save enough money to leave Ray would never become a reality. She was trapped in this farce of a marriage with no way out.

Cassandra was devastated but she refused to complain, even when Ray laid down the law, forbidding her to make friends with the other women in the trailer court. He even warned her that if he caught her talking to any of the people in the court he would hurt Jamie.

Cassandra was so afraid that if she didn't abide by Rays rules, that somehow he would carry his threat out to hurt Jamie. So she did what ever Ray told her to do. She didn't leave their small yard next to their trailer, except to go to the laundry room to do her wash. On the days she had to do washing, she kept her head lowered and didn't make eye contact, nor utter a single word to anyone. She never knew when Ray might come home at odd times to check up on her. She spent her days living in fear, afraid of what Ray might do to her, and even worse, what he might do to little Jamie.

* * *

LIFE DRAGGED BY FOR Cassandra, one day ran into the next. They had been living outside of Salinas for nine months. Jamie was growing like a weed. In spite of everything Jamie was a normal, healthy, happy baby. Cassandra made sure of that. She spent a good deal of her time playing with Jamie and teaching her things, and reading little wonder books to her to pass the time. While Jamie was taking her nap's Cassandra done things around the trailer. It was so small it wasn't hard to keep everything clean and neat, so that when Ray came home there wouldn't be anything for him to find fault with that would give him an excuse to start knocking her around again. He watched her every move as though he was waiting to pounce on her the minute she made a mistake. It kept her nerves almost to the breaking point, because she had to analyze every move she made before she made it whenever Ray was home.

Jamie was learning to crawl, and had started pulling her self up on everything in the trailer. One night after dinner while Cassandra was doing up the dishes, and Ray was sitting on the sofa watching television. Jamie was playing on the floor, she crawled over and pulled herself up on Rays pant leg holding her little arms up for Ray to pick her up the way Cassandra did, with a big smile on her little face, so proud of what she had learned. But Ray didn't pick her up, instead he slapped her. Jamie's little legs buckled and she sank down on the floor and started to cry. Not understanding why her daddy had hit her and wouldn't pick her up.

"Damn it Cassandra, get this screaming brat of yours away from me, can't you see that I'm busy?" He bellowed.

"My God Ray, she's only a baby. How could you hit her like that? Are you out of your mind?" Cassandra ran to Jamie and scooped her up in her arms, crooning to her.

"There, there sweetie, mommy's right here. Don't cry baby, Mommy loves you."

All the time Cassandra rocked back and forth on her feet, cradling Jamie in her arms, kissing her chubby cheek. Finally Jamie stopped crying, her little arms clinging tightly around Cassandra's neck.

As Cassandra stepped back out of Rays reach, she never said a word, just glared at him, hating him just a little more with each passing day.

As Cassandra got Jamie ready for bed, she vowed that she would do just about anything to prevent Ray from taking out his anger on Jamie. And if he ever hit Jamie again, somehow she would make him pay for it.

After Cassandra got Jamie settled in bed, she returned to the kitchen to finish cleaning up. Ray started to say something, but evidently changed his mind. He stood up and just walked out the door.

* * *

IT WAS QUITE LATE that night when Ray returned home, and he was drunk. Cassandra could feel fear well up inside her. This was the first time since they had moved to Salinas that Ray had gone out and gotten drunk. She prayed that he wasn't going to revert back to his old habits that he had before Jamie was born. Cassandra had secretly hoped that Ray had changed some, but it looked as though she had been wrong once again.

Long after Ray had passed out on the bed Cassandra laid there thinking. If only they didn't live so far out of Salinas, she would be able to find some sort of work so she could make enough money to get her and Jamie out of this awful situation before it was too late. Cassandra knew that if Ray had started drinking again it would only be a matter of time before the dreaded violence started again.

CHAPTER FIFTEEN

AFTER THAT NIGHT THEIR life changed drastically, Ray reverted back to the mean and hateful person he was before Jamie was born. He began patronizing the bars every night after work, staying out until all hours. He came home only when he felt like it, and would force Cassandra to have sex with him, practically raping her every night. When he was through he would roll over and go to sleep. Cassandra hated for him to touch her, he was like an animal. She had learned not to refuse him, because if she did, he would yell at her and start knocking her around. So she remained passive, and let him have his way with her. Knowing someday she would find a way out of this horrible, degrading nightmare.

*   *   *

WHAT FEW TIMES THAT Ray was home, Cassandra tried to stay busy and keep Jamie quiet and away from him. He was constantly finding fault with everything she did, and he would say hateful things to her trying to make her lose her calm. But no matter what Ray said to her, she refused to let him gourd her into saying something that would send him into one of his violent rages, and give him an excuse so he could feel justified when he beat her. Ray blamed Cassandra for all his violent rages by telling her that it was all her fault because she made him lose his temper. So she said nothing. Sometimes she could taste blood in her mouth from biting her tongue to keep from saying the wrong thing. That only made his anger worse when he couldn't make her fight back, and he would storm out of the trailer. Sometimes he stayed away for two or three days at a time before he came home again.

Cassandra never cared where Ray went, or how long he was gone. She was just glad that he wasn't around her and Jamie. It always gave her some breathing space, and a chance to try to figure some way that she and Jamie could escape from this constant nightmare that she was living in.

*   *   *

ONE DAY OUT OF the blue an idea came to her; maybe she could confide in Mrs. Flemming, she was an elderly woman who lived with her husband at the other end of the trailer court. They had met under the clothes line awhile back when she was hanging her wash out to dry. Cassandra liked the idea more and more. Glancing at the clock she noticed that it would soon be time for Ray to come home from work, so she would just have to wait to put her plan into action until the next day after Ray left for work. She was disappointed that she couldn't go see Mrs. Flemming right then, but it sure wouldn't do to have Ray come home and find her off talking to one of the neighbors. So it would just have to wait until tomorrow. Cassandra felt happy for the first time in months, and she smiled secretly to herself as she set the dishes on the table. She finally had a plan.

The next morning after Ray left for work Cassandra wanted to rush out of the house, but she decided she had better wait a little while just in case Ray doubled back for some reason. He had been in such a fowl mood this morning before he left for work that she didn't trust him. So she waited for an hour, then she bundled up Jamie and walked down to the other end of the trailer court and knocked on Mrs. Flemmings door.

⋆   ⋆   ⋆

"LAND SAKES ALIVE! COME in this house Child, out of the wind." Mrs. Flemmings face beamed with pleasure at her early morning caller. "Lordy, what a beautiful baby you have there. Do sit down, and take off your coats. I've got a fresh pot of coffee, would you like a cup?"

"Yes thank you that would be very nice." Cassandra smiled timidly, and started removing Jamie's hat and coat.

"So what brings you here child?" Mrs. Flemming asked as she poured out two cups of coffee, and a small glass of milk for Jamie.

The kindness of this gentle grandmotherly woman was Cassandra's undoing, the tears were forming in her eyes, and one slipped down her cheek as she replied. "Oh Mrs. Flemming please forgive me for bothering you so early in the morning. I shouldn't have come, but I just didn't know what else to do." Cassandra sobbed as she wiped the tears from her eyes.

"There, there, child, don't cry." Mrs. Flemming soothed as she patted Cassandra on the hand trying to comfort her. "Why don't you tell me all about it and perhaps I can help."

Cassandra sat Jamie down on the floor to play with the few little things she had brought with her, and tried to regain her composure. Then she slowly related the whole heart breaking story to Mrs. Flemming from the day she had married Ray. Making sure she didn't leave anything out. It was just such a relief to be able to confide in someone at last, and she felt so much better when she had finished pouring her heart out to this kind woman, she had held all this inside for much too long.

Mrs. Flemming was astounded by Cassandra's story, for a few minutes she was speechless. "Well Lassie, we can't do anything about this right now, but I promise you as soon as my Bengie gets home from work I'll have him go and get the county sheriff."

Cassandra jumped up from her chair scarred out of her wits, and wringing her hands, her eyes looked like a frightened animals that had been caught in the glare of someone's head lights. "Oh please don't do that Mrs. Flemming. I'm so afraid of what Ray might do to

Jamie and me if he should ever find out that I've told anyone." She begged.

"Please can't we just figure out some other way?" She pleaded.

Seeing the fear in Cassandra's eyes, Mrs. Flemming didn't want to cause the poor child any more hurt than she has already endured. "Very well child, don't you worry. As soon as my Bengie gets home I'll explain all this to him, and I just know that he will figure out some way that we can help you and little Jamie."

Cassandra hurriedly started putting on Jamie's coat and hat. As she stood up Mrs. Flemming put her arms around Cassandra and gave her a motherly hug. "Now don't you worry child everything is going to be okay. I promise you my Bengie will move heaven and earth to find a way to get you out of this horrible situation, and away from that dreadful man."

"Oh thank you Mrs. Flemming. I was praying that I could count on you to help me. Please don't mention to Ray that I was here, he wouldn't like it at all." She said as she scooped Jamie up in her arms and hastily left, running all the way back to her trailer at the other end of the court, praying that Ray hadn't returned while she had been gone.

*   *   *

THE NEXT MORNING MRS. Flemming saw Cassandra out at the community clothes lines hanging up some wash. She quickly gathered up some towels and walked to the laundry room. She thought that just in case Ray was around close by that it would look like she had some washing to do, and not purposely seeking Cassandra out. "I've got good news for you child. Bengie and I have figured out a way that we can help you." She panted, trying to catch her breath from the hasty walk from her trailer to the laundry room so as not to miss her chance to talk to Cassandra.

"My Bengie said that he has to take a load in his truck to San Jose next Friday, so if you and Jamie can be ready he will take you with him. He also said to tell you not to worry, because he won't leave until after we make sure that your husband has gone to work."

Cassandra was elated; finally her dream of getting away from Ray was going to come true. "Oh Mrs. Flemming, how can I ever thank you enough? You tell your Bengie that Jamie and I will be ready when he is."

"There's something else Cassandra, Bengie and I want to give you some money to tide you over until you get settled, and find a job."

"Oh no, I can't let you do that Mrs. Flemming, it just wouldn't be right."

"Nonsense child, Bengie and I want to do this for you. How about we just call it a loan for now, and you can pay us back when you get on your feet." She smiled, admiring this proud, independent young girl.

"In that case Mrs. Flemming, I'll accept the loan. But I promise you I will pay every cent of it back just as fast as I can. How can I ever thank you and your husband for what you are doing for my baby and me?" Cassandra said as she gave Mrs. Flemming a hug to show her appreciation.

"Don't you worry about that child. Just knowing that you and Jamie won't have to suffer anymore abuse, will be more than payment enough."

Cassandra stepped away from Mrs. Flemming. "Guess I better get back to the trailer I don't like leaving Jamie alone very long, even though she's taking her nap I still worry about her."

"One more thing dear, Bengie will stay in San Jose over the weekend and help you find a suitable apartment for you and Jamie. We just want to be sure you are safe and have a roof over your head."

"Oh Mrs. Flemming, you are so kind. How can I ever repay you?" Cassandra could feel the tears forming on her lashes, and tried to blink them away.

"Go along now child, and don't you worry about a thing. We'll be watching for Ray to leave Friday morning, then Bengie will come for you and Jamie."

Cassandra ran all the way back to her trailer eager to start putting some things together that they would take with them. As she packed various things they would need, she hid them under the bed so that Ray wouldn't see them.

Cassandra was numb with excitement; finally she was going to be able to escape from Ray at last. One more week, then she would be free from the living nightmare she had been in for so long. "Please dear God, don't let anything mess up this chance for me now that it has come so unexpectedly." She whispered silently.

But fate stepped in and changed things in her favor. Tuesday Ray came home unexpectedly in the middle of the day. He was angrier than Cassandra had ever seen him before. He was cussing a blue streak, and waving a bunch of papers in the air. The veins on the side of his neck were bulging, and looked about ready to burst at any minute.

Fear gripped Cassandra as she thought that Ray had been fired once again, and she blurted out. "What in the world has happened Ray?"

Before she had a chance to step away, Ray grabbed her by her upper arms and started shaking her so hard she thought her neck would snap.

"What the hell do you think has happened, bitch? The damn government just screwed up my life. The dirty bastards have recalled me into active duty." Then he slapped her across the face with the papers he still had in his hand. "Two more lousy months, and those bastards couldn't have touched me." He ranted, slapping her with the papers again, then shoved her down on the sofa and threw the papers in her face. "Read the damned orders they sent me. I have to report for duty the day after tomorrow in San Francisco."

Cassandra was shaking, she wasn't sure if it was from her fear of Ray, or her excitement from learning that he had been recalled to active duty. She could care less that he had to go away; she just needed to know how far away he would be from her and Jamie, and how long he would be gone. Nervously trying to hide the fact of how happy this news had made her, she asked calmly.

"Did they say where they are sending you Ray?" She rose from the sofa, not knowing if she should dance or take flight. The way Ray was still ranting and raving at her.

"Just my damned lousy luck. The bastards had to go and start that damn Berlin crisis now, and they are sending me to France for at least a year, maybe more. Who knows with those assholes in Washington?" He roared shoving Cassandra aside, causing her to fall, then stormed out of the trailer slamming the door behind him.

* * *

CASSANDRA REMAINED SITTING ON the floor where she had fallen when Ray had roughly shoved her aside when he left. She started to cry, and laugh at the same time. She was positively beside herself, and bursting with happiness to know that in just two days she would be free from Ray for at least a year. In that time she could find a job, and divorce Ray before he returned to the United States again. God had finally answered her prayers.

* * *

WITH HER EYES GLISTENING with tears, and a smile on her face, Cassandra picked up Jamie and swung her around making her giggle. Then she rushed down through the trailer court to tell Mrs. Flemming her good news.

"Child you don't know how happy this makes me to know that you and your baby will know some peace at last. Plus the government will pay an allotment for you and Jamie. It will give you something to live on, and if you are real careful maybe you won't have to find a job." Mrs. Flemming told Cassandra as she hugged her close.

Cassandra in her excitement hadn't given any thought as to what they would live on. All she had thought about was that Ray would be out of their lives, and she would have a whole year to plan a new life for her and Jamie that didn't include Ray at all. She had no idea that the government would pay her a monthly allotment while Ray was gone, and that added bonus was heaven sent. Cassandra knew for certain now that her, and Jamie were going to do just fine.

"I got to run before Ray comes back and finds me gone." Quickly she kissed Mrs. Flemming on the cheek, and ran back through the trailer court as fast as she could, carrying Jamie in her arms.

* * *

IT WAS LATE THAT night when Ray finally returned home. Cassandra was sitting on the sofa watching a movie. When Ray came through the door he threw the check book, and savings pass book on Cassandra's lap. "Here bitch, you can have these, I won't need them where I'm going."

As Ray started pulling some of his clothes from the drawers and closet that he planned to take with him, Cassandra opened the bank books and noticed that Ray had drawn out all but thirty dollars from each account, leaving her with only sixty dollars for her and Jamie to live on. "I don't understand how you could take all our money out of the bank Ray. What will Jamie and I do until my allotment comes through, or I can find a job?"

Ray just turned around and laughed. "That's not my problem bitch, I've got a war to fight."

Cassandra didn't say anymore, she certainly wasn't going to beg Ray for anything.

* * *

EARLY THE NEXT MORNING they drove to Salinas to the bus station. When they arrived Ray jumped out and got his things from the back of the pickup, then tossed his keys at Cassandra through the window. "Here bitch you might need these. And don't wreck my truck while I'm gone, or you'll be sorry." He issued one last warning before walking away, without so much as a goodbye to her and Jamie.

CHAPTER SIXTEEN

CASSANDRA SAT QUIETLY ALONE the next morning enjoying a cup of coffee while she waited for Jamie to wake up so she could feed her breakfast. It was great not having to put up with Rays verbal abuse before he left for work. The trailer was so peaceful, and no one banging around making noise. She decided to just let Jamie sleep as long as she wanted. Something Jamie hadn't been able to do since she was born, because Ray refused to be quiet in the mornings so Jamie always woke up scared, and crying. Then Ray would rant, and rave, and call her a squalling brat. He would threaten to spank her if she didn't shut up. Cassandra always intervened because she wanted to divert Ray's attention away from Jamie. Cassandra would put up with anything Ray had to dish out if it would protect her precious Jamie from his rage.

Now that Ray was gone they could both relax and feel free to do what ever they wanted, and wouldn't have to worry about Ray venting his anger on them anymore. Just thinking about how nice their life was going to be from now on brought a huge smile to Cassandra's face, and she hummed a little tune while she poured herself another cup of coffee.

* * *

JAMIE WOKE UP ABOUT nine o'clock. Cassandra fed her some cereal, and then gave her a bath. Then she put a sweater on Jamie and they casually strolled through the trailer park to Mrs. Flemmings house to see if she could use her telephone to make a collect call to her father. It was so nice to be able to enjoy the early morning sunshine, and hear the birds singing in the trees. Something they had never experienced before because they always had to rush before Ray came home and found them off gallivanting around the trailer park, as he called it. Then he would start accusing Cassandra of things she hadn't done. And the verbal and physical abuse would always follow.

* * *

FEELING A SENSE OF peace, and freedom for the first time since she had married Ray, Cassandra had a spring in her step and a smile on her face, as she went up the steps to Mrs. Flemmings porch and knocked on the door.

"Come in this house Child. My, but don't you two look just simply radiant this morning." Mrs. Flemming beamed at them as she stepped back to allow them to enter.

"I wonder if you would allow me to use your phone to make a collect call to my father." Cassandra inquired politely.

"Of course child. The phone is right there on the counter help yourself. I'll just take the wee ones sweater off while you make your call, then I'll get us a cup of coffee."

Soon as Frank Benning came on the phone, Cassandra was all chocked up just hearing her father's voice. "Oh daddy, I need your help." She wailed, and before she could say anything else, her father cut in.

"Cassy baby, has something happened to Jamie?"

Hearing the worry in her father's voice, Cassandra hastily reassured him that Jamie was okay. "No daddy, it's nothing like that. The reason I called is because Ray has been recalled back into active duty, and he left yesterday morning for France. Since he will be gone for at least a year, maybe longer, I don't want to stay here in Salinas. So I wondered if you would have time to come over and move my trailer back to Hollister."

"You know I always have time for you, and Jamie. How soon do you want me to come get you?"

"Well first I have to find a place in Hollister to park the trailer. I have Rays truck, but I was afraid that I wouldn't be able to move the trailer by myself. Plus I need to find a job as well because Ray took all the money out of the bank, including our savings, and only left me with sixty dollars. The rent here is paid for the next three weeks, so I figured if Jamie and I can stay with you and mother for a short time, I can make enough money in three weeks to rent a trailer space in Hollister."

"Cassy there is a vacant trailer space here in the court right now. I'll just go and pay the rent on it. Honey just go to the manager of the trailer court and explain the circumstances to him, and I'm sure that he will be more than happy to give you a refund for the three weeks rent. Then start getting everything ready in your trailer for the move and I'll be there first thing in the morning, is that soon enough?" Frank teased. He could hardly wait to tell Nora that their little girl was going to be living close by again.

"That's great daddy. Jamie and I will be ready and waiting. Thanks daddy, I love you." Cassandra hung up the phone, and smiled at Mrs. Flemming who was sitting near by with Jamie on her lap.

"I couldn't help but over hear your conversation child. I'm glad that you won't be going off to San Jose with my Bengie. I dreaded the idea of you and Jamie being alone in a strange town, and on your own with out a living soul to look after you." The tears of joy were slipping unnoticed down Mrs. Flemmings cheeks.

"I'm so glad that your daddy is going to come get you. It will be so much better this way child, for both of you and your darlin' little girl to be close to your own family who will look after you." She said smiling through her tears.

"Tell me child, why didn't you come and use my phone a long time ago to call your daddy?"

Cassandra's eyes filled with sadness as she explained. "I couldn't call my father while Ray was still here because I've never told my parents how badly Ray treated me. I knew that if my father ever found out about the abuse he would probably beat Ray within an inch of his life, maybe even kill him. I simply just couldn't take the chance of the consequences that my father might end up going to jail because of me. I knew in my heart that I could never have been able to live with my conscious if something like that ever happened. So I kept it to myself all this time. And I want you to promise me that you will never tell my father what I have confided to you. Daddy must never find out the truth."

"Now don't you worry about a single thing child, your secret is safe with me and my Bengie. We would rather cut off our right arm than to ever bring any hurt to you child, you are like the daughter we never had."

"Oh thank you Mrs. Flemming, I'm hoping that I can save enough money to pay for a divorce from Ray during the coming year, and be free from him when he returns to the states again."

"You just keep in touch with me and Bengie dearie. If there is ever anything that Bengie and I can do to help you and your child dearie, I want you to promise me that you will let us know immediately. If by some chance you can't come up with the money for your divorce before that dreadful man returns you just let me know, and Bengie and I will see that you get whatever you need."

"Oh Mrs. Flemming, how can I ever repay you and your husband, for all your kindness and support that you have given me. I want you to know that there will always be a special place in my heart for both of you as long as I live."

"Nonsense child, you don't owe us a thing. You just take care of yourself, and your darlin baby girl, and drop us a note occasionally and let us know how you are doing, that will be payment enough for us." Mrs. Flemming gave them both a hug.

"Now go along child and make preparations for the move so you will be all set when your daddy gets here in the mornin'. May God bless you both."

* * *

SOON AS FRANK BENNING hung up the phone he told his wife the news. "Guess what Nora? That was our little girl and she is coming home. Cassy said that Ray was recalled to active duty and she wants to come back here to live while he is gone. So I'm going to Salinas early in the morning and pull her trailer back here to Hollister."

"Oh Frank, that's great news. I can hardly wait to see Cassy and the baby again, it has been so long." Tears were running unchecked down Nora's face as Frank took her in his arms and held her close.

"Will you be okay honey? I've got to run over to the manager's office and secure that vacant space for Cassy's trailer before they rent it to someone else."

"I'll be just fine Frank, now that I know our Cassy is coming home again."

* * *

THE NEXT MORNING WHILE Frank Benning was driving to Salinas, all he could think about was how nice it was going to be having Cassy and little Jamie, living close to them again. Only God knew how much he and Nora had missed both of them these past months. Jamie must be learning to walk now; they had missed all the little things a baby does the first year.

"By God that's about to change." Frank said aloud, and started to whistle a tune as he drove along the highway headed for Salinas, and his little girl.

* * *

WHEN THEY ARRIVED AT the trailer court in Hollister, Frank and Cassandra got the trailer leveled and securely blocked. It was starting to get sundown by then and they were both tired and ready to quit for the day.

"Well kiddo, bet your mother has dinner ready for us, so how about we go see what she's prepared for us to eat. I don't know about you, but those sandwiches you fixed for us to eat on the road wore off a long time ago. I'm so hungry I think I could eat a horse." Frank put his arm around Cassandra's shoulders and smiled down at her, she could see the love for her shining in his eyes. She smiled up at her father, and then wrapped her arm around his waist, and they walked that way through the trailer court to where Nora and Jamie were waiting for them. Father and daughter, arm in arm the way it was before she married Ray. Life was going to be good again.

* * *

"YOU TWO GET WASHED up, while I put dinner on the table. I fixed meatloaf, and baked potatoes, and a salad." Nora informed them smiling, and juggling Jamie on her hip, who was reaching out to Cassandra with her chubby little arms.

"Come here sugar bug." Cassandra crooned her nickname for Jamie as she took Jamie in her arms and hugged her close.

"Go ahead and wash up first daddy while I give my little daughter a much needed cuddle." She smiled hugging Jamie close.

"Sure thing honey then it's my turn to cuddle my granddaughter, something I've been wanting to do for several months."

* * *

AFTER DINNER WAS FINISHED and the dishes cleared away; Cassandra broached the subject that she had been thinking about all day while she drove Ray's truck and followed her father pulling her trailer.

"Mom, would you mind watching Jamie for me in the morning while I go out and see if I can find a job someplace?"

"You bet I will Cassy. It will give Jamie and me a chance to get acquainted, and do a little grandmother and granddaughter bonding."

Nora agreed smiling, reaching out to tickle Jamie under her chubby little chin, making Jamie giggle wildly.

* * *

EARLY THE NEXT MORNING while Cassandra was having her coffee, and waiting for Jamie to wake up, she wrote down a few places that she thought she might check out to see if they were hiring. She needed to find a job as soon as possible because the sixty dollars Ray had left her, and the twelve dollar refund she had gotten on the space in Salinas wouldn't last for very long. She finally decided that the first place she would try was Grants Truck Stop. Cassandra had done some waitress work in the past, and the tips would really help until she got her first paycheck.

* * *

JAMIE WOKE UP AT seven o'clock. Cassandra fed Jamie her favorite cereal, Fruit Loops. Afterwards Cassandra bathed Jamie and got her dressed and ready to go to grandma's house.

"Well sweetie this is going to be a big day, wish mommy luck."

Cassandra picked up Jamie, then grabbed up the paper bag that she had put a couple of extra changes of clothes along with Jamie's favorite blanket, and a few toys, plus a couple of her favorite little wonder books, and walked through the trailer court to her mothers trailer.

Nora had seen Cassandra coming through the court, and walked out to help her.

"Goodness Cassandra, why did you try to carry everything at once, couldn't you have made two trips? Here let me take Jamie." Nora scolded reaching to take Jamie out of Cassandra's arms.

"Thanks mother, Jamie slept a little longer than I expected, and I was running a little late. I wanted to get an early start job hunting, and figured I could make it in just one trip." Cassandra explained trying to catch her breath. "Lord but that child is getting heavy. I'll be glad when she can walk better."

"You run along Cassy, Jamie and I will be just fine." Nora assured her after they had gotten everything in the trailer.

"Okay mother, wish me luck. I hope Jamie isn't too much for you today. And I promise that as soon as I land a steady job I'm going to get a baby sitter."

*　*　*

AS LUCK WOULD HAVE it when Cassandra arrived at Grants Truck Stop she learned that one of the waitresses had suddenly taken ill, and they were short handed so they hired her right on the spot. The boss told her the job paid seventy-five cents an hour, plus tips, and handed her an apron. Then he gave her a crash course on where everything was located, and pointed out to her which station was hers for the day.

Good thing Cassandra had done waitress work before because the place was packed with truckers. She wasn't acquainted with the menu so she had to look up the prices to figure the tickets, but everyone knew she was a new hire and they were all real patient with her. The day just flew by and she was surprised when the boss came over to her.

"You done a good job today Cassandra, the job is yours permanent if you want it." He informed her.

"I sure do want it, thank you sir. But what about the girl that is off sick, won't she be coming back when she gets well?"

"Brenda won't be coming back. She called awhile ago and told me she needs an operation, so she's going to stay with her parents in Los Angeles."

"Well if that's the case I'll see you in the morning. What time do you want me to start?" Cassandra inquired.

"Your hours will be six in the morning till two in the afternoon, and call me Gary. Okay?"

"Okay Gary, but only if you'll call me Cassy. Is it a deal?" She asked as she reached out her right hand to shake on it.

"It's a deal Cassy. And I might add it's the best deal I think I've made in a long time. Now get out of here before I change my mind." He ordered with a grin on his face.

"See you in the morning. Thanks again Gary for giving me the job." She waved as she went out the door.

*   *   *

WHEN CASSANDRA WALKED INTO her mother's trailer, she flopped into the nearest chair. "Gosh I'm sorry mother for leaving Jamie with you so long. I had no idea that they would put me right to work. The entire day has been like a whirl wind. I'm sorry that I didn't at least give you a call and let you know what was going on."

"That's quite alright Cassy. I sort of figured that you probably found a job and they put you right to work."

"You look as beat as I do mother, guess chasing after Jamie all day really wore you out."

"Yes I am a little tired, but it was fun. Jamie is such a good child, hardly any bother at all. I'll get used to it in time." Nora admitted.

"I'll get busy and try and find someone to look after Jamie mother, I'm afraid that it will just be too much for you to do all the time. I'm so sorry to have to burden you with baby sitting, after all it's not your responsibility, and I don't intend to let you do it for very long." Cassandra assured her mother.

"That's okay Cassy, you don't have to apologize. I really did enjoy keeping Jamie. We had a ball getting to know each other. She is such a little angel. But I must admit it will take some getting used to, the last little baby I was around was you dear, and that was several years ago." Nora smiled at the thought.

"Mom I'm exhausted, so I think I'm going to go take a hot shower and Jamie and I are going to have an early night." She said as she picked up the bag of Jamie's things.

"This time I think I'll take your advice and make two trips. I'll be back for Jamie in a few minutes."

It was only a few minutes until Cassandra was back to collect Jamie. Soon as she entered the trailer her mother told her some very good news.

"Oh by the way dear before I forget. Do you remember Doris Thomas that lives on the other side of the court? She stopped by for coffee today, and she told me that she needs to pick up some extra work to sort of help out since her husband got laid off at the plant and he had to take another job that pays less money than he was making. Anyway she said to tell you that she would love to baby sit for you for twenty-five cents an hour if you want her too. It would help you, and also help her out at the same time."

"Why that would be great mother, I was hoping that I could find someone here in the trailer court so Jamie would be close to home, and you could still see her. Yes I do remember Doris. If I remember correctly she is about twenty years younger than you are mother so I'm sure it wouldn't be a strain on her coping with a toddler, and I'm sure Jamie will love her."

"I really would love to keep Jamie and save you the expense of a baby sitter, but your father wants me to go on a trip with him in a couple of weeks. Your father and I have known Doris and Ted for a long time now; they seem like real good people, so I'm sure Jamie will be well taken care of. Doris said for you to let her know if you want her to take care of Jamie."

Cassandra was pleased that her parents were going on a trip, she had been so wrapped up in her own problems that she had completely forgotten that it was her fathers vacation time.

"That's great mother. You and daddy go right ahead and take your trip, and I don't want you to worry about Jamie and I, we'll be just fine. I'm going to go right now and see Doris before someone else hires her. Isn't it just wonderful mother how everything is working out for all of us? I've found a real good job, and the hours are great, and now I even have a baby sitter lined up." Cassandra hugged her mother and kissed her on the cheek.

"Thanks mother, I really don't know what I would have done without you and daddy. I love you both so much." She whispered softly.

"We love you too sweetie, now run along and see Doris, then you better get yourself some rest, you look positively beat." Nora said as she patted Cassandra on the back.

*   *   *

LATER THAT EVENING, AFTER she had gotten everything all squared away with Doris Thomas, who had been tickled to death to get the job for the extra money. Plus the hours fitted right in with her requirements for the time her husband was at work so everyone was pleased with the arrangements. Cassandra had fed and bathed Jamie and had her all settled into bed for the night and was feeling pretty good about everything, and life in general. She made herself some coffee, and sat down at the table with pencil and paper to make a list of the bills she had to pay each month, including the baby sitter. She figured that her allotment check would just about cover all her bills, and what she made at the truck stop would go for groceries and utilities. With any luck she could save a good part of her tips for emergencies, and hopefully one day have enough to pay for a divorce from Ray before he returned home.

Cassandra yawned and stretched, she was completely exhausted from the day's events. She picked up the things off the table and put them away, then took a shower and crawled into bed. She laid there in the dark very relaxed, knowing that she didn't have to worry about Ray coming home drunk and raping her. Never again would he be able to beat her into submission. Cassandra drifted off to sleep with a smile on her face, happy for the first time in a long time knowing that her nightmare was finally over.

Chapter Seventeen

As the days passed by Cassandra settled into her routine at home, and on the job, she was quite content with her life until the day Rays father came into the truck stop with a couple of other guys for lunch, and discovered that Cassandra was working there as a waitress.

"Well; if it isn't my son's little wife." Alex sneered, then his attitude changed and things suddenly turned ugly.

"What the hell do you think you are doing working in a place like this Cassandra? Does Ray know about this job?" Alex asked gruffly, letting Cassandra know by the tone of his voice that he totally disapproved.

"I had to get a job to support Jamie and me, not that it's any of your business." She snapped.

"Well don't think you are going to get away with it missy, I'll make damn sure I tell Ray the next time I hear from him. So if you know what's good for you young lady you'll hand in your notice, and get back home where you belong." Alex said raising his voice in anger.

When Gary Grant the owner of the truck stop heard the loud voices, he came out of the kitchen to see what all the commotion was about.

"What seems to be the problem here?" He asked as he approached the table where Alex and his companions were sitting.

"It's none of your damn business. This is strictly between my worthless daughter-in-law, and me. So just back off mister." Alex snarled as he started to rise up from his chair.

"I own this establishment, and I'm making it my business. I can't have people coming in here yelling at my employees, and upsetting the other customers, so I'm asking you and your friends to leave right now, and don't come back. If I see you in here again I'll have to call the police."

Cassandra was so embarrassed that she wanted to run and hide somewhere but her feet seemed to be rooted to the spot where she was standing, she didn't know what to do, or what to say.

"Come on Cassandra, why don't you take a little break. These fellows are leaving so they won't be bothering you again." Gary said as he guided her gently away from the table, towards the kitchen.

"You haven't heard the last of this Cassandra." Alex yelled at her over his shoulder, as his friends hustled him out the front door.

"Do you know that guy?" Gary questioned as they entered the kitchen area.

"Yes, he's my father-in-law. I'm so sorry about all this Gary, if you want to let me go, I'll understand." Cassandra responded as tears formed on her lashes.

"I'm not about to let you go honey, you are the best waitress I've got. What's his son like anyway?" Gary asked out of curiosity.

"Pretty much the same only worse." Cassandra said, wiping the tears from her eyes.

"Well don't you worry about that guy. If he ever bothers you again, you just let me know. Now go powder your nose, put a smile on your face, and get back to work." Gary said winking at her to ease the tension, and playfully swatted her on the behind with the back of his hand, much like he would if he were shooing off a child to go play.

*   *   *

THE END OF NOVEMBER Cassandra's parents decided to take another trip, Cassandra noticed their car was in front of their trailer when she arrived home from work and she thought she would let them settle in before she went down to welcome them home. Suddenly there was a knock at the door. Seeing her parents standing on the porch, Cassandra squealed and threw her arms around Frank's neck.

"Oh daddy it is so good to have you and mother home again. Jamie and I really missed you both." Then Cassandra threw her arms around her mother and gave her a big hug. Frank seemed to be beaming from ear to ear. Cassandra could tell that they had some great news for her.

"Come on in the house I'm dying to hear what all you done on your trip."

"Well Cassy we finally did it. Your mother and I just bought a grocery store, and gas station in a small logging town in southern Idaho. I'm going to retire from my job next week, and we will be leaving the end of the month." Frank told her proudly.

"Oh daddy, I'm so proud of you." Cassandra threw her arms around her father's neck, and kissed him on the cheek. "Jamie and I are sure going to miss you."

"Hold on honey, we don't plan to leave without you. There's plenty of land that goes with the place, and there are already hookups for two trailer spaces. Nora and I figured if you and Jamie want to make the move with us, then we can all be together."

Cassandra didn't even hesitate about whether or not she wanted to go with them, as she knew how much Rays family detested her, and once her parents were no longer close by, the Cartone's would probably make her life miserable.

"Oh daddy, of course we'll move to Idaho with you. I just have to give Mr. Grant a two weeks notice before I can leave. He has been so good to me; I couldn't possibly leave him short handed."

Frank was quick to respond. "There will be plenty of time to work out your notice kiddo. We won't be leaving until the day after

Christmas, as we don't take possession of the property until the first of January."

Cassandra knew that she was making the right decision, by putting some much needed distance between her and the Cartone family she would stand a much better chance starting a new life. The Cartone's wouldn't know where she was, and they wouldn't be able to tell Ray when he returned to the states. Good riddance to the whole lot of them.

Frank and Nora were happy that Cassandra and Jamie were going to move north with them because they had already made up their mind that no way in hell were they going to leave their only daughter and granddaughter alone in California to fend for themselves.

"Well baby looks like that's all settled then, we all go to Idaho. Since you have never towed a trailer before Cassy, I'll line up a tow truck driver to pull your trailer to Idaho, and you and Jamie can follow us in your pickup."

"That sounds great daddy. How much do you think that will cost? I'm a little short on money." She confessed.

"Don't worry about that Cassy, with Rays rank in the service the government will pay for one move for his family while he is overseas. Your mother and I will pay the tow truck driver when he delivers your trailer to Idaho, and you can hand it back when you get the reimbursement for the move from the government. How does that sound?"

"That sounds just fine, I wasn't even aware that the government would do that for me. What would I ever do without you and mother? There is so much for me to learn. I didn't even know that I would get an allotment check every month until the lady in Salinas told me after Ray left."

*   *   *

AS FRANK AND NORA walked back to their trailer, Frank commented to Nora.

"That's odd that Ray didn't tell Cassandra about the monthly allotment, and the moving expenses. He had to know that she would be entitled to them."

"I don't know Frank. But you know Ray, he has always been pretty selfish, and self centered. Ray doesn't think about anyone, except Ray." Nora replied sadly wishing that Cassandra had never married Ray in the first place. It hurt her deeply when the sparkle left Cassandra's eyes, but lately she had noticed that Cassandra was more like her old self since Ray shipped out overseas.

* * *

FRANK HAD BEEN BUSY tying up all the loose ends with his job before retiring, and had made all the arrangements with the tow truck company regarding Cassandra's trailer, he stopped by her trailer one evening. "Well honey it looks like we got everything all set on our end for the move. How is everything going for you? Do you need any help with anything?"

"I think I've just about got everything ready to go, except for loading the blocks into the pickup, and the suit cases with our things that we'll need until my trailer house gets up there." Cassandra smiled trying to hide how excited she was to be leaving the state of California, and the Cartone family behind once and for all

"How soon do you think we will be leaving daddy?"

"I figure in about three days, first thing Friday morning. By the way Cassy, how did it go when you left after working out your two weeks notice?"

Cassandra smiled. "A lot better than I expected. Mr. Grant wished me a safe trip, and all the happiness in the world. Said if I ever come back to this area and need a job, he would always have one for me. Then he gave me my paycheck, and an envelope. Said he couldn't handle goodbyes too well, and asked me not to open the envelope until I got home. I sure was surprised to find five twenty dollar bills in the envelope along with a note that said God bless you and your little daughter. Signed; the Grants."

When Frank saw the tears welling up in Cassandra's eyes, he put his arm around her and hugged her. " Well honey I just guess Mr. & Mrs. Grant must have thought quite a lot of you, and this is just their way of showing their appreciation for the good job you done for them." Frank gave Cassandra a quick peck on the cheek. "I better get going honey, got a few more things to do yet before Friday."

*   *   *

EARLY THE DAY BEFORE they were going to move Jamie's great grand-mother Cartone arrived along with a young woman who was driving the car that stopped in front of Cassandra's trailer. When Cassandra opened the door the young woman introduced herself as Miss. Nobel with the State of California Childs Protective Services, and informed Cassandra that this wasn't a social visit.

"We are here to pick up your child Mrs. Cartone, and place her into protective custody. I assume that you have the child's things packed and ready to go as you have been instructed to do by the court order."

Cassandra just stood there gaping; "I don't have any idea what in the world you are talking about, and you certainly aren't taking my daughter anywhere."

Miss. Nobel seemed a little disconcerted when she realized that Cassandra really didn't have any idea what-so-ever why they were at her home. So she explained what the circumstances were to Cassandra. "It has been brought to our attention that you are work-ing the night shift at a local bar, and are leaving your small daughter home alone at night while you are working. And according to the California state law that makes you an unfit mother, and I have been instructed to come and pick up your daughter and place her in pro-tective custody."

Cassandra suddenly realized that this must be a put up job by Ray's family to prevent her from taking Jamie out of the state of California.

"I regret to inform you Miss Nobel that you have been duped by a pack of lies that have been made up by the Cartone family, I have no idea how they were able to get this phony order pushed through your office to do their dirty work for them, but I can assure you that you are not taking my daughter anywhere, not now, not ever!" Cassandra paused taking a deep breath.

"For your information Miss. Nobel, I have been working for Grants truck stop for quite some time. I worked from six in the morning until two in the afternoon. I suggest that you call Mr. Grant and confirm that. As for the charge of leaving my daughter alone while I worked, that too is a lie. Mrs. Doris Thomas who lives directly across from my trailer has been taking care of Jamie for me every day while I'm at work. I strongly suggest that you take a minute when you leave my house and go and talk to her."

Then Cassandra looked directly at Ray's grandmother. "For your information you frustrated old busy body. The only place that I go at night is down to my parent's house for an occasional meal, and I take Jamie with me. She has never been left alone for a single minute. You can ask anyone in this trailer court, and they will be able to confirm that what I'm saying is the truth."

Cassandra trying very hard to control her emotions stepped quickly over to the door and swung in wide open. "Now ladies if you will excuse me, I must ask you to leave my house. This conversation is over!"

Rays grandmother, left the trailer sputtering, and fuming, because it was clearly evident that her plans had gone up in smoke.

Miss. Nobel was embarrassed that the Cartone's had lied to her, and placed her in an awkward position. "Mrs. Cartone I can't tell you how sorry I am for this terrible inconvenience, and I sincerely hope that you will accept my apologies on behalf of the State of California Child Protective Services. I was unaware that the facts that were provided to me by the Cartone family were so elaborately distorted. I want you to know that I do believe what you have told me, but for the record I have to talk to Mr. Grant, and Mrs. Thomas. Whom I'm sure will confirm your story. That way nobody can say that I didn't perform my duties according to the State Law. And further more I can assure you that you will have no further contact from our office in the future."

"Apology accepted Miss. Nobel; I understand you were just doing your job."

"Rest assured Mrs. Cartone the State of California will not take this lightly if your story checks out, and I have every reason to believe that it will. If it will bring you any comfort it is a felony to file false charges. Good day dear, once again may I apologize on behalf of the State of California for intruding in your life."

Cassandra watched as Miss. Nobel walked over to Doris Thomas's trailer and knocked on the door. Then she closed the door and sat down in the nearest chair, her legs were trembling so bad she was afraid that they would no longer hold her up. It was hard to believe that Ray's family hated her so much, that they would go to such lengths to keep her from moving out of the state with Jamie. She wondered if somehow Ray had put them up to this. Then she smiled, and thought. So much for the best laid plans. Tomorrow she and Jamie would be well on their way, and she hoped with all her heart that she would never see any of the Cartone family ever again.

*   *   *

THREE DAYS LATER THEY arrived in the little southern Idaho town, population four hundred the sign outside of town proclaimed. Cassandra decided that she already liked it here, sort of felt like she was coming home at last. Years ago before her father went to work for the company in California; they had lived on a small ranch in northern Idaho where she had grown up.

*   *   *

THE NEXT DAY HER trailer arrived, and she spent the day getting settled. That night after she had fed, and bathed Jamie, and gotten her into bed, Cassandra sat down and wrote a letter to the government to give them a change of address for her allotment checks, and to

137

forward the receipt for the tow truck for reimbursement so that she could pay her parents back the money she owed them. She knew she was going to have to be very careful with her money until she could find a job. At least parking her trailer on her father's property she wouldn't have to pay any rent that was sure going to be a big help to her financially.

*   *   *

SO FAR THE ONLY part of her plans that weren't working out, was the fact that when she tried to file for a divorce from Ray in California. She had been informed that the government wouldn't let her divorce Ray while he was overseas. Something to do with the fact there was a conflict of war going on. She was told that she would have to wait until Ray returned to the states before she could divorce him.

She decided that even though she had to stay married to Ray for the next year, she wouldn't have to worry about him inflicting any pain on her and Jamie anymore, at least for the time being she would be free.

Chapter Eighteen

C ASSANDRA HAD BEEN VERY careful not to give out her address to anyone except the government for her allotment checks. So it was a tremendous shock when she went to the small post office to collect her mail one day, and found a letter to her from Ray. She wondered how in the world he had found out where she was. The only possible way he could have found her, was through the service records, or allotment department. Even his parents didn't know that she was moving to Idaho. Cassandra wanted to run, and never look back. Her first thought was to tear up Ray's letter, and throw it away. But she decided she better open it, and find out what it said.

The whole content of his letter was cussing at her. It was full of threats of what he was going to do to her when he returned to the states. At the end he ordered her to move back to California if she knew what was good for her. Not once did he even mention Jamie, it was as though she didn't even exist.

Cassandra was shaking visibly when she finished reading Rays letter. But she was determined not to be intimidated by Ray's threats through the mail, he couldn't control her anymore and she wasn't going to let anything he had to say in a letter turn her into a scared rabbit looking over her shoulder afraid of her own shadow.

Cassandra liked her life just the way it was now, she enjoyed her freedom, and independence too much. No way would she ever go back to the way life was before when she was living with Ray. She had made up her mind that never again was she going to live in fear, or let anyone ever abuse her again. Life was too short, she had Jamie's welfare to consider now, and she wasn't ever going to let anyone hurt her child. Jamie meant more to her, than life it's self.

* * *

NOT WANTING TO TAKE a chance that the Cartone family would someday try to take Jamie away from her the way they did in California. Cassandra decided that she would take in ironing, and do house cleaning for a few people to make extra money. That way she could keep Jamie with her all the time, and not have to leave her with strangers.

Cassandra asked her father if it would be okay if she put up a notice on his bulletin board soliciting for ironing, or house cleaning work. In no time at all, Cassandra had several offers for both. She just couldn't believe how many people in the small town requested her services. And the best part of all the ones who wanted her to clean their house said it would be alright for her to bring Jamie along. And the ones who had her do their ironing, would drop their clothes off at her house on certain days, and told her to call when she was done, and they would come and pick up their ironing.

Cassandra didn't want to keep people waiting, so she would sometimes iron late into the night so that they could have their things the next day. Besides doing most of the ironing at night, Cassandra didn't have to worry about Jamie being underfoot near the ironing board. Plus it gave her more time to play with Jamie during the day. It paid off in the end, because Jamie was a very happy well adjusted child. Everyone loved having her around.

* * *

JAMIE WAS GROWING LIKE a weed; she would be two years old in the summer. Since she was barely able to make ends meet, she made most of Jamie's clothes, and only bought her shoes and underwear. Cassandra would purchase material off the bargain tables, and that saved her a lot of money on clothes. Occasionally Cassandra would even make herself a new dress. Not often, because she didn't like to waste money on her self. Jamie came first. That's just the kind of person she was, always putting the needs of others, ahead of her self.

Cassandra worked a few hours a week in the grocery store so that her mother and father could go to the bigger city close by for supplies for the store. Cassandra felt good about that, and was glad to do it. That way she felt better about not paying her parents for trailer space rent. Everybody benefited by the arrangement.

Because this small town was a real close knit community, Cassandra hadn't made any friends. She pretty much kept to herself. So she enjoyed the times that she worked in the store, as it gave her a chance to meet and talk to others.

* * *

CASSANDRA MANAGED TO STAY very busy, and the time was passing by quickly. She and Jamie never wanted for anything. Cassandra found she was happier than she had ever dreamed was possible. Life was great!

* * *

CASSANDRA SOON DISCOVERED THAT all good things must eventually come to an end when she collected her mail at the post office, and found another letter from Ray. It had been so long since he had sent that horrible threatening letter, which she never bothered to answer, hoping that he would forget about her, and leave her alone. After that one letter she had never heard from him again. In fact it had even been months since she had even given Ray a single thought. Then unexpectedly he was intruding in her peaceful life once again.

Cassandra stuffed the letter into her pocket until she decided if she would read it or not. Fear was tearing at her insides as she ran out of the post office. It was hard to believe that a year had passed so quickly.

Cassandra stopped by the store to collect Jamie, who had stayed with grandma while she had collected the mail.

"Cassy are you alright? You look like you've seen a ghost." Nora teased, not realizing how close she had hit on the truth.

"I'm fine mother; I just don't feel too well at the moment."

"You've been working too hard dear, maybe you need to go home and rest awhile. I'll keep Jamie here with me for a couple of hours, and you just have yourself a little nap."

"I think I may just take you up on the offer mother. Are you sure Jamie won't be any trouble?"

"I'm sure we will do just fine dear. I'll let Jamie help me put some canned vegetables on the shelf. Run along now Cassy and take that nap." Nora suggested.

"Thanks mother, I'll collect Jamie after awhile."

Soon as Cassandra got inside her trailer she sat down on the sofa, pulling the letter from Ray out of her pocket. For several minutes Cassandra just sat there staring blankly at the envelope, building up her courage to open it. Finally she tore open the envelope, and started reading the contents of the letter. Ray started the letter off by telling her that he was being discharged from the service and was coming home. He wrote that he had been doing a lot of thinking the past few months, and he realized how terribly wrong he had been in the way he had treated her in the past, and he vowed that he was a changed man now, and never again would he abuse her in any way. Ray said he was really looking forward to coming home to her and Jamie and starting their lives over.

There were no threats of any kind, or any signs of anger displayed in the letter at all. He talked about little Jamie, and wondered if she would remember him. He even elaborated that he was bringing Jamie a real special gift to show her how much he loved her.

Cassandra was so confused, Ray's letter just didn't seem to be written by the same man she knew, and hated. In fact the letter was so nice, it made her wonder if by chance someone other than Ray had written the entire contents of the letter for him.

*   *   *

CASSANDRA JUST DIDN'T KNOW what she was going to do about this drastic change of events. It had been her intention to divorce Ray as soon as he returned to the states. She sure never thought that Ray would seek her out when he came home. In fact she prayed that he would just return to California to his parents, and leave her alone. Now it looked as though things weren't going to happen the way she had hoped.

Was it really possible that during this past year overseas something happened to change Ray's way of thinking, and he really had changed? Could they really put the past behind them, and start over again for Jamie's sake.

Cassandra didn't know what to make out of all this. She was thankful that she had never mentioned to her parents anything about her plans to divorce Ray. That way there wouldn't be any explaining to do, should she decide to try to start over with Ray, and give their marriage one last chance to survive.

Cassandra even wondered what she would do if Ray hadn't changed, what if he was just telling her what he thought she wanted to here. And as soon as he was established here, he would revert back to the way he was before he went to France.

Cassandra kept weighing the pros, and cons of taking Ray back. Should she give him another chance for Jamie's sake? Or should she just tell him right out that she wanted a divorce. Cassandra didn't want to deprive Jamie of her father if there was the slightest chance that Ray really had changed. But then on the other hand if Ray was lying to her, could she put her and Jamie's life on the line again. Spending every day living in fear, wondering when he would fly into a rage that could cause serious consequences for her, and possibly to Jamie as well.

No matter how hard Cassandra tried, she just couldn't keep that question from haunting her.

*   *   *

THE NEXT FEW DAYS passed in a haze, Cassandra still hadn't decided what she was going to do about Ray. Her nerves were on edge, and she couldn't seem to keep her mind focused on anything. She couldn't eat, and when she went to bed, she had nightmares from the past and would wake up scared and drenched in sweat. Her safe happy world was crumbling down around her, and she didn't know what to do to prevent it from happening.

Cassandra worried that what if Ray didn't like it here in this little town, what if he couldn't get a job in the lumber mill. What then, would he insist that they move back to California. Cassandra just couldn't bare the thought of having to go back there, and have to give up the happy peaceful life she had here. And moving away from her parents just didn't bare thinking about. Having them close by was a great comfort to her. She felt safe and secure, knowing that they would always protect her.

Chapter Nineteen

T HE DREADED DAY OF Ray's home coming finally arrived. The Greyhound bus always stopped at Benning's Corner Store. Ray got off the bus, entered the grocery store as though it was an everyday occurrence. "Hello Nora, you're looking good as always."

Nora had been rearranging one of the shelves, and had her back to the door so she hadn't seen Ray when he came in, and couldn't keep the surprise from showing on her face as she turned around and greeted him. "Well look what the wind blew in, welcome back Ray. Does Cassy know you're here?" Nora asked, wondering why Cassandra wasn't here with Jamie to greet him.

"No, I just now arrived on the bus. I thought I would surprise them."

"Goodness I didn't know it was time for the bus, he must have been running early today." Nora replied a little flustered having not seen the bus stop.

"Yeah I guess he was. Nora where can I find Cassandra? Does she live far from here?" Ray inquired nonchalantly.

"You mean you don't know where Cassy lives?" Nora questioned in a surprised voice. She wasn't aware that her daughter had never written to Ray since he went away.

"No, I guess she must have forgotten to send me directions." Ray lied

"Cassy lives just up the hill within walking distance of the store. It's the trailer house with the picket fence around it. Frank built that for Cassy so Jamie could play in the yard. It's the same trailer she had, so I'm sure you'll recognize it when you see it."

"Thanks Nora, guess I'll go and get re-acquainted with my family. I've been away from home a long time. Sorry I can't stay and visit but I'm sure you understand." Ray smiled as he left the store.

*　　*　　*

Jamie was sitting on the couch watching her favorite cartoon, and Cassandra was on her hands and knees mopping the kitchen floor when a shadow suddenly blocked out the sunlight from the screen door. Glancing up she saw Ray standing on the porch looking through the door at her, fear washed over her, she couldn't seem to find her voice, all she could do was stare up at Ray from her position on the floor, hoping that she wasn't really seeing him, that it was just a figment of her imagination, and her eyes were just playing tricks on her.

"Well Cassandra, are you going to invite me in, or are you just going to let me stand out here on the porch?" Ray smiled teasingly to soften his words.

Cassandra scrambled up from the floor and pulled her blouse down over her shorts stammering nervously. "Sorry I keep the latch on the screen so that Jamie doesn't fall out the door." But she refrained from unlatching the screen, she wasn't sure if she wanted to let Ray into the house or not. So she just stood there staring at him through the door.

Ray must have seen the fear in her eyes, and he spoke softly. "It's okay Baby, you don't have to be afraid of me. The past is past, I told you in my letter that I'm a changed man, and I will never hurt you again. I promise you all I want is a chance to make it up to you, and Jamie."

Cassandra just stood there as the past flashed through her mind, how many other times had she heard those very words.

Ray must have known what was going through her mind. "I know you probably don't believe me honey. All I'm asking for is a chance to prove to you that I really mean it this time. I just want my family back, and I promise to do everything in my power to make you happy. So please, I'm begging you Cassandra to give me that chance."

Against her better judgment Cassandra unlatched the screen door and stepped back allowing Ray to enter.

As Ray came in the trailer he sat his duffel bag down by the door and walked over and sat down by Jamie and smiled as he picked her up and placed her on his lap. "Hi sweetie, you probably don't remember me because you were so little when I left, but I'm your daddy."

Jamie immediately started squirming, and then started to cry. "Mommy, Mommy."

Cassandra quickly reached out and took Jamie into her arms. "I'm sorry Ray; Jamie just isn't used to strangers picking her up."

"That's alright Cassandra you don't have to apologize, I understand that I am a stranger to Jamie. But I want to correct that. I'll just have to be patient and let her get used to having me around." He smiled as he reached up and ran his finger softly down Jamie's little cheek. "Its okay sweetie, don't cry daddy won't ever hurt you. I love you, and I will always be here for you."

Cassandra sat down in a chair by the table, holding Jamie securely on her lap, Jamie had stopped crying but she kept looking over at Ray as though she expected him to grab her again. Secretly Cassandra was glad that Jamie hadn't taken to Ray right off, and he had his work all cut out for him to not only regain her trust, but he also had to gain Jamie's trust as well. And from past experiences that was sure going to take some doing on his part, and time would tell if he had really changed, or if he was just putting up a good front on their first meeting in a little over a year.

Acting as though nothing had happened between him and Jamie, Ray nonchalantly asked. "So what are the job prospects like in this quiet little town?"

"Well about all there is here is the lumber mill, or ranches to work on. And if I remember correctly you weren't all that fond of ranch work, so I guess that just leaves the mill." Cassandra smiled to take the sting out of her words.

Ray looked thoughtful for a few seconds then smiled. "Well guess I'll just have to go over to the lumber mill first thing in the morning and see if they are hiring."

"The mill starts up at six every morning except on week ends, and since this is only Wednesday they will be running tomorrow." Cassandra watched Rays face as she spoke to see what sort of reaction she would get in response to her mentioning that he get an early start. Remembering how he hated to go job hunting before noon when they had first gotten married. But Ray's response surprised her.

"Well I guess I'll be there when they open for work then. Seems like I vaguely remember someone told me a long time ago, that the early bird gets the worm." Then he winked at her knowingly to let her know it was her words that he was referring to.

"Well then since we have the prospect of a job out of the way, how about the three of us taking a little ride and you can show me how to get to the lumber mill, and show me around town. Maybe we can even find somewhere to get a bite to eat while we are out, sort of a little home coming celebration. How does that sound to you?"

Cassandra was surprised that he was actually inviting her out, like he really cared about her opinion. "That sounds like a good idea, only we will have to come home right after lunch so that Jamie can have her nap."

"Let's get started so we'll have plenty of time, sure don't want my little girl to miss her nap." Ray smiled as he winked at Jamie.

It didn't take long to drive around and show Ray the town, and how to get to the entrance to the mill.

"This sure is a nice quiet little place, I think I'm really going to like living in this little town. I just hope I can get on at the mill. Looks like that little restaurant there by the post office is the only one around here, so guess that's where we will have lunch."

"There is a bigger place up the canyon about fifteen miles, but we won't have time to go there today and still get back in time for Jamie's nap." Cassandra informed him, hoping it didn't set him off.

"The restaurant here in town will be fine; we can try the other place when we have more time. I can't have my little girl missing her nap." Ray smiled letting her know that he understood, and didn't mind that they had to be home early.

*   *   *

SOON AS THEY GOT home Cassandra put Jamie down for her nap, and then put on a pot of coffee. They sat at the table drinking coffee and really talking for the first time in the three years they had been married. Cassandra couldn't believe that Ray was actually listening to what she had to say.

Then Ray told Cassandra about some of the other countries he had visited while he was on his tour of duty, and how much he was looking forward to starting over again, and how important it was to him to get a second chance to get to know his family. He could sense the uneasiness in Cassandra, and he assured her that they would just take one day at a time, and that he had no desire to push her into anything she didn't feel comfortable with until she was ready to take their marriage into the next phase. He just wanted her to relax, and give them a chance to know each other all over again. And down the road when she felt more comfortable with him then they could think about the romance side of their marriage.

Cassandra was relieved to know that he wasn't going to force her to have sex with him right away. She just hoped she could believe him on that score. But time would tell when it was time for them to go to bed. She wasn't too fond of the idea of having to sleep with him, but he was her husband so she couldn't very well ask him to go to a motel on his first night home. So being assured by him that sex wasn't on the agenda right away she guessed she could endure sharing her bed with him for the time being until she made up her mind about trying to make a go of her marriage, or getting the divorce she had wanted every since the night she married him.

CHAPTER TWENTY

THE NEXT MORNING CASSANDRA woke up when she heard a rustling sound by the side of the bed; she glanced at the clock and saw that it was only five o'clock. When she saw that Ray was already up and getting dressed, she jumped out of bed reaching for her robe.

"That's okay honey, you just stay in bed. I thought I would just run down to that little restaurant and grab a cup of coffee before I run over to the mill office."

"Really Ray I don't mind getting up and fixing you some coffee and breakfast before you leave."

"I know you don't honey, but let me pamper you a little bit. Okay? You can fix me some breakfast when I get back." Ray smiled at her as he went out and closed the door softly behind him.

Cassandra laid there not knowing quite what to make out of this new Ray. She was afraid to trust him, even though he had kept his word about not touching her and had kept to his side of the bed all night just like he had promised. It sure was going to take some time for her to get used to this new Ray, he had never been this considerate or kind spoken to her in all the years they had been together, and she wondered how long it would be before he reverted back to his old ways. It was hard for her to believe that Ray could change this drastically in one short year.

Cassandra decided just to be on the safe side that she wouldn't put too much trust in this new Ray, she wasn't going to let herself be lured back into a false sense of security like she had in the past. This time she would make damn sure that she didn't fall for Ray's sweet talk and promises until he had actually proven to her that he was a changed man, and not just giving her a snow job until he got back into her good graces again. This new Ray was almost too good to be true. Especially after knowing what a bastard he was in the past.

*   *   *

CASSANDRA HAD JUST GOTTEN out of the shower, and dressed. She was making up the bed when she heard the sound of Rays pickup driving up in front of the trailer.

"Well baby good news, I got the job as a mill Wright in the molding department. I start work tomorrow morning." Ray told her excitedly giving her the thumbs up sign.

"That's great Ray!" Cassandra hoped she sounded enthused. Somehow she had secretly hoped he wouldn't get a job, and that he would decide to go back to California, and she could tell him she wasn't going with him, because she wanted a divorce. In her heart she knew all she really wanted was to be free from Ray, she had no desire to stay in this marriage. If only she didn't have to consider Jamie, she didn't want to deprive Jamie of her father, and that was all that kept her from telling Ray to leave the minute he had set foot on her porch yesterday.

Putting her thoughts aside she asked. "How about me getting Jamie up and dressed, and then I'll fix us all some breakfast?"

"Sounds like a good idea babe, is there anything I can do to help?"

It was a good thing that Cassandra had already turned to get Jamie up because she was stunned by his offer to help. "Not a thing Ray, but thanks for offering." She hoped that her surprise didn't show in her voice.

While Cassandra was dressing Jamie, and starting breakfast, Ray sat on the couch looking at the newspaper he had picked up off the door step when he came in. "This little home town paper sure doesn't have a hell of a lot to say does it?" He asked as he folded it up and placed it on the small end table by the couch.

"Well in a town of four hundred people there just isn't all that much going on around here to write about. That's why we only get one newspaper a week." Cassandra smiled as she set the plates on the table. "Breakfast is ready you two."

Ray scooped Jamie up off the floor on his way to the table. "You heard your mama sweetie its time to eat."

Jamie started to squirm the minute Ray picked her up and was puckering up to cry.

"Come here Sugar Bug and mommy will put you in your high chair so you can have some good old scrambled eggs and toast." Then she playfully poked Jamie in the tummy. "We got to feed that tiger in there." Jamie started to giggle the way she always did, and the tense moment passed.

"How come she always wants to cry if I come near her, or pick her up?" Ray asked in a surly voice. His tone of voice was a sound from the past and chills raced down Cassandra's spine.

"Oh Ray just be patient, she'll come around once she gets to know you, you have to remember she was just a baby when you left and now you are a stranger to her. You just have to give her a little time."

"I'm sorry honey; guess I'm just trying to rush things a little. I'll try to be more patient with her." Ray smiled, but the smile looked more like a sneer.

Cassandra pushed her plate back, she had lost her appetite seeing the look on Rays face, and the past came rushing back in her mind, for a split second the old Ray had surfaced once again.

"Don't tell me you are full already Cassandra, why you have hardly touched the food on your plate."

"I've had all I want right now; guess I'm just not as hungry as I thought I was this morning." Cassandra smiled as she started to get up and take her plate to the sink.

"Well the least you can do is sit here and talk to Jamie and I until we finish our breakfast, can't you?" Rays voice was just a shade off from being an order instead of a request.

"I'm sorry Ray, guess I just wasn't thinking there for a second. I'm not used to having someone else at the table. Habit I guess." She responded as she sat back down in her chair.

"Well you better start getting used to it babe, because I'm not going anywhere for a long time." Ray replied softly, and smiled to take the sting out of his words.

* * *

WHILE CASSANDRA CLEANED UP the dishes Ray sat down on the floor with Jamie to play with her toys, he was talking softly to her. Jamie was staying just out of his reach so there was no contact between them. She didn't quite know what to think about the big stranger sitting there playing with her toys. Ray picked up a little ball and rolled it to Jamie. Cassandra could see a smile tugging at the corners of Jamie's mouth, she loved to play roll the ball. But just as Jamie started to touch the ball rolling towards her, Ray suddenly reached out and grabbed Jamie's hand as it closed over the ball and pulled her over onto his lap trying to cuddle with her. This startled Jamie and she started to scream and tried to get off Rays lap, but Ray tightened his grip so she couldn't get free. "Come on Jamie, daddy's not going to hurt you, he just wants to love you."

Jamie started screaming. "Mommy, mommy, make the man let me go."

Cassandra rushed over and took Jamie out of Ray's arms. "There, there, sweetie, its okay."

Jamie stopped crying as soon as she felt her mother's arms around her.

"You have her spoiled rotten Cassandra. You shouldn't run to her every time she whimpers. I wasn't going to hurt her." Ray stated none too gently.

"I know that Ray, but Jamie doesn't. You just scared her when you suddenly reached out and grabbed her onto your lap." Cassandra explained softly, trying not to irritate Ray anymore than he already was, hoping to defuse the tension.

"How in the hell can I get to know her for Christ's sake if all she does is scream for you every time I touch her?" Ray said heatedly, and then softened his tone. "I'm sorry Cassandra I didn't mean for that to come out the way it did." He apologized. "I just get so damn frustrated that my own daughter doesn't know me."

"Just give it some time Ray. I know that in time Jamie will get used to having you around, it's just that for most of her life it has just been the two of us, and she is so little she doesn't understand." Cassandra explained as she put Jamie down and unlatched the screen door. "Why don't you go out side and play for a little while sweetie so mommy and daddy can talk." Soon as Jamie left the porch Ray blurted out.

"Well things have damn sure got to change around here; I won't tolerate my own daughter being afraid of me. How could you let such a thing happen Cassandra?" Ray asked in an accusing voice.

"Yes things certainly will have to change Ray, and you are the one who has to make the changes." Cassandra shot back.

"Just what do you mean by that statement Cassandra?" Ray demanded to know.

Hearing the tone from the past in Ray's voice, Cassandra decided it was time to lay her cards on the table and let the chips fall where they may. "Well if you remember you really weren't much of a father to Jamie from the time she was born. How many times did you ever hold her in your arms? She was almost three weeks old before you even seen her."

"And whose fault was that, you let your damn parents take over." He accused.

"Don't you remember why I went to stay with my parents Ray? Well let me refresh your memory, it was because you back handed me and knocked me out the door when I was eight and a half months pregnant, then drove off and left me lying there bleeding to death."

"I'm sorry about that, I was scared and didn't know what to do.

That's all in the past Cassandra, let's just forget it and try to start over."

" I'll never forget the way you treated me before you were recalled, and I want to make it very plain to you right now Ray, that in order for us to make this marriage work you have got to realize that I'm not going to tolerate your treating me like you did in the past. If you can't learn to control your temper, and treat Jamie and me with a little kindness and respect, then this marriage is never going to work." Cassandra stated watching the expression on Rays face as the anger was building up.

"That was a long time ago, things are different now." Ray stated vehemently.

"Yes things certainly are different now Ray. I've regained my self respect, and my independence, and I've been standing on my own two feet for a little over a year now, and raising a baby by myself. I've struggled to make ends meet with no help from you what-so-ever. I've found out how good it is to be happy, and to be able to go to bed at night knowing that I have nothing to fear. I enjoy being able to pick my friends, and talk to them any time I want. And you know what Ray? I like the way my life is right now, and not you, or anyone else is ever going to change that, or take it away from me again. Do you understand what I'm saying Ray?"

Ray just sat there not looking at her, or saying a word. He didn't like what he was hearing, but he managed to refrain from letting his anger get the best of him.

"I understand what you are saying Cassandra, and I plan to do everything in my power to make it up to you for the past. I've got the job at the mill now that I hope will work out so we don't have to move away from here." He said quietly, all signs of his anger had seemed to vanish.

"I'm willing to try and make this marriage work for Jamie's sake Ray. So I hope that you will find a way to make this job work, be-cause if you don't, and you decide to move, I think it's only fair to tell you that Jamie and I won't be going with you!"

CHAPTER TWENTY-ONE

T HREE YEARS HAD PAST since Ray returned from France. In that time they had managed to live a fairly normal life together, and probably to the outside world they appeared to be a normal happy family. But deep down Cassandra had this niggling doubt in the back of her mind that something just wasn't right because she still couldn't feel like she could trust Ray. The past kept coming back to haunt her, and she remembered all the times that Ray had treated her nice one minute, then beat the hell out of her the next.

Cassandra knew in her heart that she didn't love Ray when they got married, and she didn't love him now. In fact she very much doubted that she would ever be able to love him. She still wanted a divorce, and wanted more than anything for things to be the way they were the year they were apart. She just wasn't happy living with him in the same house, and sharing his bed. The love making was still pretty much the way it had been in the early part of their marriage. Ray satisfied his needs, but left her wanting, and wondering if this was what sex was all about, how come so many people stayed together for so many years, because she didn't enjoy it at all. Maybe it was just her, she didn't have anything to compare it to because Ray was the only man she had ever slept with in her entire life.

So many times Cassandra wished she hadn't agreed to try to save this marriage just for Jamie's sake, and had simply told Ray when he came home that she wanted a divorce. Now a divorce wasn't an option, because as long as Ray continued to treat her and Jamie okay she no longer had any grounds for a divorce.

It was too late, life was passing her by and there wasn't anything she could do about it. Jamie would soon turn six years old on her birthday next month, and would be starting school in the fall.

*　*　*

RAY HAD MADE MANY friends at the mill; he bought a 30-06 rifle and went hunting with his friends almost every weekend. A couple of nights a week he went and played poker with some of the guys.

*　*　*

THEN THE UNEXPECTED HAPPENED, Ray started coming home late from work most nights, he would be moody, and had started drinking again. They had started hiring women to work at the mill, and she had heard rumors that Ray was running around with a few of them. People tried to protect Cassandra from knowing the truth. But in a small town of four hundred people word got around pretty fast. A couple of times she had even seen another woman with Ray in his truck, but he had explained that he was just giving her a ride home and there wasn't anything for her to worry about.

Cassandra resigned herself to trying to make the best of a bad situation, and tried not to let the town's people know how embarrassed and humiliated she was, hoping that if she acted like everything was okay the rumors would stop before Jamie got hurt by the gossip. But she recognized Ray's pattern of conduct from the early years. First there were signs of moodiness. Then the drinking and abusive language started, along with the womanizing. It was only a matter of time before Ray reverted back to his old self.

He was starting to harass Cassandra by finding fault with everything she did or said, and tried to pick a fight with her every chance he got. He wanted her to get angry so he could have an excuse to lash out at her. When ever there was anyone else around he would belittle her in front of them and try to make her look stupid. How she hated it. But she refused to let Ray provoke her, and she kept silent. She knew from past experience that when Ray was like this, the best thing for her to do was keep her mouth shut and try to stay out of his way. And by no means would she give him any cause to lose his temper, because she knew from past experience how violent he could be, and she knew in her heart that she could never endure going through that again.

As for Ray running around with other women she could care less, because at least he left her alone. Her flesh crawled when ever he touched her. Ray was still like an animal, and his brand of love making left her cold, bruised, and unsatisfied.

She knew that it was only a matter of time before the abuse started again, and as soon as Jamie started school she was going to apply for a job at the mill. She knew that the wages they paid at the mill would be good enough that she could make it on her own, and have no trouble supporting herself and Jamie. Then when Ray started handing out physical abuse as well as the verbal abuse she would have grounds for a divorce. She had made up her mind that never again would she subject herself to living a life of fear and abuse as she had in the past. Life was just too short!

* * *

RAY RETURNED LATE FROM a weekend hunting trip with his friends, and he was so drunk that his buddy had to help him into the house.

"Cassy I'm sure sorry about this, we tried to keep him from drinking so much, but you know Ray he doesn't listen to anyone." Brad apologized.

"I understand Brad, once Ray sets his mind on something wild horses couldn't stop him from doing what he wants." Cassandra smiled, but the smile didn't quite reach her eyes.

"Just tell me where to put him Cassy, do you want him on the bed or the couch?"

"The bedroom if you can get him there, Lord knows how long it will take for him to sleep this off, and I would prefer that Jamie didn't see him like this when she wakes up."

Then Ray started trying to pull away from Brad. "What the hell do you think you're doing?" He bellowed as he gave Brad a violent shove into the table, catching Brad completely unaware.

Brad regained his balance and took a hold of Ray again trying to help him to the bed. "Come on Ray old buddy time for you to sleep it off."

"Leave me alone you bastard." Ray yelled trying to break free of Brads hold on him. "Where the hell am I anyway?" He slurred breaking loose from Brads hold on him.

"You're home old buddy, I'm just trying to help Cassy get you into bed so you can sleep this off." Brad said once again trying to take hold of Rays arm.

"Where's my gun you bastard? I'm gonna blow that bitches head off." Ray swung his fist at Brad, but Brad ducked and Ray sprawled on the kitchen floor out cold.

"I'm sorry as hell about this Cassy, let me call Randy to come in and see if we can get Ray into bed for you."

Cassandra was scared and badly shaken by the events that had just taken place, and all she could do was nod her head.

With Randy's help the two of them got Ray onto the bed. "I'll go out and get Rays rifle and then we'll get out of your way Cassy."

"No Brad, just keep the rifle for now, you can return it to Ray later." Cassandra blurted out, her fear clearly visible in her voice.

"Yeah guess that would probably be best just in case Rays comes out of it before he has a chance to sober up." Brad agreed as he and Randy left.

* * *

CASSANDRA LAY DOWN ON the couch and pulled an afghan over her, but she knew that she wouldn't get a wink of sleep for fear that Ray would wake up. She shivered thinking about the look on Rays face when he said he would blow her head off. Thank God she told Brad to keep the gun for now, and bring it back some other time because after that out burst from Ray, the last thing she wanted in the house was a loaded gun for him to get his hands on.

Laying there on the couch, Cassandra thought it was bad enough just having a gun in the house. Ray always tossed it on the bed when he came home from hunting, and she always made sure that it was unloaded before she put it on the top shelf of the closet where it would be out of Jamie's reach. Ray was too careless with his rifle and she always had to make sure that it was unloaded and put away. That always made Ray mad but damned if she was going to allow someone to get hurt because of Ray's carelessness, especially Jamie.

She thought about how that always seemed to provoke Ray, and he would show his anger by storming out of the house, then he would head for the bar and get drunk, and usually he managed to pick up what ever single woman was available that he happened to take a fancy too, and end up spending the night with her.

Cassandra thought about what a constant embarrassment it always was for her when some of the people would go out of their way to tell her about the things Ray did, some of them had been her friends before Ray came home from France. Cassandra couldn't understand why everyone seemed to side with Ray, they even went so far as to tell her it was all her fault that Ray done some of the things that he did, because if she was a decent wife to him then he wouldn't have to find his pleasures in the arms of another woman.

It seemed that Ray had everyone fooled into believing that he was a sweet, kind and gentle person. He made sure that nobody ever saw the mean, selfish, possessive, controlling person that he really was. He had even had her fooled the past three years with his sweet talk and lies. But she wasn't fooled anymore, everything he had said to get back into her good graces, were all lies, he hadn't changed at all. He was still the mean hateful person he had always been, and Cassandra knew he would never change

* * *

THE NEXT MORNING WHEN Ray finally got up Cassandra confronted him. "You have got to stop this drinking Ray. I can't stand the humiliation any longer, and the whole town is talking about your drinking and womanizing, and I'm just not going to tolerate it anymore, I have Jamie to think about "

Rays arm shot out and he back handed her across the face. "Look bitch you don't have any say in the matter. I'll do as I damn well please, so get off my back."

But Cassandra wasn't backing down. "I know now that you are still the same mean bastard that you always were Ray, and I know that this marriage isn't going to work out because you will never change. I want you to pack your things and get out."

"I'm not going any where bitch. This is my house and I'm staying right here, so you might as well get used to the idea." He sneered.

"Okay have it your way Ray, if you won't leave, then I will, and I'm taking Jamie with me."

Ray grabbed Cassandra by the upper arms and started shaking her. "You aren't going any where bitch. And if you leave, you will go without Jamie. Because there is no way in hell that I'll ever let you take my daughter." Then he punched Cassandra in the face knocking her back down on the couch. As Ray stood there glaring down at her, Cassandra thought that he was going to hit her again.

"Go a head hit me again Ray if that's what you want to do, but it won't change my mind. Jamie and I are still going to leave if I have to crawl out of here on my hands and knees."

Ray walked over to the door, and then turned. "I warn you bitch if you take my daughter I'll kill you."

Cassandra was devastated; she didn't know what she was going to do. No way was she going to leave without Jamie. There must be some way she could force Ray to move out, and somehow she would find a way no matter what she had to do. She made up her mind that this time she would go to her parents, and tell them everything. Even ask them to help her if she had to in order to protect Jamie from harm.

Chapter Twenty-Two

Two days later Cassandra took Jamie across the street to play with the little boy that lived there. The two children were practically inseparable; she and her friend Lucy took turns having the children play at each others house. This gave each of them a chance to run any errands they might have knowing that their children were in safe hands.

* * *

By the time Cassandra got home and put her groceries away it was time for Jamie to come home. As she walked across the street she noticed that the children weren't out side playing in the yard. She went up and knocked lightly on the door. Lucy opened the door saying. "Come on in Cassy I've got a fresh pot of coffee on."

"Thanks Lucy but I'm running a little late. I just came over to collect Jamie and I have to get right back and start dinner, Ray will be home soon."

Cassandra noticed the color drain from Lucy's face, she seemed rather shocked.

"God Cassy you mean you didn't know?"

Cassandra started to tremble. "Know what Lucy, has something happened to Jamie while I was gone?"

"Heavens no Cassy, nothing has happened to Jamie, her father came over about a half an hour ago and picked her up. Sure hope I didn't do anything wrong."

Cassandra could feel the panic rising up inside of her. "Of course you didn't do anything wrong Lucy. I guess it just slipped my mind that Ray was getting off work early today and said he would pick up Jamie and take her for a little ride up the canyon to see the squirrels and chipmunks. You know how much she enjoys that, but I still better run and get dinner started they should be coming home anytime now." Cassandra hated lying to her best friend; it left a bad taste in her mouth. Turning quickly she darted down the front steps hoping that Lucy hadn't seen the fear in her eyes. "Thanks for watching Jamie today." She called back over her shoulder as she rushed across the street.

* * *

ONCE INSIDE HER TRAILER Cassandra sat down to wait, worrying about where Ray had taken Jamie. Why had he left work early, he had never done that before. Two hours passed and there was still no sign of them. Finally Cassandra couldn't stand the waiting any longer so she ran out and jumped in the old pickup they had kept when Ray bought a new pickup a couple of months ago. She started driving up and down the streets looking for Rays red ford pickup, it was loaded with chrome and he kept it washed and shining all the time, you couldn't miss it because it stood out from all the other vehicles in the small town.

The longer she drove the more worried she got because she couldn't find Rays pickup anywhere in town. Then the thought that they may have had an accident on the winding road up the canyon entered her mind and she started praying. "God please don't let anything happen to Jamie."

Cassandra decided to go back home and see if perhaps somehow she had just missed them on one of the side streets, and that they were back home waiting for her.

Soon as she turned into the driveway past the big trees she could see that there was no sign of Ray's pickup. Almost at the breaking point, Cassandra ran in the trailer and called the sheriffs office to see if there had been any accidents reported in the canyon in the past few hours. "No Mamm there hasn't been an accident reported anywhere in the county in the past twenty-four hours. Why do you ask?" The Deputy inquired.

"My husband picked my daughter up from the baby sitters at two o'clock this afternoon and said he was taking her for a ride. It has been eight hours, and there hasn't been any word from them since, and I can't find his pickup anywhere around town. I've simply looked every place I can think of." Cassandra told him tears chocking up her voice.

"Please can't you help me, I'm so afraid something terrible has happened to my daughter."

"Just a minute Mamm while I get the Sheriff on the line."

Cassandra thought sure an hour had passed, when in fact it had been only seconds until she heard Sam's voice on the line.

"Sheriff Sam Waters, how may I help you?" He inquired with a voice of authority.

"Oh Sam I'm so glad you were there. This is Cassandra Cartone." She slowly and sobbingly told the Sheriff about the events that led up to her call.

"Oh please Sam can you do something to help me, I just know that something awful must have happened to Jamie." Cassandra wailed beside herself with worry.

"Now Cassandra please just calm down, I'm sure Jamie is okay. Ray probably just took her into the city to see that new Disney movie. So why don't you just relax and stop worrying. Rays not going to let any harm come to Jamie. So just be patient I'm sure that they will probably be home before you know it." He consoled her in a fatherly sort of way.

"But Sam you don't know Ray like I do. You have no idea what Ray is capable of doing."

"What do you mean by that Cassandra is there something that I should know that you aren't telling me?" Sam questioned.

"Oh Sam it's a long story, I've never told a living sole. Just please believe me and do something to help me find Jamie before it's too late."

"I don't know what you are hiding from me young lady, but one of these days real soon you and I are going to have a long talk about this."

"Sam please, just promise me that you will help me find Jamie, I'm begging you to do something now before it's too late. I'm out of my mind with worry, and I won't be able to relax until Jamie is safely home again." She pleaded.

"Officially Cassandra my hands are tied, there isn't a damn thing I can do until they have been missing for forty-eight hours. But unofficially I will see what I can find out. You just stay by the phone and if I find out anything I'll call you immediately, and if they return you call me at once. Is that understood?"

"Yes Sam, I'll do as you say. I just want Jamie back." She sobbed.

"Okay honey, now please try not to worry, I'll get a hold of Jay and put an alert out for everyone to be on the look out for Ray's pickup." As Sam hung up the phone he wondered what in the hell was going on in the Cartone family. He had known Cassandra and her parents every since they had moved to the valley, and she was one of the most stable and upstanding young ladies he had ever met. He knew that there was more to this than she was letting on. He had a gut feeling that what ever was driving her to this over wrought state had more behind it than she was telling him. What it was he had no idea, but he was damn sure going to find out and get to the bottom of it. Why was Cassandra so worried about Jamie being alone with her dad? There sure was a hell of a lot more to this story than what she had told him on the phone.

"Jay put out an alert to be on the look out for Raymond Cartone's red ford pickup, I don't want it stopped, I just want to know where the hell it is." Sam barked out the order.

* * *

CASSANDRA MADE A POT of coffee and sat on the sofa watching the clock on the wall in the kitchen. The time seemed to stand still, and then she started pacing back and forth. Her eyes went from the clock to the telephone. What was Ray up to now, and what was his purpose of taking Jamie and not even calling her? One thought after another flashed through her mind. She wouldn't put anything past Ray, he was evil through and through, and he was capable of doing anything that he could to bring her pain. He hadn't changed at all, he was still the same mean and hateful person he had always been, and now he was using Jamie as a pawn to show Cassandra that he still held the upper hand, and she would toe the mark and jump to his tune just like she always did before he went to France. She knew; beyond a shadow of a doubt that Ray was capable of even hurting little Jamie if it suited his purpose. "Oh dear God please don't let Ray harm Jamie, please protect her until she is safely back in my arms." She prayed, hoping with all her heart that God would hear her prayer. Glancing at the clock Cassandra noticed that it was three in the morning and Ray and Jamie were still missing, and the phone hadn't rang. She was bone tired from worry and stress and slowly sleep over came her.

* * *

WHEN CASSANDRA WOKE UP it was seven in the morning. She grabbed the phone and frantically dialed the Sheriffs office and asked for Sam, who came on the phone at once.

"Good morning Cassandra, did Ray and Jamie make it home alright last night."

"No Sam; there hasn't been any sign of them, and Ray hasn't called. I'm so worried; I just know that something awful has happened. My daughter may be hurt and laying in a ditch some where, and I'm not there to help her. Please can't you do something?"

"Now hang on there Cassandra, get a hold of yourself. I've had people looking for Ray's truck all night, and so far there hasn't been a single trace of them. But I promise you if they are anywhere in this county or the State of Idaho, I'll find them! You just continue to stay by the phone and I'll call you just as soon as we find them."

* * *

SEVERAL DAYS HAD PAST, and still there was no word from Ray. The Sheriff had called daily to tell her that there still wasn't any trace of Ray's pickup. But he had filed a missing persons report for both Ray and Jamie, and had people from his office and the State Troopers still on the lookout for him.

Cassandra was half out of her mind with worry, what awful thing had Ray done with their daughter. Why hadn't someone been able to find them yet? They couldn't have just disappeared off the face of the earth. Finally out of desperation Cassandra called Rays parents. She was bluntly told that they hadn't seen Ray or Jamie, and had no idea where they were, and ordered her to leave them alone, and not to ever call them again.

Cassandra placed a call to Sam at the Sheriffs office and told him about the conversation she had with Ray's parents. About how cold and uncaring they seemed to be, they hadn't shown any emotion about the fact that Ray and their granddaughter had been missing for several days. She had the feeling that they knew where Ray was with Jamie and was keeping it from her.

"Rest assured Cassandra I'll get on the phone and have someone sent out to the Cartone place and see if maybe that's where Ray is. I'll call you and let you know what I find out. "

"Thanks Sam, I want you to know that I really appreciate all that you are doing to help me find Jamie."

Cassandra was cleaning up the kitchen when the phone suddenly rang. Jamie had been missing for a week now; she snatched up the phone praying that it was someone that would tell her where Jamie was. It was one of Rays brother-in-laws that lived somewhere in southern California. He told her that Ray had dropped Jamie off at his house in the middle of the night a couple of days ago and he had been trying to locate Cassandra to tell her where Jamie was and that she was alright, and was crying for her mother. Fred told Cassandra that he didn't know what the problem was between her and Ray, but he and his wife didn't want to be mixed up in the middle of things. But he felt that a child belonged with her mother, and he would do everything in his power to see that Jamie was safely returned to Cassandra.

"Just give me your address Fred, and directions to your house. I'll throw a few things in a suitcase and leave here within the hour and come collect Jamie myself. I can't tell you Fred how very much I appreciate your calling me. I will always be grateful to you for being so kind."

"You drive careful Cassandra, and don't worry about Jamie we will take good care of her until you arrive. I'm going right now and tell her the good news that her mommy is coming to get her."

"Thanks Fred, I'll be there just as soon as I possibly can. If I leave right now I should be there sometime late tomorrow afternoon. Please tell Jamie mommy loves her."

*   *   *

CASSANDRA PLACED A QUICK call to the Sheriffs office and asked for Sam Waters.

"Sam I know where Jamie is so you can call off the search. I'm on my way right now to go get her."

"Where is Jamie Cassandra, let us handle this in case there is trouble."

"She's in southern California; Ray dumped her at one of his sisters and took off, my brother-in-law called me a few minutes ago." She explained.

"I still think you should let the police handle this Cassandra." Sam insisted.

"No Sam, I need to go and get Jamie myself. She has already been through enough, she's scared, and with strangers. Jamie needs me now more than ever before Sam, please don't stop me. This is something that I just have to do on my own. I'll call you when I get back."

About twenty minutes after Cassandra had received the call from Fred, she was putting her suitcase into the pickup when Ray drove into the yard in a brand new blue dodge pickup. No wonder the police hadn't found him, Ray had traded trucks. Ray jumped out of his truck and ran over to Cassandra and grabbed her by the upper arm.

"Where the hell do you think you're going Bitch?"

Cassandra didn't take time to answer him, she jerked free of his hold on her arm and jumped in the open door of her pickup and quickly locked the door. Ray grabbed the door handle as she started the truck, but she slammed it in reverse and stepped on the gas as hard as she could. Ray had no option except to turn loose of the door handle or be drug down the road. Right now Cassandra was so mad that she didn't care if he was run over or not. She was going to go get her daughter in California, and nothing, or no one was going to stop her.

*   *   *

IT TOOK CASSANDRA FIFTEEN hours to make the trip to California, she only stopped for gas, and grabbed something that she could eat while she was driving, she was on a mission to get her child and she wasn't wasting any time along the way. The longer she drove the more she hated Ray for taking Jamie away from everything she knew, and dumping her on perfect strangers. Fred and Ellen had never seen Jamie before, except for a picture of her when she was a tiny baby. Cassandra hoped that some day Ray would rot in hell for what he had done to her and Jamie.

* * *

FINALLY THE LONG TRIP was over and Cassandra was pulling into Fred and Ellen's driveway. Just as she jumped out of the truck the front door of the house opened and Jamie rushed out running to her mothers out stretched arms. "Mommy, Mommy." It was a joyous reunion for both of them.

"I can't begin to tell you two what this means to me Fred. Someday maybe I can repay you somehow."

"Nonsense Cassandra you don't owe us a thing, we only did what any self respecting person would do under these circumstances."

Cassandra started to put Jamie in the truck. "Come on sweetie we have a long way to go to get back home."

"You two aren't going anywhere this late in the day, Ellen and I would like you to spend the night, have a meal and a good nights sleep, then you can get an early start in the morning. How does that sound?" Fred offered.

"To tell you the truth Fred it sounds wonderful. I want you to know that Jamie and I really appreciate all you have done for us."

* * *

EARLY THE NEXT MORNING just as dawn was breaking, Cassandra said her farewells to Fred and Ellen, settled Jamie in the seat next to her, and headed the truck north for the trip back to Idaho. It was almost sundown when they arrived back home. The last place they had stopped for gas Cassandra had gotten her and Jamie something to eat. Jamie was almost asleep when they pulled up in front of the trailer, and Cassandra heaved a sigh of relief when she saw that Ray's truck wasn't there. She carried Jamie into the trailer and tucked her into bed. Then she made a pot of coffee and sat down to relax from the long drive. As Cassandra sat there drinking her coffee she made up her mind that somehow she had to force Ray to move out of the house. There was no way that they could ever live together after what he had just done. Their farce of a marriage had been doomed from the start, she had never loved Ray, and now she knew beyond a shadow of a doubt that she could never trust him again. His sweet talk and promises were as worthless and rotten as he was.

*   *   *

CASSANDRA WAS UP EARLY the next morning, Jamie was still sound asleep. The coffee had just finished perking and she was pouring herself a cup when she heard a vehicle pull up in front of the trailer. Cassandra knew that none of her friends would be coming by this early in the morning, so it had to be Ray. She felt the old fear churning in her stomach. Then anger took over, he had some nerve. How dare he come back here after what he had done? She had a firm grip on her emotions by the time the door opened and Ray came in the trailer.

"Well I see you made it back home okay. How was your trip to California, and how is Jamie?" He said nonchalantly as though the trip had been planned by mutual agreement between them before she left.

"Why should you care? You rotten son-of-a- bitch. How could you take our little daughter clear to California and dump her with strangers like she was nothing more than a sack of garbage?"

"Oh come on baby don't make such a big deal out of this, Jamie wasn't hurt none, it was only a little joke. Besides you both got a little trip out of the deal, so why can't you just be satisfied with that? After all there wasn't any harm done." Ray sneered.

"It may have only been a joke to you Ray, but personally I don't see anything funny about it. You showed me just how mean, uncaring and hateful you can be. And I find that what you have done to Jamie is simply unforgivable. I want you to pack your things and get out of this house now, and don't ever come back."

"Surely you don't mean that honey, let's just talk about this, shall we?"

"There is absolutely nothing to talk about Ray. This time you have gone too far, I want you out of this house and out of my life once and for all!"

"You're just upset baby, and tired from the trip. Surely you don't mean what you're saying right now because you're angry with me. Let's just give it a few days and think it over."

"I've already had plenty of time to think things over all the way to California and back. I've had enough of your beatings to last me a life time. I'm fed up with your drinking and womanizing, and being the talk of the town. And now after what you done to Jamie, that was the final straw. I want a divorce Ray. Now do I make myself clear?"

Ray just stood there in silence, and then he smiled. "Haven't we been happy here for a few years honey before I started drinking again?"

"If you want the honest truth Ray, I have only been happy twice in all the time we have been married. Once when Jamie was born, and the year you were in France. It was pure heaven that year without you in my life, and I really liked who I was, and was enjoying my life here with Jamie until you decided to come back. I moved here hoping that somehow you would never bother to find me. But you did, and I took you back into my life for Jamie's sake because I thought you had changed. But you haven't changed Ray, and you never will. I realize that now and I want a divorce. I can't put it any plainer than that. It's over Ray, so you may as well accept it. You aren't going to change, and I'm tired of living in fear and humiliation."

Ray stood there with a hurt look on his face, and then he humbled himself and started crying. "Please don't do this to me Cassy. I need you and Jamie in my life. I was drinking and you made me so mad. I figured the only way to get even was to take Jamie away from you. I know that's a damn poor excuse and if I could turn back the clock and undo what I done, I would. I really didn't mean to hurt you or Jamie. I just wasn't thinking straight at the time." He stopped and wiped his eyes. "Please baby, just give me another chance. I promise I will never take another drink, and I will never hurt you or Jamie ever again. Only please don't send me away Cassy, I know I done a terrible thing, and I'm sorry as hell. I love you and Jamie, and I want to be a good father to her, someone she can be really proud of as she grows up. So please just give me one more chance honey, I promise I'll make it all up to both you and Jamie. I just need you to trust me. I promise that you will never be sorry. Please baby, let me prove to you that I can be a good husband and father."

Cassandra had never seen Ray cry before, and she wondered if he was just putting on an act, or if he really was sincere this time. Seeing Ray humbling himself this way had her totally confused. Her first thought was to stick to her guns and throw him out on his ear. But what if he really did mean it this time, and if she threw him out it would deprive Jamie of her father. Hoping that she wasn't adding another mistake to her collection, and not wanting to go through a divorce for Jamie's sake, Cassandra made up her mind.

"Okay Ray, I'll give you one last chance. But I warn you that if you screw up and go back on your promise, or lay a hand on Jamie or me ever again, there won't be anymore chances."

Chapter Twenty-Three

Jamie started school in the fall of 1965; the house was empty with out the sound of her chatter and giggling. Cassandra found that she had too much time on her hands, and she needed something to keep her busy now that Jamie was in school or she would go out of her mind. Cassandra knew that the mill had started hiring women and decided to go and see if she could get a job there. As it turned out getting on at the mill was a lot easier than she had thought, the foreman hired her on the spot.

"Looks like this is your lucky day Mrs. Cartone, it just so happens one of my employees in the cut up plant quit yesterday and I need someone right away. So guess the job is yours if you want it."

"Oh thank you Mr. Harvey, you have no idea how much getting this job means to me."

"Well I hope you can handle the work Mrs. Cartone, you are such a tiny little thing and all. But you're welcome to give it a try, but if you can't keep up with the lumber coming off the belt I'll have to let you go."

"I promise you won't be sorry you gave me a chance Mr. Harvey, I'm stronger than I look, and I'm a good worker."

" Okay be here at eight o'clock in the morning ready to work, that means dressed in blue jeans, long sleeved shirt, high top steel toed boots and a pair of gloves." He instructed taking in her sleeveless blouse, peddle- pushers, and open toed sandals.

"Yes sir, Mr. Harvey you can be assured that I will be dressed appropriately for the job." She promised.

"Just be sure that you are, and perhaps you can also do something with that long hair of yours, can't take a chance of it getting all tangled up in one of those belts." He replied gruffly as he walked away, mentally thinking that he must be out of his mind to hire this delicate little thing to work in the mill. Was it the fact that she seemed so desperate to get the job, or was he just getting soft in his old age?

*　　*　　*

CASSANDRA WAS SO EXCITED about getting the job that she never even noticed Ray as she passed through the area of the mill where he was working. As she left the mill parking lot she glanced at her watch and decided that she still had time to drive over to the larger town that was only twenty miles away and buy herself the required work clothes that she was going to need for her new job.

*　　*　　*

THE PURCHASE OF THE jeans and shirts were the easy part, while the boots were something else. She had been to just about every store in town and was about to give up when finally one of the clerks suggested that because she had such a small narrow foot, she might try the children's shoe department and maybe she could find some boys boots that would fit her. It was almost noon when she finally found a pair of boy's boots with a steel toe in a size four, and a D width, which of course they were much too wide for her foot. The clerk suggested that maybe she could ware two pair of socks in them to make them fit better. Since they were the only pair of boots in the entire town that even came close to fitting her, Cassandra decided to purchase the dreaded boots because no way was she going to let this job get away from her. At the same time Cassandra wondered if the reason the mill foreman had given her this job was that he knew darn well that she would never be able to find the required boots.

As Cassandra headed for home, she started to laugh. "Well Mr. Harvey you may have thought that you were letting me down easy thinking that there was no way I could find any boots. But I fooled you Mr. Harvey, I found the damn boots. You have yourself a new employee now, whether you want me or not!" Cassandra grinned when she realized that she was talking aloud. "Yahoo." She yelled, and stepped on the gas.

* * *

JUST AS CASSANDRA PULLED into the driveway another thought crossed her mind, this new job would also make her independent of Ray, and should he go back on his promise and start handing out abuse again she wouldn't have to put up with it anymore because now she had a good job that would support her and Jamie, and she decided that this was only the beginning. Now she would start on rebuilding her self esteem, and regaining her independence because never again was she going to feel trapped out of fear.

* * *

CASSANDRA PUT ALL HER new clothes away soon as she got in the house. Then while she waited for time to go pick Jamie up from school she put on a pot of coffee, and picked up the telephone and called her good friend Marlee.

The phone rang several times, and then Cassandra heard a breathless "Hello."

"Oh Marlee I hope I didn't disturb you, sounds like you are out of breath."

"That's okay Cassy; I was out getting clothes off the line when the phone rang. What's up kiddo?"

"Marlee, do you remember me telling you awhile back, that I was thinking about trying to get a job over at the lumber mill? Well I went over there this morning, and they hired me on the spot. I start work tomorrow."

"That's great Cassy, I'm so happy for you."

" Marlee would it be imposing on you too much to watch Jamie for me, it would only be for two hour's in the morning, take her to school, and pick her up at night and keep her for another hour until I get off of work, and I'll pay you for your trouble."

"Nonsense Cassy, I have to take Ginger to school and pick her up every day so it won't be any extra trouble for me. Besides Ginger and Jamie get along so well together it will give them both something to do. I won't hear of you paying me to look after Jamie a couple of hours a day. What are friends for?"

"Thanks Marlee, you don't know how much I appreciate this. I'll bring Jamie by your house in the morning a little before six o'clock."

It was late that night when Ray got home; he and a couple of his friend's had gone dove hunting after work. The first thing Ray always done when he came home from hunting, was walk straight through the trailer, and toss his gun down on the bed. The gun was always loaded so Cassandra would have to unload it and put it high up in the closet so that Jamie couldn't ever get to it. Ray was so careless with his guns, but no amount of preaching on Cassandra's part could ever change his ways, so to save trouble Cassandra just made sure that the gun was never left on the bed for more than a minute after Ray came home. As she passed him in the hall he grabbed her by the arm.

"Where the hell are you going Cassandra?" He spoke harshly.

"I won't be a minute Ray; you know how I hate having your gun left on the bed."

"Forget about the damn gun. I want to know what the hell you were doing over at the mill today."

"I went over and applied for a job in the cut up plant, and I got hired. I start to work in the morning." She answered proudly.

"Oh no you're not, I forbid you to work at the mill. So you just get your ass over there first thing in the morning and tell them that you changed your mind."

"Ray I refuse to let you do this to me again. I'm taking that job with or without your permission. I need it so that I can feel like a whole person again. I don't want to be totally dependent on you, or anyone else for that matter. Besides now that Jamie is in school I have a lot of time on my hands with nothing to do. So I'm taking that job and I'm going to keep it!"

Cassandra could tell right away that Ray didn't like it one bit that she would deliberately disobey his orders. Before she could say anything else Ray grabbed her by the shoulders and started shaking her so hard that she was afraid her teeth were going to fall out. Then he back handed her so hard that she would have fallen to the floor had she not grabbed onto the kitchen cupboard to prevent her from going all the way down. As she tried to regain her balance, Ray jerked her away from the cupboard and hit her again, this time with a doubled up fist. But instead of falling she stumbled towards the bedroom down the hall. Before she could get her bearings Ray struck her again, and she fell on the floor beside the bed, and her right elbow struck something hard on the bed. She could see Ray charging down the hall towards her and from the hateful look on his face she was afraid this time he really would kill her. At that moment she realized what her elbow had come in contact with….Rays gun…Glancing up she saw Rays hands reaching for her throat… in a split second Cassandra knew that it was kill or be killed. In one fluid motion she jerked the rifle up under her arm, and rammed the barrel of the 30-06 into Ray's stomach as hard as she could from a sitting position and pulled the trigger. Silence permeated the dull click as the hammer fell on an empty chamber. For the very first time Cassandra saw fear in Ray's eyes because he didn't know the gun was empty. Without a single word Ray backed away, then turned and walked out of the trailer.

*   *   *

CASSANDRA WAS NUMB WITH shock as she realized what she had almost done. She sat on the floor by the bed, staring wide eyed at nothing as the reality set in, rocking back and forth cradling the rifle in her arms like a baby, crying her heart out. She cried for all the years of physical abuse that she had suffered at Rays hands. She cried because she never should have married him in the first place, and she cried because she knew that she was capable of killing Ray if she had to in order to protect herself and Jamie. She had to end this farce of a marriage and put a stop to this living nightmare once and for all before it was too late, and someone was killed

Cassandra slowly got up from the floor, carefully put the rifle on the top shelf of the closet, then walked out and sat down on the couch. Her mind retraced the events that had just taken place, and fear shot through her. She knew that beyond a shadow of a doubt that after what had taken place tonight that there was no going back, and she was afraid that both she and Jamie's life would be in danger if they continued to live with Ray in the same house.

Cassandra felt a chill run up her spine as she recalled how quick she had been to pull the trigger. She didn't hesitate a single second before she squeezed that trigger. In her heart she knew that the next time she might not be as lucky, and the gun would be loaded. Horrified at her thoughts she cried out. "Oh God what if I had killed Ray just now, there wouldn't be anyone to take care of Jamie!"

*   *   *

CASSANDRA HAD NO IDEA when she had fallen asleep on the couch, she had been too afraid to go to bed for fear that Ray would return. She woke up cramped and cold around five o'clock the next morning. "Oh Lord." She moaned when she saw the clock, if she hurried she would just have time to shower and get Jamie ready for school, and drop her by Marlee's before she had to be at work.

*   *   *

AS CASSANDRA WALKED THROUGH the mill to the department where she was supposed to work she noticed there was no sign of Ray anywhere. She breathed a sigh of relief knowing that she wouldn't have to face him right now. In fact Cassandra never saw Ray at all during the work shift that day. She picked Jamie up after work and went home feeling apprehensive, wondering if Ray would be waiting for them.

When Cassandra turned into the driveway relief washed over her when she saw that Ray's truck wasn't there.

"Come on sweetie let's go inside and get your clothes changed, and then mommy will get supper started."

"But daddy isn't home yet."

"That's okay honey, daddy might not be here for supper tonight and I'm starved."

"But mommy we have to wait for daddy." Jamie wailed.

"No baby we don't have to wait for daddy, he wasn't at work today so he must have had some business to take care of. But just in case we will set a place for him at the table." Cassandra promised to appease Jamie.

*   *   *

RAY HADN'T SHOWED UP by the time Cassandra had supper cooked, so she and Jamie sat down to eat alone. Cassandra noticed that Jamie kept glancing over at the vacant place setting at the end of the table where Ray always sat, but she never said anything until after they had finished. "Mommy, why didn't daddy come home tonight?"

"Jamie you know there are a lot of times that daddy isn't here, and pretty soon he may not be coming home at all and there will just be the two of us like the time that daddy was over seas." Cassandra explained.

"But why mommy, doesn't daddy like us anymore?" Jamie asked tears welling up in her blue eyes.

"I'm sure he does sweetie, but daddy just has other things to do sometimes. Now wipe your eyes Jamie and help mommy clear the table, after we get the dishes done I'll help you with your bath, then I'll finish that story I was reading to you. How does that sound?"

Cassandra smiled making light of the tense moment while she was trying to get Jamie's mind off Ray being gone.

* * *

JUST AS CASSANDRA WAS tucking Jamie into bed the telephone rang. "Goodnight baby, you go to sleep, okay?" Cassandra kissed Jamie on the cheek and went to get the telephone.

"Hello."

"Well it sure took you long enough to answer the phone, where the hell were you?" Ray grumbled.

"If you must know Ray, I was putting Jamie to bed." Cassandra snapped so as not to let fear creep into her voice.

"Come on honey is that any way to talk to your old man?"

"Just how do you expect me to talk to you Ray after what you did last night?"

"Oh forget about last night Cassy, it was nothing, just a little misunderstanding that's all. Hell you ought to know me well enough by now Cassandra to know that I don't really mean the things I say when I get riled up." He coaxed.

"Well it may have been nothing to you Ray, but it certainly was something to me, I could have killed you last night if that damn gun hadn't been empty." Cassandra said heatedly.

"I just called to tell you that I was on my way home, I should be there in a few minutes."

"No Ray I don't want you to come home. Its over between us, you can come and get your things Saturday."

"You can't mean that baby; I need you in my life. I promise you it won't ever happen again." He pleaded.

But Cassandra was going to stick to her guns, she was sick of Rays sweet talk, and lies. This time she was turning a deaf ear to his pleading and crying, this time it was over and wild horses couldn't change her mind. She didn't care what people thought, her only concern was for her and Jamie's safety. And the only way she could make sure that Ray's abuse would stop was to end this farce of a marriage once and for all.

"I do mean it Ray so you might as well accept it. I don't love you; in fact I never did love you. I just want you out of my life for good."

Rays loud boisterous laugh came over the phone. "Oh Cassy, Cassy, what am I going to do with you? You know you need me, so I'm coming over."

" Please don't come here Ray. I promise you this time the gun is fully loaded, and I will use it if you step one foot on this property. Get it through your thick skull that I don't want you anywhere near me, now or ever! It's over!" She warned.

"Just give me another chance baby. Let me prove to you that I can be a good husband, and father. I promise nothing like this will ever happen again."

"No Ray, no more chances. I can't live this way any longer, and I won't let Jamie grow up being afraid of her father." She paused. "I also had the locks changed Ray, so I'll leave your things out on the patio. And please don't get any ideas about trying anything foolish because the sheriff will be here too." Cassandra's hands were shaking as she hung up the phone.

* * *

CASSANDRA PICKED UP THE phone and dialed the sheriffs office, when Sam answered she quickly explained to him what had been going on in her life for the past nine years, and the events about the gun that had finally led to her decision to end her marriage. Then she made the sheriff promise her that he wouldn't say a single word to her father about all that she had told him because she didn't want her parents to ever know how badly Ray had treated her through the years.

"I always knew there was something about Ray that didn't quite meet the eye Cassandra, but now it all makes sense to me and I want you know that I won't divulge your confidence to a living soul if you don't want me too. I'll see you on Saturday so don't you worry about a thing."

"Thanks Sam you don't know how much I appreciate this."

"I think I do Cassandra, and I want you to know that I think you are a remarkable woman, and you can always count on me."

* * *

THE NEXT DAY CASSANDRA avoided going anywhere close to the area of the mill where Ray worked. But she could feel his eyes on her from across the distance that separated their work areas; she refused to glance his way as she didn't want to even make eye contact with him. She felt like a fly under a microscope and her flesh crawled in fear of what Ray might try to do.

* * *

WHEN THE FIVE O'CLOCK whistle blew to signal the end of the day, Cassandra sprinted through the mill like the hounds of hell were after her. She jumped into her vehicle and rushed out of the parking lot just as the rest of the employees came out of the building. She drove to Marlee's to pick up Jamie.

Marlee answered her knock at once. "Hi Cassy, come on in and have some coffee."

"I can't today Marlee I'm sort of in a hurry." She answered nervously.

Marlee knew instantly that there was something bothering her friend, because they always shared a cup of coffee when Cassandra came to collect Jamie after work.

"Care to talk about it Cassy? You know I'm a good listener."

"I know you mean well Marlee, but honestly I just need to get Jamie and go home right now. But I'll tell you all about it real soon." She promised.

"Okay Cassy I'll go get Jamie, the girls are playing in the back yard right now."

Jamie came running around the corner of the house and launched herself into Cassandra's arms. "Mommy, mommy, come see Ginger's new puppy. He is so cute."

"I don't have time sweetie." Seeing the hurt look on her daughters face was almost her undoing. "But I promise I'll see the puppy Monday night. Okay baby?"

Jamie's face brightened with a big smile. "Okay mommy just as long as you don't forget, cause he is just so cute you gotta see him."

* * *

ALL THE WAY HOME; Jamie kept up a constant chatter about the puppy. She was really excited about it. "Do you think daddy will let me have a puppy mama?"

"Well not right now honey, but maybe real soon we'll see about getting you a puppy of your very own." Cassandra promised as she turned into the driveway breathing a sigh of relief when she saw that Ray's truck wasn't there.

* * *

CASSANDRA STAYED UP MOST of the night packing up Ray's belongings. She didn't want anything left for the next morning, she just wanted to get all the boxes and things that belonged to Ray out of the house and stacked on the patio so that there would be no reason for him to come into the trailer for a single thing.

* * *

JUST AS CASSANDRA SET the last box down she heard a vehicle drive into the drive way, she was so frightened she ran into the trailer and shut the door and locked it. Then she looked out the front window and discovered that it was the sheriff.

Breathing a sigh of relief that it wasn't Ray, she rushed to the door to invite Sam in, but he declined. "Thanks Cassandra, but for all intents and purposes it's best if I just stay out here and make it more official and not a social call."

Cassandra started to step out side but the sheriff stopped her. "I think it would be best Cassandra for you to stay in the house until Ray comes and picks up his belongings, that way he will know that you mean business this time and he will be dealing with me in the future."

"Okay sheriff if you think that is best, I'll stay out of the way."

"Believe me Cassandra it's the only way. I intend to put the fear of God in Ray and let him know in no uncertain terms that if he ever steps foot in your house again, or lays a hand on you I'll put his ass in jail and throw away the key!"

* * *

CASSANDRA SAT IN THE chair facing the front window, the sheriff had walked back to his car and stood leaning against the front fender smoking a cigarette while he waited patiently for Ray to arrive. She could hear the clock on the wall ticking off the minutes, and each minute seemed like an hour. She was trembling not knowing what was going to happen when Ray showed up. She knew he would be furious when he saw the sheriff there waiting for him.

* * *

THE TIME DRAGGED BY, Cassandra was starting to think that Ray wasn't going to come. Jamie woke up and padded barefoot out to the living room where Cassandra was, rubbing the sleep from her eyes. Cassandra almost jumped out of her skin when she heard Jamie's voice. "Mommy what is that cop doing out in front of our house?"

Cassandra not wanting to alarm Jamie calmly replied. "That's the sheriff honey; he's just waiting for daddy to arrive so that he can talk to him."

Jamie yawned very wide, and still rubbing her eyes she said. "Oh." And that seemed to satisfy her curiosity.

" It's way too early for you to be up honey, why don't you go back to bed and sleep a little bit longer and when you wake up again mommy will fix you some pancakes, how does that sound to you sweetie?"

Cassandra swooped Jamie up in her arms, and carried her back to bed. As she gently laid her down she could see that Jamie was almost back to sleep again, she tucked her in and kissed her softly on the forehead.

*   *   *

JUST AS CASSANDRA GOT back to her place by the window she saw Rays truck pull up out front. She watched as the sheriff moved away from his car and walked over to speak with Ray. She couldn't hear what they were saying but she could tell from the angry look on Rays face that he wasn't too pleased by what Sam was saying to him. She saw Ray double up his fist, and at first she thought that Ray was going to punch the sheriff, but he must have changed his mind on that score and slammed his fist onto the hood of his truck, then walked over to where Cassandra had stacked his belongings and started tossing the boxes and things none to gently into the back of his truck.

When everything was loaded Ray jerked open the drivers door and got behind the wheel, started the truck, gunned the engine a couple of times, then threw gravel from the drive way as he tore out of the yard.

Cassandra saw the sheriff walking towards the trailer and opened the door before he had a chance to knock. "Do you think he will be back Sam?" She asked fear showing in her voice.

"Don't you worry Cassandra; I doubt very much that Ray will give you anymore trouble. I really laid the law down to him and I told him exactly what was going to happen if he comes back here and tries to bother you again in the future. I'm leaving now Cassandra. But you be sure and call me if you need me, you hear?"

"I hear you Sam. Thanks for everything, and I do mean everything." Cassandra smiled as tears formed in her eyes.

"Now don't you go fretting girl about anything, I promise Frank will never learn about this from me, everything you told me in confidence will remain just between you and me. And I'm sure your secret is pretty safe, because I doubt very much that Ray will ever have the guts to tell your father."

Chapter Twenty-Four

Early the next morning while Jamie was still asleep Cassandra walked down to her parents house, since it was Sunday and the store was closed she knew that she could talk to her parents with out any interruptions. She wanted them to hear it from her and not get a distorted version from the town gossips.

*   *   *

"Well this is a pleasant surprise Cassy. Pour another cup of coffee honey our little girls here." Frank said as he stepped back from the door allowing Cassandra to enter.

"What brings you calling so early in the morning? Frank inquired as Cassandra sat down in a chair at the end of the table.

"I have something to tell you and mother before you hear it through the grapevine." Cassandra wasn't going to tell her parents everything, but she wanted to be the one to tell them that she and Ray had split up.

"Daddy, Ray and I have split up; I'm going to get a divorce just as soon as I can save up the money." Cassandra stated looking him directly in the eye; she had always been able to talk to her father about anything.

"Gosh honey we never realized things were this bad between you and Ray, are you sure this is what you want to do?"

"I'm sure dad, we don't have a life. Ray runs around with his buddies all the time, drinking and chasing around with every woman in town. Sometimes he doesn't even come home at all for an entire weekend. It has been very embarrassing for Jamie and me for a long time now. But Jamie is getting older now and she hears the kids at school talking about all sorts of things that they hear from their parents. I just don't want her to grow up knowing her father is a liar and a cheat. Friday night after a terrible argument I told Ray to get out, and that I wanted a divorce. He left mad, and later he called me and threatened me. I told him that he could pick up his belongings the next day. He wasn't very happy about that, so I decided to call Sam and asked if he would come and over see things until Ray had picked up his stuff and left." Cassandra breathed a sigh of relief that finally she had been able to tell her story in a believable way without divulging anything that would cause her father to go after Ray.

"That explains why Sam's car was up at your house so long yesterday. I saw his cruiser parked in front of your trailer when I went to the post office and wondered about that. But I decided that you would tell us in your own time."

"Yes, there sure isn't much that goes on in this small town that someone doesn't see or hear about." Cassandra agreed "The town gossips will have a field day with this, that's why I came down so early this morning. I wanted you both to hear the truth from me before anyone had a chance to put their own spin on things they don't know anything about."

"Are you going to be okay financially Cassy?" Frank inquired with a worried look in his eyes.

"I think so dad, I have a real good job at the mill, and a good babysitter who won't take a dime from me to look after Jamie while I'm at work, so I'm sure I can manage okay. Course it may take me a little time to save the money for my divorce, but that's alright. In time it will all work out in the long run." Cassandra smiled to show that she wasn't worried, making light of the situation as she didn't want her parents to worry about her.

"I sort of had a feeling that some day you would realize you and Ray didn't have a future. God when I think back to all the times he ran out on you before he was recalled back into the service it made my blood boil. But I didn't want to interfere so I kept my mouth shut. Then when he came home from France I thought perhaps he had changed and things were going to be alright for the two of you. But apparently that was short lived, as soon as he went to work here and became acquainted with some of the local people; I've noticed the past few years he has changed. And I don't mind admitting that I haven't been too happy about the way he has changed, the drinking and womanizing to name a few. But I knew it wasn't my place to say anything, so I've tried to stay out of it knowing that one day you would do what was right for you."

"I know daddy, I made a terrible mistake when I married Ray, and I have wished so many times that I had listened to you and had never married him in the first place. But once we were married I tried to make the best of my marriage. Then when Jamie came along I tried so much harder to make the marriage work for her sake." Tears rolled down Cassandra's cheek. She couldn't hold them back any longer.

"Don't cry honey, your mother and I will always be here for you anytime you need us."

"I know that daddy; you have always been there for me. It's just that I have made such a mess out of my life."

"No sweetie you gave it your best, and that's really all anyone could do. I have known for a long time that you weren't very happy, but I just didn't feel I had any right to tell you how to run your life. That was your decision. Now that you have decided to end your marriage to Ray, your mother and I will support you any way we can, financially or otherwise."

"Thanks daddy." Cassandra stood up and threw her arms around Frank's neck and hugged him tightly.

"Thanks for the coffee, I better get back to the house before Jamie wakes up and wonders where in the world I am."

* * *

THE FIRST WORK DAY after she and Ray split up she was a little hesitant when she dropped off Jamie on her way to work, not knowing what Marlee might have heard over the weekend. Taking a deep breath she knocked on the door.

"Come on in Cassy, got time for a quick cup of coffee?"

Cassandra glanced at her watch. "Yeah I am a little early this morning so guess I do have time for a quick cup of coffee." She sat down in the nearest chair as Marlee quickly reached for another cup from the cupboard.

"Coming right up gal." Marlee smiled as she sat the coffee down on the table in front of Cassandra.

"I guess you have probably already heard the news through the grapevine that Ray and I have split the sheets." Cassandra inquired as she looked down at her coffee cup.

"Yes I heard about it. You know how this town is, every time someone farts, the phones start ringing." Marlee cleared her throat then proceeded to clue Cassandra in about what she was told by one of the towns gossips.

"The preachers wife could hardly wait for the sheriff's car to leave your place before she was on the phone spreading her version of what she deemed was the honest to Gods truth. She said Ray caught you with another man and he dumped you. She said the sheriff was there to help him get Jamie."

Cassandra was fuming, the nerve of that woman to make up such a story and spread it around town.

"The old biddy sure got it wrong my friend. The real truth is that I kicked Ray out on his ass, and had Sam come over just in case I needed some protection, you know what a vile temper Ray has and I must admit that I'm a little bit afraid of him." Cassandra took a swallow of her coffee.

"Marlee I'm going to tell you something that I have never told a soul until now, and I want you to promise me that you won't breathe a word about this to a living soul. I don't want my parents, especially my father to ever find out the real truth about the living hell that my marriage has been all these years living with Ray."

"You know you can trust me with anything Cassy, you are my best friend and I would never divulge anything that you tell me in confidence to a living soul. You have my solemn oath on that."

"Thanks Marlee. To be quite truthful Ray has two sides to him, one that he portrays to the public, and the one that he exercises at home. He has been beating me for years, and I like a fool kept putting up with it trying to keep our family together for Jamie's sake. But last week was the final straw and I would have killed him if the damn rifle hadn't been empty. That's when I realized that I had finally had enough, and that I was capable of killing Ray to protect Jamie and myself. So I called Sam told him everything that has happened to me in the past nine years, even some things that I haven't told you, horrible things that would be beyond your comprehension, and I don't have time this morning to go through it all. But for the record it was me that called the sheriff to be there for my own protection when Ray came to get his belongings."

Marlee was sitting there open mouthed and wide eyed, amazed at some of the things Cassandra had just told her.

" My God Cassy, how have you managed to put up with all this crap for so many years and still stay with that no good bastard?"

"Believe me dear friend it sure hasn't been easy." Cassandra smiled to relieve the tension, as she glanced at her watch jumping to her feet.

"Gosh I better get going kiddo or I'm going to be late for work."

Cassandra hugged Jamie. "You be a good girl today sweetie, mind Marlee, and mama will see you tonight. Okay?"

"I'll be good mommy. Will you promise to look at Gingers puppy tonight?"

"Yes sweetie I promise to take time and see this terrific puppy soon as I get off work."

Cassandra motioned for Marlee to step out on the front porch with her where they wouldn't be over heard by Jamie.

Cassandra handed her friend an envelope. "Marlee I want you to give this note to the teachers, it's giving them strict instructions that nobody, and I do mean nobody but you are to pick Jamie up from school. I don't trust Ray not to try to take her away like he done once before. He doesn't really want Jamie as much as he would like to hurt me. So promise me that you won't let anyone take her except for me."

"You go on to work Cassy, and try not to worry. I'll protect Jamie with my life, just as I would with Ginger."

Cassandra threw her arms around her friend's neck, giving her a big hug. "Thanks Marlee, I knew I could count on you."

Running down the steps Cassandra jumped in her vehicle and waved goodbye as she backed out of the driveway.

* * *

ALL DAY LONG CASSANDRA worried about Jamie. She hadn't seen Ray anywhere in the mill all day. When the five o'clock whistle blew she was running through the mill to her car, she couldn't wait to see if Jamie was alright. Pulling into Marlee's driveway she breathed a sigh of relief when she saw both Jamie and Ginger playing with their dolls on the front porch. Cassandra jumped out of the pickup, and started running towards the house; just as Jamie came flying down the steps screaming. "Mommy, mommy, come see Gingers puppy."

"Okay sweetie lets go see this puppy, I can hardly wait, I've thought about nothing else all day." She lied.

The puppy was an adorable buff colored Cocker Spaniel, he bounced around the yard from one little girl to the other like a little ball of fluff.

"Isn't he just the cutest thing you ever saw mama?" Jamie squealed. "Oh please mama can I have one just like him for my very own? Mrs. Peterson still has one left and she said that I could have it if it was okay with you. Please, please, say yes mommy and I will be the happiest little girl in the whole world." She begged.

Cassandra was speechless, and started to hedge. "Oh sweetie I don't think that would be such a good idea right now. Who would take care of it while you are in school and I'm at work?"

"Marlee said that if you decide to let me have the puppy that she wouldn't mind if you brought both me, and the puppy to her house every day and he could play with Gingers puppy in the back yard while we are in school." Jamie explained trying hard to convince her.

Cassandra glanced at Marlee for conformation, and Marlee nodded her head in total agreement. "Well it sure looks as though you two are ganging up on me. So guess I'm out voted. You can have the puppy." She conceded.

"Oh you are just the best mommy in the whole world." Jamie squealed with delight running to her mother and throwing her arms around her hips hugging her tight.

"Can we go get him now mommy, huh, can we mommy, please, please." She wheedled.

"I'm not sure if now is a good time honey, we don't even know if Mrs. Peterson is home."

"I'll run in and make a quick call Cassy, won't take a minute." Marlee offered as she ran towards the house.

Jamie was standing with her fingers crossed behind her back; her eyes squeezed shut very tight, as though she was praying for a miracle. And she remained that way until Marlee returned.

"Well kiddo we're in luck, Mrs. Peterson is home, and she said that you can come right over and get the puppy."

Jamie let out a war hoop that probably could be heard for miles and started dancing around the yard. Then realization set in, and she ran towards Cassandra.

"Come on mama lets go before you change your mind." She said pulling on Cassandra's pant leg.

"I'm not going to change my mind sweetie, but it is time for us to be going."

All the way to Mrs. Petersons house Jamie kept up a nervous chatter about the new puppy she was about to get. "What should we name him mommy? Ginger named her puppy Taffy, cause he's the same color as a piece of candy." She explained how Ginger chose the name for her puppy.

"Why don't we just wait until we see the puppy honey, then we can pick a name that will suit him. How does that sound?"

When they arrived at Mrs. Peterson's house, she was waiting for them on the front porch with a squirming bundle of buff colored fluff in her arms.

Jamie let out a squeal. "Oh look there he is mommy, hurry and stop the car." She was so eager and excited that Cassandra was afraid that Jamie would open the door before the car was at a complete stop.

"Don't open that door Jamie until I shut the engine off." Cassandra ordered.

"I won't mommy, but please hurry, I can't wait to hold my very own puppy."

Soon as the car stopped Jamie flew out the door, just as Mrs. Peterson put the puppy down on the ground and he ran straight to Jamie. She scooped him up in her arms and hugged him to her chest planting a huge kiss on the top of his head. Cassandra had never seen Jamie this excited about anything before and her heart swelled with the love she had for her daughter.

On the way home Jamie laughed and squealed every time the puppy licked her on the face. "Oh thank you mommy for my very own puppy, he is so cute."

"Have you decided what you want to name him?" Cassandra asked.

Jamie shook her head negative, and looked very thoughtful for a few minutes before she spoke. "I thought about muffy, but that sort of sounds like a girls name, so I guess I will have to think of something else."

"Well maybe I can help honey. Since he is sort of buff colored, what about calling him Buffy, that's close to Muffy." Cassandra suggested.

"That's a neat name for him mommy." Jamie held the puppy up and looked him right in the face, and very seriously told the puppy. "Your name is Buffy." The puppy started licking Jamie in the face and she giggled. "I think he must like his name mommy, he won't stop kissing me."

Chapter Twenty-Five

Getting the puppy for Jamie turned out to be a God send, he kept Jamie so occupied that she didn't seem to notice too often that Ray was never around. The time was flying by; Christmas came and went with no sign of Ray. Occasionally Cassandra saw him in other parts of the mill during the work shift but he never tried to seek her out, and he hadn't called the house a single time since the sheriff had talked to him the day he collected his belongings, and Lord only knows how thankful she was for that.

Cassandra dropped Jamie at Marlee's every morning, and collected her after work, Jamie would keep up a constant chatter about all that had happened during the day, and her school work wasn't suffering by not having her father around. In fact Jamie rarely mentioned him at all, and her report card showed straight A's. Cassandra was so proud of her daughter. Their life was so peaceful without Ray that it made her wish that she had kicked him out of the house long before she did.

The town gossips were still trying to spread things around about what they liked to think happened between her and Ray, but eventually someone would set them straight and soon the gossip died out. Even the kids in school had stopped saying mean things to Jamie and she just bubbled with happiness all the time.

*   *   *

THE END OF JANUARY the nightmare started again, and caused Cassandra's whole world to collapse.

*   *   *

CASSANDRA GOT OFF WORK at the regular time and drove to Marlee's to pick up Jamie, when she arrived she knocked on the door but nobody answered her knock. She tried the door and when it opened she found Marlee in tears, with Ginger and the two puppies on the sofa in the front room, there was no sign of Jamie anywhere.

"Marlee what's happened? Where's Jamie?" She screamed as she ran to her friend, knowing that something awful had happened.

Through her tears Marlee sobbed out her story. "Oh Cassy I tried to call you at work as soon as I found out, but the mill office was already closed."

"Found out what Marlee? Come on pull yourself together and tell me where Jamie is."

"I don't know where she is Cassy, Jamie was gone when I went to pick up the girls." She wailed.

"Well did you ask the teacher? What did she say?" Cassandra was trying to be calm for her friend's sake, but fear was eating at her insides.

"All the teacher could tell me was that Jamie's father and grandmother collected Jamie around noon time. They showed her a note signed by you giving them permission to take her out of school for her grandfather's birthday party at their house, and that you were going to drive straight into town after you got off work." Marlee started crying again. "Oh Cassy I can't tell you how sorry I am, Jamie was in my care and I let this happen to her."

"This is not your fault Marlee, so please don't blame yourself. It's okay. I'll just drive into town and get Jamie and bring her home if you don't mind keeping Buffy for awhile."

"Gary will be home soon Cassy, he can take care of Ginger and the puppies and I'll go with you." Marlee offered.

"I really do appreciate your offer Marlee, but this is something I have to do by myself. I don't know how much trouble the Cartone's may give me when I get there to pick up Jamie and I may have to call in the police. I don't want you involved in this so I better just go alone."

"Oh Cassy don't go by yourself, please let me go with you." Marlee pleaded.

"It will be okay Marlee, please don't worry. I promise I will call you when we get back home." Cassandra promised.

*　*　*

CASSANDRA RUSHED OUT OF the house to her car and headed into town, driving as fast as she could without breaking the speed limit too much, the last thing she needed right now was to get stopped by the cops. It seemed like the thirty miles to the Cartone house took forever. It was just like the Cartone's to pull something like this. She prayed that Ray hadn't kidnapped Jamie again. When she arrived the house was in total darkness, and it didn't appear that there was anyone at home, but she jumped out of the car and rang the doorbell anyway. It seemed that an eternity passed as she stood there on the door step, when there was no response to her ring she realized her suspicions that Ray had indeed kidnapped Jamie again were true, and she started crying as she ran back to her vehicle and headed for home, she had to get a hold of Sam as soon as she possibly could and report Jamie missing to the authorities.

*　*　*

PULLING INTO THE DRIVEWAY in front of her trailer, Cassandra jumped out and ran into the trailer and grabbed up the phone and quickly dialed the sheriff.

"Sam here, how can I help you?"

"Oh Sam you've got to help me, Ray and his parents have kidnapped Jamie again." She wailed.

"Slow down Cassandra, and pull yourself together. Tell me exactly what has happened." He instructed.

"Today Ray and his mother gave Jamie's teacher a forged note saying that they had my permission to take her out of school under false pretenses that I would be joining them later after work for a birthday party for Jamie's grandfather. I rushed into town as soon as Marlee explained to me what had happened, only the house was in darkness and there wasn't anyone at home."

"Did you and Ray ever get a divorce Cassandra?" Sam questioned.

"No, not yet Sam. I've been trying to save up the money for the divorce."

"Then it's pretty much the same as the last time Ray took Jamie Cassandra, about all I can do is put out an all points bulletin for the state of Idaho and find out if they are still in this state. According to the law if there isn't a divorce decree showing that a Judge has granted you custody of Jamie, then we can't charge Ray with kidnapping. The way the law reads right now Ray is Jamie's father and he has as much right as you do to take her anywhere he wants to." He explained patiently.

"Oh Sam what am I going to do. You know Ray is only doing this to get back at me, he doesn't want Jamie, he just wants to hurt me, and force me to take him back."

"I'm real sorry there isn't a hell of a lot that I can do Cassandra, my hands are tied by the law. As long as you and Ray are still married the law says that you both have equal rights to Jamie."

"I know you would help me if you could Sam. I was just hoping that maybe the laws might have changed since the last time Ray stole Jamie."

"I wish I could do more for you Cassandra. Just keep a tight rein on your emotions, and hope in your heart, and if I find out anything I'll call you right away."

Cassandra hung up the phone and slumped into a chair as all the pent up emotions poured from her heart, praying that somehow she could find Jamie before any harm came to her.

* * *

EVEN THOUGH IT WAS late at night Cassandra just couldn't stand being alone, she pulled her coat back on and ran down to her parents house and banged on the door.

Frank opened the door, and seeing Cassandra standing there in the dark crying was almost his undoing. "Cassy what in the world has happened? Is Jamie sick?" He asked as he pulled her into his arms to comfort her. " Looks like my girl needs a hug."

"Oh daddy I need your help. Ray and his mother stole Jamie out of school today at noon. I've been into town but there isn't anyone at home at the Cartone's. I called Sam as soon as I returned home, and he told me there isn't anything he can do because Ray and I have never gotten a divorce yet." She sobbed into his shoulder.

"Let's go in the house out of this cold, I'll make a pot of coffee and you tell me everything from the beginning and we'll see if we can figure out where we can go from here."

Nora emerged from the bedroom tying the belt on her robe. "Who is it Frank?"

"It's Cassy dear, Ray has taken Jamie again." Frank answered as he helped Cassandra out of her coat. "How about brewing a pot of coffee Nora, I'm afraid we are going to need it."

"Now Cassy start at the beginning and let's see what we can come up with."

Cassandra repeated the whole story to her parents, trying to hold back the tears, but not doing a very good job of it.

"Cassy have you tried to call Rays sisters, or anyone else that you can think of yet?"

"I just called Sam so far. After hearing that there isn't much that he can do according to the law, I was so upset that I just came down to talk to you dad."

"You've done the right thing Cassy, because I'm going to do everything in my power to help you find Jamie." He assured her.

"I'm glad tomorrow is Saturday because that will give me two days to call around and see if I can find out anything from some of the relatives. Fred helped me last time this happened." Cassandra said taking a sip of her coffee."

"That's a good place to start honey, but I doubt if it will do very much good this time. Since Fred helped you last time he may have been left out of the loop on this occasion. But it damn sure won't hurt to give him a try just in case."

"Daddy what am I going to do if we can't find Jamie?"

Seeing the fear and desolation in Cassandra's eyes at the thought of never seeing her daughter again was tearing the heart right out of him. "Don't you worry baby we'll get Jamie back." Frank promised as he held Cassandra close to his chest.

"But Daddy we don't even know where to start looking and the law can't do a single thing to help us." Cassandra sobbed.

"Just don't give up baby, I'm going into town tomorrow and see Alex, and I'll beat the hell out of him if I have to until he tells where that worthless son of his has taken Jamie. Come hell or high water I'm going to get some answers before I come home."

"Oh Daddy please promise me you won't do anything that will get you thrown in jail. I couldn't bear losing you and Jamie both." She pleaded as the tears streamed down her face.

"Don't you worry about that honey, I'm not about to do anything that stupid, but I know damn well Alex and Rita know where Ray has taken Jamie and I'm damn sure going to find out one way or the other." Frank assured her. "Now dry those eyes and lets all get a good nights sleep. I'm sure things will look a lot better in the morning."

"Cassy would you like to spend the night here with us." Nora asked softly. "It won't take me but a minute to make up the couch for you."

Cassandra blew her nose, and wiped the tears from her eyes. "Thanks mother, but I think I'll go back home just in case someone tries to call me about Jamie."

Chapter Twenty-Six

After a sleepless night, and groggy from too much coffee, Cassandra kept watching the clock so she could start making her phone calls to see if she could find someone who might have some idea where Jamie was. She didn't want to call and wake anyone up. First she called Rays parents only to discover that their phone was no longer in service. Then she called Fred and Ellen in Southern California, Fred answered the phone. "Fred this is Cassandra. Ray and Rita took Jamie out of school around noon yesterday with a forged note from me on the pretext that it was for a birthday party for Alex. I drove into town soon as I found out, but the house was dark and there wasn't anyone at home. I just now tried to call them and found out that their phone had been disconnected. Do you have any idea what is going on? "

"Gosh no Cassandra, this is the first I've heard about this. But I promise you one thing if Ellen and I can find out anything at all about what is going on I'll call you right away. Damn those people don't they have any idea what they are doing to Jamie, and you too for that matter. I can't begin to tell you how sorry I am. I know you must be half out of your mind with worry. But I'll make some calls and see if I can find out anything. I'll get back to you." Fred promised.

"Thanks a lot Fred you don't know how much I really appreciate this."

*   *   *

NEXT CASSANDRA CALLED RAYS sister in Washington State. But she drew a blank there as well, Nadine denied having any knowledge that Jamie was even missing, and said that her parents had gone on vacation, but had no idea where they went.

*   *   *

HAVING HAD NO LUCK with any of Ray's family, Cassandra decided to call some of Ray's friends to see if perhaps one of them knew about Jamie. But they all said the same thing, that all they knew was that Ray had quit his job at the mill Thursday night when he told them that he found a better job some place else, but they said he never disclosed to them where the job was. Ray had just told them goodbye, and he would see them around.

*   *   *

FRANK WASN'T ANYMORE SUCCESSFUL than Cassandra was, he drove into town to see Alex and Rita only to find some guy putting up a **For Sale** sign on the property. Frank called the number on the sign, but there was no answer. The people who lived next door to the Cartone's said they had seen them loading a u-haul truck early Friday morning and the Cartone's had pulled out about three o'clock Friday afternoon.

*   *   *

"DADDY IT JUST DOESN'T make sense that Rays sister would tell me that Alex and Rita had gone on vacation. Surely Nadine knew that they were selling their house and moving."

203

"There are a lot of things that don't make any sense to me about this whole damn thing baby. But we'll keep trying until we get some answers. Some where out there someone knows something, so we'll just keep digging until we find where Jamie is and bring her back home again."

"Daddy I know that this wasn't a spur of the moment thing, the Cartone's must have been planning this for quite some time. Ray quitting his job the night before, and Alex and Rita putting their house up for sale. Plus the fact that Ray and his mother took Jamie out of school right after lunch. That gave them plenty of time to get out of the State of Idaho before I got off work and found out Jamie was gone. Marlee said she called the mill office at four o'clock but the girl always goes home early on Fridays. Ray knew about that. Now I know why Ray wasn't at work on Friday. I didn't pay too much attention to him being gone, because there were a lot of days that he didn't show up for work."

"I sure do agree with you Cassy, but that doesn't give us much to go on." Frank put his arm around Cassandra's shoulders and hugged her close. "Just hang in there honey, sooner or later the Cartone's will slip up and someone will hear something. I just hope it won't be too long before we find Jamie."

*   *   *

THE DAYS TURNED INTO weeks, and the weeks turned into months. Cassandra was getting more and more depressed as she worried about where Jamie might be, was she okay, was she getting enough to eat, did she have a warm bed to sleep in. Was the person who had Jamie taking good care of her, and giving her love and comfort? These thoughts were in her mind constantly. She couldn't sleep, and had no appetite, she was losing weight, but she kept working at the mill hoping that one day she would pick up some sort of information that would help her find Jamie.

*   *   *

ONE NIGHT SHE WAS on her way home from the mill, when she decided on the spur of the moment to stop at the liquor store. Why she had no idea, because she had never had a drink in her entire life. She just sat there staring at the front of the building, but she never left her car. Then she backed out of the parking lot and continued on home. The next night she did the same thing, only this time she went in and purchased a bottle of whisky. When she got home she set the whisky bottle in the center of the table and just sat on the couch staring at it. All she could think about was Jamie, would she ever see her daughter again. The amber color of the whisky was calming to her. Then one night she decided to try the whisky. She just sipped it a little at a time. The more she sipped the calmer she felt. Jamie had disappeared in January, and now it was almost the end of April and this was the first time that her mind was relaxed and numb to her loss.

*   *   *

CASSANDRA WAS DRINKING MORE and more every night as the days and weeks passed, now she was making a regular nightly stop at the liquor store for her bottle of whisky to help her make it through the night. She was living on whisky and cigarettes, and only a sandwich for lunch every day. She had stopped going by to see her parent's weeks ago, when they called she made up some excuse about being busy, or else she acted like she wasn't home and never bothered to answer the phone. Most of the time she just told them that she wanted to stay close to her phone in case someone called about Jamie, she was afraid that if she wasn't home that she would miss a call.

Frank and Nora thought that she just needed some time to adjust, and they didn't put any pressure on her. One night Sara Jones, the lady that owned the liquor store stopped in late to pick up a few groceries and when she seen Cassandra's truck go by. She made a remark to Frank and Nora. "There goes my best customer." She picked up her bag of groceries and left. "See ya later." She called over her shoulder as the door shut behind her.

Frank was stunned when he saw it was Cassandra. He was shocked to find out that Cassy had been going to the liquor store, and wondered when she had started drinking. He decided it was time for him to find out what was going on. If Cassandra was drinking she was in pretty deep trouble and he knew that she needed him now more than ever before.

"Hold down the fort Nora, I'm going to run up and see Cassy for a minute."

*   *   *

CASSANDRA HAD JUST STARTED to pour herself a much needed drink when there was a knock on the door. Setting the bottle and half filled glass down on the drain board by the kitchen sink she went to see who was there. "Hi daddy, come on in." She tried to sound cheerful when she opened the door so Frank wouldn't know how depressed she really was.

"I was just going to fix me a drink dad would you like to join me?" She offered.

Frank stepped inside the trailer. "No thanks Baby, but I think we do need to have a little father daughter talk." He said as he walked over and picked up the bottle of whisky and half filled glass in each hand and started to pour them both down the drain at the same time.

When Cassandra realized what her father was doing she made a grab for the whisky bottle. "Oh daddy what are you doing? Please don't do that daddy." She screamed, trying to wrestle the bottle away from him. "Let go of the bottle daddy you don't know what you are doing, I really need this."

"No you don't Cassandra, you just think you do." Frank yelled trying to keep hold of the bottle while the last of the whisky disappeared down the sink.

"I do need it daddy; it's the only way I can make it through the nights." She whispered as she slowly sank down on the floor at his feet in total defeat.

Frank slowly lifted her up and cradled her in his arms as he led her over to the couch and sat down holding her on his lap. "How long has this drinking been going on honey?"

"I don't know daddy, two or three month's maybe. I can't remember."

"Why did you start drinking baby? Why didn't you come to your mother and I Cassy? We would have helped you through this without the whisky."

"I just didn't want to bother you with my problems daddy."

"Honey, when are you going to learn to let your mother and I help you once in a while? That's what parents are for. If you don't let us know what is going on, we can't help you."

"Oh daddy I've really made such a mess of my life. I just miss Jamie so much, and I can't find her. I don't even know if she is alright, or even alive. My life is just meaningless with out Jamie; at least the whisky numbed my mind so I wasn't constantly thinking about her."

"Baby I know how terribly you must miss Jamie. But honey drinking yourself into a stupor every night isn't the right thing for you to do. You are living on whisky, cigarettes and coffee, you've lost so much weight that you are ruining your health. If you don't pull yourself together honey when we do find out where Jamie is you won't be in any shape to go and get her. So promise your old dad that you will stop drinking, and start taking better care of yourself. If not for yourself, at least do it for Jamie." Frank knew that if he could get Cassandra to make him a promise that she would never go back on her word.

Cassandra moved off Franks lap and sat huddled on the end of the couch wiping the tears from her eyes, and not saying a word. Frank didn't say anything either, he figured he would just give Cassandra some time to mull things over in her mind. He was glad he had been able to get the whisky poured down the sink before Cassandra had a chance to drink any of it. At least she had a clear mind at the present, and he prayed that she would come to terms with what she was doing to herself, and make the right decision.

*   *   *

AN HOUR PASSED WITHOUT either of them saying a single word. "Okay daddy I promise. We'll try it your way for a while and see how it goes." She whispered in a soft voice.

"That's my girl." Frank said as he pulled her close, and gave her a hug.

"Tell me daddy what do we do now? Where do we go from this point on?" She asked sadly.

Frank looked at his watch. "Well I guess the first thing we are going to do, is go help your mother close the store. Then we are all going to go for a ride up the canyon and have a good meal, maybe stay and listen to the band for awhile and relax a little. How does that sound?"

"Can we change the plans a little daddy? If we are going out to eat I would like to take a shower and change. I'm a little grubby after working all day."

Frank felt uneasy about her request and he must have taken too long to reply as he sat there beside her.

"Don't worry daddy there isn't anything in the house to drink except for coffee and water. I made you a promise and no matter how bad things get around here I will keep that promise." She assured him as she watched the doubt in his eyes turn to pride.

"Okay honey, you get showered and changed while I go help Nora close the store. Will a half hour be long enough for you?" Frank asked as he stood up and walked to the door.

"That will plenty of time daddy, I'll be ready and waiting." She smiled at him as she closed the door.

Frank noticed that the smile didn't quite reach her eyes and he knew that his little girl would never be truly happy until she had her daughter back home safe, and sound again. Frank knew deep down that he would move heaven and earth if he had to before he would ever see his daughter's beautiful blue eyes smiling again, or know a moment's peace until he could make her dream of getting Jamie back become a reality.

Chapter Twenty-Seven

Time slowly passed; Cassandra was gradually getting her life back on track again. Every night since she made the promise to her father she would go home after work and shower and change and go down to the store and help out until closing time, then all three of them went to her parents trailer where they had supper and watched television or talked until ten o'clock when Cassandra would go home and crawl into bed.

In time the demons were starting to fade away. Instead of wallowing in self pity the way she used to, now she was planning for the day that Jamie would come home. She had even managed to gain a few pounds, and with all the good food her mother cooked every night her skin had filled out and the dark circles under her eyes had vanished, she was learning to smile and joke again, almost back to her old self except for a haunted look in her eyes when she thought no one was noticing. Deep down in her heart she wondered if she really would ever see Jamie again.

Every night Cassandra prayed to God and begged him to help her find Jamie safe and well. Knowing that with each day that passed Jamie was out there some where crying for her mother. Each night Cassandra vowed that she would never give up her search for her daughter, even if it took the rest of her life, she would never give up hope.

*   *   *

EVERYDAY WHILE CASSANDRA WAS at work she hoped that someone would drop a hint of where Jamie might be, but maybe nobody really knew because there was no mention of Jamie or Ray. She hoped that she would gain some information through the small town grapevine, but that never became a reality. Maybe Marlee or her husband had heard something, she decided to go visit them after work, she hadn't seen or talked to either of them since the night Jamie disappeared. In fact Marlee still had Buffy; Cassandra just couldn't deal with seeing the puppy knowing how much it was a part of Jamie, that's why she hadn't had any contact with Marlee since that fateful night. They were all such a huge reminder of her life with Jamie. So she had kept her distance from her friend.

*   *   *

WHEN THE FIVE O'CLOCK whistle blew Cassandra ran out to her truck and drove to her parent's store. "Hey dad is it okay if I skip supper tonight? I thought it was high time I went and paid a visit to Marlee and checked on Buffy. I want to apologize for not even talking to her or picking up the puppy. I just hope she will understand and forgive me."

"Sure its okay honey, you don't have to ask our permission to go visit your friends."

"Thanks dad. You know this is really awful of me, but for some reason it completely slipped my mind about Buffy. I just remembered the puppy today. God I sure hope Marlee isn't too mad at me after all this time of not even calling her."

"Honey I'm sure Marlee won't be mad at you. Matter of fact she has been in the store almost every day for months to ask about you. She hasn't called you because she knew you were having a hard time, and felt partly responsible for what happened to Jamie. Your mother and I explained that it wasn't her fault, and that there weren't any hard feelings. We asked her to just be patient, and you would come around in time."

"Boy what a relief to hear that. I have to admit that I have been in my own selfish little world for so long wallowing in self pity that I never gave my best friend a single thought. God what a mess I've made of my life."

"That's all behind you now honey. I'm sure Marlee will be very happy to see you, so run along now and don't keep her waiting any longer."

* * *

CASSANDRA DROVE TO THE other end of town to where Marlee lived, and when she turned into the drive way her friend came bounding down the front steps with two cocker spaniels close on her heels. Cassandra jumped out of her truck and threw her arms around Marlee and the two of them were squealing with delight like a couple of teenagers. Both of the dogs were barking and jumping up on them eager to share in all the excitement.

"Gosh but you are a sight for sore eyes Cassy. I've missed you so much these past months."

"I've missed you too Marlee. I just got lost for a few months. I can't tell you how sorry I am for not even picking up Buffy. Thanks so much for taking care of him for me, and please forgive me for everything."

"Nonsense Cassy, you don't have anything to be forgiven for. I know how hard it has been for you these past months and your mind was on other things. Besides Buffy hasn't been any trouble at all. Just look at him, hasn't he grown like a weed?" Marlee knew instantly that she had said the wrong thing. "Oh Cassy please forgive me, I never meant to cause you any pain. I just spoke with out thinking."

Tears were shimmering in Cassandra's eyes and she stooped down and took Buffy in her arms and reality set in as she realized that Jamie had probably grown just as much.

"Oh God Marlee if Buffy has grown this much, I wonder how much Jamie has changed since I saw her last. Will I even recognize Jamie the next time I see her? If I ever see her again, it has been so long."

"Of course you will dear friend. And you stop talking like that Cassandra; I know in my heart that you will see Jamie again. You just have to be patient. I know how hard this is for you, but you can't ever give up hope of finding her. "Marlee assured her." Come on Cassy lets go in and have a cup of coffee like old times."

* * *

IT WAS THE LAST week in June and Cassandra was taking her lunch break in the employee lunch room when Brad and Randy came in and sat down with their lunch buckets at the table directly behind her.

"Well Brad old buddy how was your vacation to Canada?" Randy inquired.

"It was great, the wife and I had a real good time. That country is really beautiful; we hated to have to come home. By the way Randy bet you can never guess who I ran into when I stopped for a six-pack of beer at a store in Cascade on our way home. It was our old hunting buddy Ray Cartone."

Cassandra was glad she had her back to their table so they wouldn't know she had heard them. She wanted more than anything to start turning cartwheels or dancing around the room. But instead she remained silent and decided to linger a little longer over her cigarette and coffee in hopes of hearing a little more about Brads meeting with Ray.

"Tell me Brad, what's that old son-of-a-gun doing these days. Randy asked eagerly.

"Said he was working at the mill there in Cascade, but he was sort of in a hurry and couldn't talk very long because he was on his way to Spokane. Something to do with some papers he had to sign to get his kid into a Catholic boarding school or something like that. I was paying for my beer and didn't catch it all."

"Well I'll be damned. Funny how small this old world really is, you running into Ray after all this time while you were on vacation." Randy said shaking his head.

Cassandra decided she had heard enough, if she didn't get out of the lunch room real fast she doubted that she would be able to contain her excitement for much longer, and she sure didn't want Brad and Randy to know that she had been listening in on their conversation.

* * *

AS THE AFTERNOON SHIFT seemed to drag on and on, it was really working on Cassandra's nerves to keep her excitement from showing. There were so many people working at the mill that had taken Rays side when they split up, that she knew beyond a shadow of a doubt that she must try to continue being the way she had been all these months since Jamie disappeared, just doing her job and showing no kind of emotion what so ever. She didn't want anyone to know that she had finally gotten the information that she needed so she could go and get Jamie. Other wise someone might tip Ray off that she now knew where Jamie was and he would move her some place else.

* * *

FINALLY THE FIVE O'CLOCK whistle blew to signal quitting time. Cassandra had to hold herself in check to keep from running. She knew she had to saunter out to her car the same way she did every night. It took all her self control to appear normal. Somehow it seemed like her truck was miles away from where she had parked that morning.

Soon as she got into her truck she let out her pent up breath and just sat there for a couple of minutes until she stopped trembling.

Then she started the engine and willed herself to drive slowly out of the parking area that was posted at five miles per hour.

*   *   *

CASSANDRA PULLED UP NEXT to the back of the store where she always parked so that her truck was out of the way for customers to park. She walked around to the front door and looked around to see if there were any town people inside before she said anything, she was in luck her parents were alone in the store.

"Daddy you aren't going to believe this but I got lucky and found out where Jamie is." She said as she danced around the store.

Frank and Nora both rushed to her and they all hugged in the middle of the store.

"That's the best news we've had in a long time baby, how in the hell did you find out?" Frank asked eagerly.

"I was having lunch and a couple of Rays old hunting buddies came in and sat down behind me. One of them had been on vacation and had run into Ray accidentally in a store in Cascade where Ray is evidently living now. Ray told him he didn't have time to talk as he was on his way to Spokane to sign some paper to put Jamie in a Catholic boarding school. So I figure Nadine and Larry have had her all this time." She explained.

"Can you believe that sorry son-of-a-bitch would do such a thing to his own daughter, he doesn't want her, he just wants to keep her away from you Cassy?" Frank raged.

"I know daddy, it breaks my heart to think how callus Ray is. But I'm going to go get her before that happens. School doesn't start until September so Jamie will be at Nadine's for at least another six weeks or so. I figure I have some vacation time coming so I'll go into the office in the morning and tell them that I want to take next week off. I only have tomorrow and Friday to work before I can leave, so I'll use that time to pack a few things and I can leave here early Saturday morning."

"Good I'll be ready to go with you, I'll find someone to come in and help Nora while were gone."

"Daddy I'm sorry but I have to go alone, I don't want anyone to even get a hint that I know where Jamie is so we all have to keep things to the normal routine so that someone doesn't tip Ray off about my plans. He has a lot of friends here in town that figured everything was my fault, and I'm quite certain that a few of them know where Ray is, and has known where Jamie is as well."

"Honey I know you're right, but I hate to see you make that trip alone. Do you think maybe your friend Marlee might go with you. Everyone knows what good friends you are and I doubt if anyone would think too much about you two girls taking a little trip together." Frank suggested.

"That's a good idea daddy, I think I'll run down and see if Marlee would like to take a little trip with me. I know she won't tell anyone where we are going."

*　　*　　*

CASSANDRA JUMPED OUT OF the truck and ran up the steps and rapped on Marlee's front door.

"Hey kiddo if you aren't just beaming from ear to ear. Come on in and tell me what's got you so excited."

"Oh Marlee I know where Jamie is, and I have a favor to ask of you."

"That was the next thing on my list of to do things for today, grant one special favor." Marlee teased.

"So tell me how did you find Jamie, and what can I do to help you?"

"I over heard a couple of Rays old hunting buddies in the lunch room today, and one of them had ran into Ray when he was on vacation last week. Anyway to make a long story short I think Jamie is at Ray's sisters in Spokane, Washington. I'm leaving on Saturday morning very early, my plan is to go and steal Jamie back. Daddy doesn't want me to make the trip by myself, and I wondered if you would go with me if it's at all possible for you to get away. We should only be gone a couple of days, but I'm going to ask for a weeks vacation so nobody will suspect anything. This has to be kept strictly confidential because I know Ray has someone here that keeps him informed on what goes on around here."

"Well you don't have to worry about Gary and I on that score. We would both like to see Ray rot in hell for what he has done to you and Jamie."

"I'm glad for your support Marlee, but do you think you can go with me?"

"I'll ask Gary, he's off for the weekend so he could take care of Ginger, and the live stock. So I don't see any problem why I can't go with you."

"Is Gary home now so we could find out for sure Marlee? I really need to know right away, other wise I'm going to have to figure out something else."

"Yes he's out back doing some chores. I'll go get him and we can get this squared away right now." Marlee said as she started to the back door. "Grab yourself a cup of coffee kido, I'll be right back."

Cassandra barely had time to pour herself a cup of coffee and sit back down when both Marlee and Gary came into the kitchen.

"Congratulations Cassandra, Marlee told me you know where Jamie is. I can't tell you how happy I am for you. So I came in to personally give you my permission to take Marlee with you on this jaunt."

Cassandra jumped up and ran and threw her arms around Gary and gave him a big hug. "Oh thank you Gary, you will never know how truly much this means to me. I'll be forever in your debt."

"Nonsense Cassandra, you don't owe me a thing. I'm just happy that you now have a pretty good chance of getting Jamie back home where she belongs, and I'm glad that you consider us good enough friends to let us have a part in helping you."

The tears started to stream down Cassandra's face.

Gary put his arm around Cassandra and hugged her. "Hey why all the water works honey, this is a happy occasion."

"I know Gary, but these aren't sad tears, they are tears for happy." Cassandra explained. "You have no idea how long I've waited for this day to come."

"No, but we have a pretty good idea." Gary said as he started to leave. "I got to get back to work so I'll leave you two alone to plot your strategy." He winked at both of them as he went out the back door.

CHAPTER TWENTY-EIGHT

SATURDAY MORNING CASSANDRA WAS up and dressed and had her suit case in the truck by two-thirty, she jumped in and headed for the other end of town to pick up Marlee.

They decided that leaving this early in the morning there wouldn't be anyone up to see which way they went. Frank and Nora were going to tell anyone that asked where she had gone on her vacation, that she went to Las Vegas, Nevada to see some friends.

* * *

CASSANDRA PULLED UP TO Marlee's house and she and Gary came out with Marlee's suit case, tossed it in the back of the truck, Marlee kissed Gary goodbye, and they were off in minutes.

* * *

THEY DROVE BACK TO the other end of town and headed for the canyon, as luck would have it they never saw a single car on the road. So far everything was going according to plan.

"So tell me Cassy what are your plans for when we get to Spokane?"

"I'm thinking that the first thing we will do is gas up the truck so we'll have a full tank of gas when we get to Nadine's. I decided to play the vacation part to the hilt. I'm going to tell Nadine that we were just driving through and stopped in to see Jamie, and if she is there, then I'm going to ask nicely if perhaps I can take her for an ice cream so we could visit a little while. I'm going to tell Nadine that I will bring Jamie back in an hour, because we want to get back on the road as soon as possible."

"Sounds like a good idea so far. What do you plan to do if she lets you take Jamie for an ice cream?"

"Well I figured the mileage, and I think if Nadine falls for my story, then soon as I get Jamie in the car I'll just drive slowly until we are out of sight of her house, then I'm going to head straight for the Washington/ Idaho boarder. I figure that by the time the hour is up we should be well inside the state of Idaho and we'll be out of the Washington State Troopers jurisdiction. I plan to take a secondary back road out of Spokane that is a shorter distance to the boarder. They won't be expecting me to do this, and I figure it will buy us a little extra time."

"I'm impressed Cassy. You sure you didn't work for the C.I.A. sometime in your former life." Marlee teased.

"No to tell you the truth, dad and I spent some time with the road atlas last night and planned out our escape route." Cassandra confessed smiling.

"How will you find the secondary road after you leave Nadine's?"

"Dad and I thought about that to. I'm going to go into Spokane on it so there won't be any chance for error."

It was a piece of cake going in on the back road, as luck would have it; it wasn't too far from the road to Nadine and Larry's house. That was more than Cassandra and her dad had bargained on. Cassandra couldn't believe her luck.

"Wait until I tell dad about this when we get home." Cassandra said grinning from ear to ear. "So far, so good."

"Now all I have to worry about is nothing going wrong when we get to Nadine's."

"Keep an eye out for a gas station Marlee; we have to make sure we have a full tank. Nadine's should be close by according to the street signs."

Cassandra was driving slowly enough so she could turn in when they came across a gas station. "If we're lucky I hope we can find a station on this side of the street, other wise we'll have to go around the block."

"Oh there's a Standard station coming up on the next corner Cassy."

"Good; step number two has worked out in our favor." Cassandra surmised.

They pulled in and a man came right out to help them. "What can I do for you young lady." The portly fellow inquired.

"Would you fill it up with Ethel please, and check the oil." Cassandra asked politely.

"Sure can little lady. Looks like that windshield could use a little cleaning too, you girls been traveling far? Sure is a lot of bugs on it." He teased heartedly.

"Yes sir, we're on vacation, and figure to head up and have a look at Canada while we are this close. I got some relatives in Seattle that we'll probable spend the night with." Cassandra responded figuring she would lay a little backup foundation just in case this friendly guy was a friend of Larry's. And just might put two, and two together seeing the Idaho license plates on the truck.

Cassandra paid for the gas and as they pulled out of the station Marlee started laughing. "Boy that was some whopper you laid on the guy at the station. What was all that for?"

Cassandra smiled. "Well I don't know that guy from Adam. Thought it might buy us a little insurance. In case he's a friend of Larry's."

"What a terrific idea Cassy. I'm impressed." Marlee looked at her friend with pride in her eyes. "What ever made you come up with that lie so fast right off the top of your head?"

"Well Marlee if you had been tricked, and screwed around as much as I have by the Cartone's in the past ten years, you would learn how to cover your ass in advance the way I have, and try to stay one step ahead of them if you can."

Marlee looked at the map. "Turn left at the next corner Cassandra, that's our street."

"Okay here we go." Cassandra said as she turned onto the street to Nadine's.

"Marlee just so there is no hang ups, no matter what I say, you just go along with it. Okay?"

"Sure thing kido, you're in the driver's seat."

Cassandra started to tremble; she knew she had to regain control of her emotions if she was going to pull this thing off. As she pulled into the drive way she took three deep breaths to help her relax. Being this close to getting Jamie back and screwing it up at the last minute would be the last straw.

Cassandra got out of the truck and walked up the walk and rung the door bell.

Nadine opened the front door; she looked shocked to see Cassandra standing on the porch. "Hello Cassandra what brings you here?"

"I was driving through on vacation with a friend of mine and thought I would stop by and see Jamie."

Jamie must have been close enough to hear Cassandra's voice, and she came running and pushed past Nadine and launched herself into Cassandra's arms screaming.

"Mommy, mommy I knew you would come for me. I just knew it."

"Oh baby it's so good to see you again." Cassandra crooned holding her little daughter close for the first time in six months.

"Would you and your friend like to come in?" Nadine offered.

"That would be nice Nadine, only I'm afraid I'm sort on limited time, I have to be in Seattle tonight so I only have about an hour. But I would really appreciate it if I could take Jamie down to the drug store for an ice cream cone and visit with her for a little while alone before I bring her back."

"Well I'm not sure if that would be a very good idea Cassandra." Nadine hedged.

"I'm her mother Nadine; surely you can let me spend an hour alone with my daughter before I leave." Cassandra said sweetly, and smiled.

"I promise I'll bring her right back. Surely that isn't asking too much under the circumstances, is it?"

Nadine appeared to be struggling with her inner self. "Oh I guess there isn't any harm in letting you take Jamie for some ice cream, if you promise to bring her back in an hour." She finally relented.

"Oh I promise Nadine. I just want a little time alone with my daughter; it has been so long since we have had a chance to be together."

Cassandra took Jamie by the hand and started down the walk to-wards where her truck was parked. She had to pace herself so as not to break into a dead run for the truck.

"See that you keep your word Cassandra and bring Jamie back in an hour." Nadine called after her.

Cassandra helped Jamie into the truck and when she saw Marlee she squealed and launched herself into Marlee's arms. "Oh Marlee I thought I would never, ever see you and mommy again."

Cassandra climbed into the truck and called out the window. "We'll be back before you know it Nadine, and thanks a lot." As she backed out of the drive way and pointed the front of the truck back towards town. She could see Nadine standing on the porch in her review mirror.

"Boy this was easier than I thought it would be Marlee."

Cassandra went down about a mile from Nadine's house until she came to the highway marker for the secondary road she planned to take, and made a left turn away from the direction of town.

Jamie noticed. "Mommy you made the wrong turn, the ice cream place is the other way." She said and started giggling.

"I know sweetie, we aren't going to town for ice cream. I decided to take you some place else instead." She smiled at Jamie and stepped down on the gas as they were out of the city limits now and she needed to put some much needed distance between her and Spokane and reach the state line before the hour was up

"But where are we going mommy. Is it a surprise?" She asked excitedly.

Cassandra laughed and tickled Jamie in the tummy. "Yes it is a surprise sugar bug."

Jamie giggled. "Oh I love surprises mommy, but there isn't any place out here to get ice cream, and we're getting father away from town all the time mommy." Jamie had a frown on her face. "We really aren't going to get any ice cream are we mommy? You tricked me just like daddy and Aunt Nadine did." And she started to cry.

Cassandra slowed down and pulled off the road for a few minute's and took Jamie into her arms. "Mommy wasn't trying to trick you sweetie, she tricked your daddy and Aunt Nadine. Mommy is taking you home with her where grandma and grandpa Benning are, and we will never have to be apart again. How does that sound baby?"

"Do you really mean it mommy, are you really taking me home with you?"

"I sure am baby, so dry your eyes, and I want you to know that no one is ever going to take you away from mommy ever again. I promise."

"Oh thank you mommy, that's just what I've wanted for ever such a long time now. But every time I asked daddy or Aunt Nadine to take me home, they told me that you didn't love me anymore, and they told me I wasn't ever going to see you again."

"They lied to you sweetie, Mommy has been looking for you for months, but I had no idea where you were. It was only a couple of days ago that I found out so I came and got you just as soon as I could. So dry your eyes and let's get back on the road we are losing some very precious time. We have to hurry so nobody can catch us. Okay?"

Cassandra pulled back onto the highway. "Mommy I just knew way down in my heart, that you still loved me." Jamie whispered as she snuggled close to Cassandra.

*   *   *

"WELL GUESS YOU CAN relax some now Cassy, we're coming up on the state line I can see the marker up ahead." Marlee said excitement showing in her voice.

"Guess the Gods are smiling on us Marlee. We got this far without a hitch in our plans; sure hope things continue to run in our favor. We still have to get through Cascade without Ray spotting my truck. I think we may find a motel at the town before we get to Cascade and hold up there until the wee hours in the morning after the bars close. That way we just might be lucky enough to slip trough Cascade undetected. Because I'm quite sure by now that Nadine has figured out that we didn't go for ice cream. She has probably already notified Ray if he has a telephone. Guess we'll just have to hope for the best, and cross that bridge when we come to it."

"Boy you sure pulled a fast one on Nadine, Cassy. I want you to know that I'm very proud of you. You done great; pulled that off without a hitch. Just like a real pro." Marlee commented trying to contain her laughter.

"Yeah I guess I have to agree with you on that one Marlee, it was pretty slick wasn't it?" Cassandra mentally patted herself on the back for a job well done.

CHAPTER TWENTY-NINE

IT WAS AROUND ELEVEN-THIRTY that night when Cassandra spotted the motel sign blinking on and off, just down the road on the right. "Looks like this will do for a little rest. What do you think Marlee?"

"Looks fine with me, my old bones could sure do with a stretch."

"Yeah we have been going pretty steady since we started out; we could all do with a rest." Cassandra replied turning into the entrance to the log cabin motel. She glanced down at Jamie who was fast asleep snuggled into her side.

"Sit tight for a minute Marlee while I go get us a room. Jamie might be scared if she wakes up and I'm not here." She said as she stepped down out of the truck without waking Jamie. "Poor little tyke, she's out like a light."

Cassandra came right back. "We're in number three." She handed Marlee the key as she slid behind the wheel. "Think you can get both the bags out of the back while I carry Jamie?" She asked as she pulled up in front of cabin three.

Cassandra set her travel alarm for three o'clock in the morning; it wouldn't give them much sleep as they would have to get back on the road. None of them undressed, Jamie didn't have anything but the clothes on her back, and Cassandra and Marlee were just too tired to bother. They were only going to be here for a few hours anyway.

* * *

SEEMED LIKE CASSANDRA HAD barely closed her eyes and the alarm went off. She jumped out of bed. "Hey Marlee wake up, time to rise and shine."

Marlee sat up rubbing her eyes. "What time is it Cassy?"

"It's three o'clock, time for us to hit the road." Cassandra said as she closed her suit case, and started wrapping her coat around Jamie.

Before Cassandra could say anything Marlee grabbed up the two suit cases.

"Right, I know the drill. I'll take the bags while you carry Jamie." She said winking at Cassandra.

* * *

"CASCADE STRAIGHT AHEAD LET'S hope that lady luck is still in our corner." Cassandra said and felt a chill of apprehension race down her spine.

Just as they entered the north end of the town both girls were holding their breath as they slowly went through the town of Cascade at the posted speed limit of twenty-five miles per hour. It was so early in the morning, that there wasn't a sign of any people, or vehicles. Cassandra spotted a police cruiser parked in front of an all night truck stop on the south end of town. She glanced at the door as she passed, but there wasn't any sign of the cop coming out. She exhaled loudly. Then she started to laugh when she realized that she had been holding her breath all the way through town.

"What are you laughing about Cassy?"

Cassandra glanced over at her friend. "Do you realize that I just drove through town holding my breath? I was so afraid that any minute Ray would spot the truck and take out after us."

Cassandra kept a close eye on the rear view mirror to see if the cop car pulled out from the truck stop. By now they were at the end of the city limits and there still wasn't any sign of another vehicle. She stepped on the gas and leaned back and relaxed. They should be home by late afternoon if their luck held out.

*   *   *

IT WAS ALMOST FIVE o'clock that night, when they pulled up at the back of Benning's Corner Grocery. Jamie was jumping up and down in her excitement to see her grandparents.

"Hurry mommy so I can get out." She squealed.

"Okay Sugar Bug, there you go." She patted Jamie on the rear as she darted around the corner of the building yelling. "Grandma, Grandpa I'm home."

*   *   *

THE SIGHT THAT GREETED Cassandra's eyes as she entered the store was almost her undoing. Frank was holding Jamie in his arms and she was hugging them both at the same time and kissing first one then the other.

"Boy you sure made good time Cassandra. You must have really pushed that old truck of yours." Frank commented as he walked over and wrapped her in his other arm.

"We sure did. Everything went like clock work just the way I hoped it would."

"Can I use your phone Nora?" Marlee asked. "I want to call Gary and let him know that I'm back in town and will be home in a few minutes."

"Sure Marlee, go right ahead." Nora said as she moved the phone over closer so Marlee could use it.

"Cassy why don't you go ahead and run Marlee home, I know Gary is anxious to see her." Nora suggested. "Jamie can stay here with us while we close the store and we can get all the details of your trip over supper."

"Good idea mom. Hope you're fixing something good because I'm sure hungry, we had a quick bite of breakfast in McCall but just a few snacks since. I know Jamie must be starving."

* * *

WHILE THEY WERE EATING supper Frank asked. "So what are your plans now Cassy?"

"To be quite honest daddy I'm afraid I never thought of anything beyond just getting Jamie back home." She confessed.

Frank cleared his throat. "We don't mean to interfere in your life honey, but your mother and I have been kicking a few things around while you were gone."

"I would very much like to hear your idea daddy. And just for the record you and mother can interfere all you want because I need a lot of help right now so that Ray can never do this again."

"Your mother and I thought that since you have the next week off from your job it might be wise for you to stay here tonight, and in the morning you can leave Jamie here with Nora while you and I go into town and see Ralph Jennings. He has been our attorney for the past few years and I know he will help you with all the legal stuff. Also we have decided the only way to prevent Ray from stealing Jamie again we will give you the money to pay for your divorce."

"I really appreciate that daddy, but first let's see how much it will cost, and then if I don't have enough in the bank, I'll borrow the balance from you and mother." She smiled.

"Okay baby, I just wanted you to know that you wouldn't have to wait if you were short of money."

"I've been saving everything I could since Ray and his mother stole Jamie. There was only one thing in the whole world that I wanted and that was to have my little girl back home with me where she belonged."

* * *

THE NEXT MORNING CASSANDRA and Frank drove into town and saw Ralph Jennings, and he called a friend of his who was a Judge and had him issue a restraining order that prevented Ray and his entire family from being able to come within five hundred feet of both Jamie and Cassandra. Then they worked out the details of the divorce, and filed the necessary papers to start the divorce proceedings. The Judge set a court date for the middle of January due to the six month waiting period in the State of Idaho.

* * *

RALPH JENNINGS ASSURED CASSANDRA that because Ray had taken Jamie away from her twice, and both times he had dumped her with relatives was a clear indication that he had no desire to keep her himself. So he was pretty confident that the Judge would grant Cassandra full custody of Jamie.

* * *

ON THE DAY OF her court date Cassandra told her parents that she was going to go by herself, with only Marlee along as her character witness when she went before the Judge. She knew she was going to have to explain to the Judge about Ray's abuse. She hadn't discussed any of that with Ralph, while her father was with her. But she had called the attorney soon as she got home and told him the complete story, and made him promise that he would never tell her parents the truth about how Ray had treated her.

* * *

WHEN THE JUDGE HEARD her tragic story he stipulated the terms of Cassandra's divorce were due to extreme, physical, and mental cruelty, and granted her total custody of Jamie.

*　*　*

AS CASSANDRA DESCENDED THE courthouse steps she felt a tremendous feeling of peace come over her as she realized her living nightmare was finally over, she was free of the past, no more sweet talk and lies; no more threats, and nothing or nobody were ever going to hurt her or Jamie ever again.